MARCEL
THEROUX

The Paperchase

'Exquisitely calculated ... very satisfying'
JOHN LANCHESTER, AUTHOR OF *THE DEBT TO PLEASURE*

Marcel Theroux was born in Kampala in 1968. He was educated in Britain and America and now lives in London. His first novel, *A Stranger in the Earth*, is available in paperback. *The Paperchase* is his second novel.

Also by Marcel Theroux

A Stranger in the Earth

THE

Paperchase

MARCEL THEROUX

An *Abacus* Book

First published in the United States of America by
Harcourt Inc., in 2001, as
The Confessions of Mycroft Holmes: A Paperchase
First published in Great Britain by Abacus in 2001

Typeset in Ehrhardt by M Rules
Printed and bound in Great Britain
by Clays Ltd, St Ives plc

Abacus
A division of
Little, Brown and Company (UK)
Brettenham House
Lancaster Place
London WC2E 7EN

www.littlebrown.co.uk

ONE

THE NEWS OF MY UNCLE Patrick's death came as a shock, not because it was sudden, but because I had assumed he'd been dead for ages.

Patrick dead. Father was all the telegram said. My first reaction was: Patrick who? And then I remembered.

If I'd given him any thought over the preceding years I'm sure I would have realised he was still alive, albeit in a world that had ceased to bear any relation to mine. It's just that I'd been doing my best to forget everything about my family, and though I got Christmas presents every year from Aunt Judith in Boston, I was succeeding pretty well at it.

Of course I remembered Patrick – he'd just been tucked away in a distant compartment of my mind like an odd sock: present but incomplete. After all, a person doesn't slip out of the world like a blip off a radar screen. A life ends with a death. The telegram was conclusive: it completed him. *Patrick dead.*

And then a strange thing happened: the news of his death resurrected him in my imagination: the Patrick that was in me, the faint but indelible stamp of him that *was* me. Whole sections of my memory became active for the first time in years. It was like discovering a false bottom in a suitcase; or that my tiny flat in Clapham had grown an extra storey overnight. I thought about Patrick and his crazy old house on Ionia and, strangest of all, I began to miss him – a man I had not clapped eyes on for almost twenty years.

I was in a mood to be maudlin, anyway. I had been working night shifts for months, getting in at eight in the evening and going home twelve hours later. In the quiet hours of the early morning, no one wanted to talk and there was nothing to do except stumble around the newsroom reading the newspapers or, in my case, fret over the choices that had got me there. I lived in twilight, going home each morning in sunglasses to protect my tired eyes. And the darkness seemed to have settled over every aspect of my life.

The incoming American President had inaugurated his term in office with airstrikes in the Middle East and we had been told to expect more. Extra journalists and editors had been summoned to cope with the increased workload at night, because the management had calculated that the United States would time hostilities to coincide with its evening newscasts.

'Are we at war yet?' said Wendy, the news editor, as she arrived for work on the evening I got the telegram.

I told her we weren't.

'That's good, because I didn't have my tin hat in my bag.' She sat down at her terminal and began peeling an orange and prising it into bits with her stubby thumb as she read the handover. She was a great believer in the power of vitamin C to mitigate the effects of too many night shifts.

I wasn't the only one who seemed to have forgotten Patrick.

I trawled the wires thinking that the death of the author of the Oscar-nominated *Peanut Gatherers* deserved at least a mention, but there was nothing. He had been silent too long. Like me, the obituarists must have assumed Patrick had been dead for a decade. The telegram was in my pocket. I touched it instinctively as if to confirm that he had indeed existed.

It was a very quiet night. The rumour of war had made all other news irrelevant. Watching our newscasts, you got the feeling that the world's concentration had narrowed to a small point, a beam of attention that excluded everything apart from a handful of politicians and journalists. But though we continued to report what they said, in reality nothing was happening. It was television's way of twiddling its thumbs, but with more menace. It was the pregnant silence between lightning and a thunderclap.

It wouldn't make much difference to me, however. War or no war, my duties would be the same. My job was to write the twenty seconds of talk that precedes a news report, the bit where the newsreader looks serious, or mildly amused, depending on the story, and addresses the camera. And sometimes I wrote the words that appear magically under someone's head when they're being interviewed. And sometimes I produced a guest from the make-up room and showed him through the labyrinth of corridors to the studio. And occasionally I might write a whole report to fit pictures that had arrived by satellite. When this happened, my name would appear at the beginning of the piece followed by the word 'reporting' – a word which probably overstates the journalistic value of the hundred or so words I had cobbled together from wire stories. And at the end of the piece I would sign off: 'Damien March, BBC News', which – because it didn't mention a location – implicitly acknowledged that I was 'reporting' on the events in Prague, or Sarajevo, or wherever, from the bowels of Shepherd's Bush. Once I had dreamed of being 'Damien March, BBC News, Madrid', or 'Damien March, BBC News, on board the USS

Saratoga', But I was never more than Damien March, BBC News, and often less.

Very early on, I lost that zest for the work that marked people out for promotion. Every six months or so, there'd be a new face on the night shift: always young, nearly always a man, usually wearing a tie, and clearly just passing through our newsroom en route to higher things. I envied them their unquestioned sense of purpose – the feeling, I suppose, that they knew what they wanted, and they were becoming it. They all shared the certainty that sooner or later they would be Someone on TV, which, let's face it, is the principal ambition of just about everyone right now. I sometimes think we are all souls in limbo, waiting hopefully to join those who have been eternised on the box.

I recognised myself in these people – getting in early, going home late, working through lunch – but as I had been years earlier. To them I was just an old lag. To me, they were sleep-walkers. I thought if you bumped them hard enough they would wake up, as I had, and feel disoriented, and not under-stand how or why they'd got there. Some time in the last five years, my ambition had faded away, and though I still went through the forms of my job, I'd given up expecting it to answer the question: Who am I? After ten years in television, I was remembered chiefly by my colleagues as the person who had done that report on the transvestite Thai kickboxer. And that was five years ago.

At three o'clock in the morning I had my lunch break. The canteen looked like the mess room of the *Marie Celeste*. I helped myself to a sausage that was as brown and shiny as old varnish, and a scoop of scrambled eggs the texture of carpet underlay. Another tray clattered onto the metal runners beside mine. It belonged to Tom, a former colleague who had been promoted onto the national breakfast show. He was also a new father.

'How's Niamh?' I said. 'How's it being a dad?'

Tom didn't like the look of the food on offer and asked for an omelette. 'Being a dad? It's the most wonderful, exasperating, inspiring, you know, all the clichés you can think of, thing that you can imagine. It's just incredible.'

'I can't imagine,' I said. 'I can barely keep myself in clean underpants, never mind a dependant.'

'It gives you an amazing strength,' he said, as we waited at the till while the woman who had made the omelette wiped her hands on her apron and came round to ring up the contents of our trays. 'I feel like I'm able to go out into the world because I have that base. Leaving in the evening, looking at Niamh and Tara in that bed – it brings out the caveman in me. It makes me want to go out and club a bear or something.' Tom handed his loyalty card to the cashier to be validated. 'Six more stamps and I get a free breakfast,' he said.

'You're the first hunter-gatherer I've heard of who carries a canteen loyalty card,' I said. 'What are you going to have for your free meal? Woolly mammoth?'

'You should get one of them, gobshite. You might as well get something for free.'

'I don't want to think about eating thirty of these between now and September. Look at it. They should be dropping fried bread on Iraq instead of bombs. Far deadlier.'

'You will eat them, though. I've seen you eat twice that many. Chuck us a napkin.'

'Yes – but I don't want to *plan* on it. It's a commitment thing. You're married, you wouldn't understand.'

My palate was sleepy and inert at that time in the morning and I liked to shock it with English mustard on the sausage and Tabasco sauce on the scrambled egg. That tingle was the most reliably pleasurable feature of my entire life at that time. Sometimes I accidentally overdosed, and the mustard on the roof of my mouth gave me the feeling that someone was removing my nasal hair with a blowtorch. It made it painful to talk, so when Tom asked me what my news was, I was telegraphic in my replies. 'Not much,' I said, 'uncle died.'

'Oh, Jesus,' he said. 'I'm sorry.' He paused, realising that his consolations had exceeded my grief. 'Your uncle?'

'Patrick. Writer. Lived in the States. Hadn't seen him in years.' The burning sensation had mellowed into a tolerable buzz.

'I always forget you're a Yank,' said Tom.

'Yeah, me too.'

'You don't seem so upset.'

'You know me, I keep it all locked up inside.'

Later that morning, I returned a guest to reception and walked back up the stairs to the seventh floor to find that dawn had happened: London was bathed in a greyish light, as unflattering as the neon tubes in the newsroom. From the seventh-floor landing I watched a Hammersmith train labouring silently through a veil of drizzle.

I breathed on the glass of the window and rubbed off the mist with my sleeve. It seemed odd that until recently Patrick and I had been inhabiting the same planet. But we had: Ionia wasn't Never-Never Land, it was over there – three thousand miles west of the kebab shops outside Shepherd's Bush station.

I went back to the newsroom and told Wendy I was feeling ill. Something had been threatening me for days with symptoms that were almost indistinguishable from the disorienting effects of night shifts. I had the ghostly sensation of being at one remove from my own body, as though I were trying to operate it by remote control.

'Yes,' she said. 'You look a bit peaky.'

That's funny coming from you, I thought. In spite of all those oranges, she had the night worker's vampiric pallor. I suspected that she flew home at dawn and went to sleep in a box of dirt. 'I wondered if I could go home early,' I said.

'That should be okay. Just check Fergus is all right for the seven o'clock bulletin.'

As I travelled back home on the underground in my sunglasses, a deep gloom settled over me. *Patrick dead.*

I never slept well after night shifts, and I was dreading lying awake through the morning, so I took two of the Temazepam that Laura had left in the bathroom cabinet along with a travel-size pot of moisturiser. I don't know if it was the flu, or the pills, or something more deep-seated still, but I slept right through the day and woke up at 3 a.m. the following morning. I was feverish and confused. I wasn't really *thinking* in any accepted sense of the word: I felt as though I was being made to watch clips from a movie about my life called *Damien March: The Low Points*. At that hour, and in that state, it seemed to have been nothing but wrong turns. I was thirty-five – which seems young now, but didn't then – without anything I could call a relationship, and doing a job that I didn't enjoy. Equally, of course, I wasn't destitute, disabled or – as far as I knew – terminally ill. But at three o'clock in the morning, the glass is always half-empty.

In a moment of fevered inspiration, going to Patrick's funeral suddenly seemed like the only way I had of reminding myself who I was. I couldn't face a long conversation with Dad on top of everything else, so I called my aunt in Boston, guessing that, with the time difference, she would still be up. She was, and she seemed pleased to hear from me.

She said Patrick had died suddenly of a heart attack, alone on Ionia, some months short of his sixty-fourth birthday. He had been out jogging.

Judith said his body had been discovered at the side of the running track by a member of the Junior Ionics – not, as you might think, a doo-wop group, but the local high-school baseball team.

Patrick had died of a massive myocardial infarction. He had been estranged from his family for years. His death was sad and premature. But no one has the final say on the genre of their demise, and Patrick's also contained elements of comedy. His toupee had become detached from his pate and was found alongside his body. The boy who saw it first mistook it for a puppy lying loyally beside its fallen master. But though Patrick had owned many animals over the years (African geese, peahens, a pony, a goat, a sheep named Bessie, a parrot,

four cats, dozens of chickens), he had always had an aversion
to dogs.

Judith said she would understand if I couldn't make it to the
funeral. No one was expecting me to come. She imagined I'd
be far too busy. In fact, she gave me so many opportunities to
opt out that I began to wonder if she was going herself. For
my part, I was possessed by a dangerous certainty about what
I wanted to do. I told her I'd be there, and then hung up the
phone.

My body clock was by now totally skewed. I decided to
administer a knock-out dose of two more sleeping pills, which
I chased down with a toothmug of red wine. I lay down again,
and my body appeared to dissolve from the feet upward. I fell
asleep and dreamed about Ionia.

First, I found myself floating just outside the window on the
seventh-floor landing of Television Centre. Instead of falling,
I began to rise, slowly at first, but then so quickly that my eyes
watered from the wind. As I looked down, the frozen traffic on
the M25 seemed to twinkle like one of the rings of Saturn. Up
ahead, I could see the Bristol Channel, separating the pig's-
head outline of Wales from the long shank of southwestern
England that points into the Atlantic. As I drifted west across
the sky, I watched the channel empty into the dark mantle of
the Irish Sea. I was moving fast but silently, like a weather balloon sweeping along the upper atmosphere – over Eire, past
the deserted crofts of the Great Blasket Islands, and through
the edge of the giant shadow that had been travelling westward
ahead of me: night itself rotating around the planet. It was suddenly chilly, like diving into the deep cold currents of a lake.
The scattered fragments of the Azores passed by me on the
left, and I came to the lights of America's eastern coastline. At
its northerly end, the tiny arm of Cape Cod flexed around its
bay. Ionia, Patrick's home, was a tiny comma of rock and
trees and sand dunes just off its triceps.

The island was lying bathed in darkness. Along the main
roads, the seasonal businesses hadn't opened – yet. The ice-

cream stores were shuttered; the mini golf courses weather-beaten from winter. The wind was still whipping up white caps on the sound and hammering the screen door with the broken catch. But watching it, you could sense that in a few weeks the rhythms of summer would have taken over: the sporadic knocking of new homes being constructed; buzz-saws pruning trees and bushes; the smell of tanning cream and sawdust; clams sizzling in the deep-fryer; nose-to-tail traffic from Boston on Friday afternoon; sailboats ruffling the cold blue water of Cape Cod Bay; twice the number of ferries making the crossing to the island; gleaming brown skin on the public beaches; a song – no one yet knew which one – that would play on the radio until it marked that summer as indelibly as the blue anchors on the harbour-master's forearms.

TWO

THE PERSONNEL MANAGER, a jug-eared Irish bruiser called Graham Toohey, gave me compassionate leave. He sounded relieved when I said it was my uncle that had died.

'I thought for a moment it might have been your brother,' he said.

No such luck, I thought.

'I loved *The Omega Man*.'

'Well, I'll be sure and tell him,' I said.

I couldn't get on a direct flight to Boston at such short notice, so I ended up flying into Newark that night and renting a car.

The transatlantic flight finished off my flu and the strangely purposeful behaviour that had accompanied it. I found myself waiting for the courtesy bus outside the arrivals terminal and wondering what on earth I was doing there. It was nine at night by the time I'd finished the paperwork for the rental car, and the thought of the journey ahead made me regret having come. The car seemed as vast and awkward as a yacht. After adjusting the mirrors and starting the engine, I tried to signal to turn left out of the parking lot, but only managed to switch on the wipers, which scraped to and fro sporadically over the bone-dry windscreen all the way through Manhattan, while I muttered, 'In this country, we drive on the right,' to myself as a mnemonic.

The sight of Manhattan coming into view across the Hudson cheered me up. It looked like a – like a what? – something jewelled and glittering. It was my first glimpse of the city in ten years. And there was something a bit sad about seeing something you were part of getting along fine without you. It was like bumping into a former lover who is wheeling a baby in a pushchair: life goes on in your absence.

My last memory of the place was of me and my brother Vivian lugging packages to the vast all-night post office on Thirtieth and Eighth to be sea-freighted back to England. I had given my brother a hug and handed him the keys to my studio flat on West Twenty-first Street. It had been cold, because I remember a very black homeless man was lying above a steam vent to keep warm. The smoke seemed to billow around him, as though he were the remains of spontaneous combustion, or a burnt offering.

Somewhere between New Haven and Providence I had had enough of driving. The radio and periodic blasts of air from the open window weren't enough to keep me alert, and I found myself dropping off at the wheel. I didn't feel ready to join Patrick in the funeral home, so I pulled off the interstate and found a motel. I can't remember the name of it. Was it an Econolodge? A Comfort Inn? A Motel 6? A Knight's Inn? A Day's Inn? A Budgetel? An E-Z Rest? Whatever it was called, it had a huge glass window draped in orange cloth and fronting the parking lot, a remote control stapled to the bedside table, which was scarred with cigarette burns, and a wide, saggy bed, like the back seat of a limousine, from where I continued to steer the rental car in my dreams, carefully guiding it down the right-hand lane of the highway.

The funeral home was fiercely air-conditioned. The only person without goose pimples was Patrick, peering out of the hatch of his coffin, his face waxy, his hairy fingers entwined over his chest and padlocked with a rosary. His nostrils were more cavernous than I remembered; his features greyer and more jowly. His blond wig had been decorously arranged over the top of his papery head. I had once been so used to Patrick's weird hair – the wigs followed experiments with comb-overs, transplants, weaves, and pate-dye – that I was surprised when people drew attention to it. I took his appearance for granted and somewhat resented people who didn't. No one pointed out men wearing baseball caps, or beards. Why point out the wig?

But seeing him after so long, with his old grey face on the pillow, I saw why people had been so surprised. 'Wig' didn't really do it justice. I kept thinking of the word 'syrup' from 'syrup of figs' – the Cockney rhyming slang for a wig. Patrick's was a golden syrup flowing over his head. It was the hair of a surfer, or a 3-D Jesus, and it looked decidedly odd on a man of sixty-three whose natural hair colour had been raven black.

I touched the back of Patrick's hand gingerly and made the sign of the cross, and said a Lord's Prayer up to 'Give us this day our daily bread', which was all I could remember. My hand was drawn to the golden curls of his wig. Almost inadvertently, I found myself giving it a valedictory pat. The sensation of the wiry hair on my fingers stayed with me for the rest of the day.

The people around me seemed oblivious to the presence of the corpse. The only sign that they were aware of it was in the hushed tone of their voices. No one appeared to recognise me either. Being ten years older was like being in disguise. I retreated to one of the side tables to get a drink and bumped straight into my father.

'Well,' he said, 'how kind of you to have come, Vivian.'

How kind of you to have come: he said it so precisely that it threw me for a second, it didn't even sound like English.

'Damien, Dad,' I said. 'I'm Damien.'

'Damien! Well . . . The two of you . . . so very alike now. You've filled out.'

He was wearing a dark suit and one of his Jermyn Street cravats. He looked, I thought, like a Hollywood English butler – something he was probably aware of himself. His hair was greyer, but there was still a good deal of it. It makes nonsense of genetics that Dad should have so much hair and Patrick so little. But age had made them more alike in other ways – the jowly faces, cartilaginous noses, the same shaggy eyebrows with the odd overgrown hair poking out of them: stalks of wheat in a windowbox. Dad's was a fuller version of the face in the casket.

'Work is making me fat,' I said.

'Really? I always found it kept me thin.' He patted his paunch. 'I gather you're still at the Beeb?'

'Still at the Beeb,' I said. 'Still at the Beeb.'

'Jolly good.' To my shamelessly Anglophile father, 'Working for the BBC' was right up there with 'took silk', 'reading Greats', and 'someone in the City'. I had never managed to explain to him that the BBC I worked in was a kind of high-tech post office, full of underappreciated people grumbling about the pay and conditions.

At that moment, I had the feeling I always had talking to my father: the feeling that he was looking down on my life from very high up without too much interest. He was outwardly impressive, like the deity of a pre-Christian religion: a totem pole, or a King Log, an Ark that you carried around the desert to intimidate your enemies. But it was a bluff. He couldn't intercede for his people. The box was empty. Even his sonorous, mid-Atlantic voice seemed to have a wooden echo.

'Seen anything of old' – he checked himself for a beat – 'Vivian?'

'We haven't spoken for a couple of years,' I said, trying very hard not to make it sound like a rebuke.

'Ah!' boomed the voice of the Ark. His shaggy eyebrows flew upward like divots, but he said nothing further. He knew that if he asked too many questions, he ran the risk of unearthing tiresome information.

The body was buried the following morning on the family plot in West Dennis. It was a bright May day. At the last minute, one of the readings in the service was reassigned to me, because I had come the farthest to attend it. My brother Vivian had not bothered to turn up.

My steps echoed through the church as I walked back to my pew from the lectern. My ears were still blocked up from the flight, and the effort of projecting my voice made me light-headed.

My father then read an extract from the Book of Common Prayer. I had to admit it sounded good. His foghorn of a voice filled the room:

'The days of our age are three score and ten,' he read. 'And though men be so strong, that they come to fourscore years, yet is their strength then but labour and sorrow; so soon it passeth away and we are gone.'

Aunt Judith was sniffling into a handkerchief. I was shocked how grey and old the four surviving siblings looked – even from the back.

'O teach us to number our days,' my father went on, 'that we may apply our hearts unto wisdom.'

The reception was held at Patrick's house, which meant catching the ferry to Ionia after the service. A few people didn't have time to make the extra trip. Patrick's mother, my nonagenarian grandmother, wasn't considered strong enough to go. As I kissed her cheek and said goodbye, I could hear my voice reverberating tinnily through the amplifier in her hearing aid.

Ionia sits in the Atlantic a few miles off the coast of Massachusetts. It's less than an hour from the mainland, but in the middle of the sound the sea floor drops off sharply. The water there is as blue-black as open ocean, and for a couple of minutes you are out of sight of either shore.

I went up to the top deck to get away from the funeral party. Sitting together in their dark clothes on the orange plastic seats of the ferry, they looked like a group of missionaries.

The breeze from the island carried the scent of pine trees. A small boy clattered up the stairs hugging a box of Crackerjack popcorn, eager for a first glimpse of land. And suddenly, Ionia's low hump had broken the straight line of the horizon. From the lee of the shore, a gust of wind blew through me like the draught from an open window.

We reached Patrick's house in taxis from Westwich. A catering company had laid out tables on the lawn by the summer kitchen and were serving a sickly seafood chowder.

The house stood alone at the top of a slope that rolled down to a tidal marsh and the sand dunes beyond it. It was built of wood, with white sides and jet-black shutters. Inside, it smelled of timber and books and wax polish. I was startled by familiar details – the stone in the library with the woman's face painted on it in coloured ink; the narwhal's tusk; the sky-blue velvet love seat in the sitting room; an idealised self-portrait of Patrick like a languid Byron, with high cheek-bones and lots of hair. Seeing them again I felt the exhilaration of the lucid dreamer: as though by remembering them I had brought them into existence.

I felt a kind of reverence for the place – it was full of relics, after all. The house was Patrick's life's work. In the absence of a family, it was all he had to project himself into the future. It was the sum total of his life's choices. And what choices!

Patrick had hoarded all sorts of junk: records, books, ice-cream scoops, mechanical banks, marbles, playing cards. But among the worthless detritus that had accumulated over decades were some treasures. For every twenty battered old cookery books, there might be a first edition of *Vile Bodies;* for every fifty records by Bob Seger and the Silver Bullet Band, you would find an original Sun pressing of Elvis Presley; for every gimcrack scrimshaw, a netsuke, or a Victorian doll. And the confusion, the clutter, the mixture of art and trash reflected him exactly. The house was Patrick.

I went upstairs and found my cousin Tricia rummaging through one of the upstairs cupboards. I wanted to see what was in there too, but I had a vision of Patrick bristling with anger: he was intensely private, and the sight of Tricia digging through his possessions, and almost sweating with excitement, would have undoubtedly hastened the myocardial infarction that killed him. She pounced on an antique shawl and wrapped herself in it. She said she wanted it to remember him by; but there was a fuck-you in her voice. It occurred to me that Patrick's family had all been slightly afraid of him. He had consistently excluded and offended them. If any one of us had turned up while Patrick was alive, he would probably have hidden in one of the upstairs rooms and not bothered coming down. And people had grown fearful of him. By returning to the house, by gawping at it like tourists, by taking his things – and by the end of the day, everyone had something – his family were saying: You don't scare us any more. But it was a boast: they were slightly jumpy – a group of children striking poses by a dead tiger.

Patrick's study took up one end of the top floor of the house. The ceiling was open to the eaves and a library ladder on casters led up to a gallery where Patrick kept his reference volumes. I pulled out books in no particular order: something about knots, one on seamanship, another on phrenology, an Esperanto grammar.

A forbidding wall of black filing cabinets lined one side of the lower room – these held his record collection. Beside them, a hatch in the floor concealed a narrow set of stairs down to the kitchen.

I sat on Patrick's leather swivel chair and admired the view.

The room's only windows faced north. A ribbon of sea was visible glittering beyond the dark band of trees. Through a telescope, the surface of the ocean seemed to snap and ripple like a flag in the wind. Direct sunlight rarely entered the room. It was cool and dim, like a cavern, or a wine cellar, and haunted with the smell of books and wood. A potbellied stove warmed the study in winter.

Snatches of conversation drifted up from the gathering beneath the window.

What I was hoping to find was a fountain pen. I had a picture of myself back in London, keeping a diary and using a relic of Patrick's life to record the minutiae of mine, but the only objects on top of the desk were a row of green box files and a human skull with pencils in its noseholes.

The leather chair creaked and yawed back as I leaned over to open the drawers. I looked in a couple – with the prickling selfconsciousness of a man walking knowingly into the ladies' toilets. They held only stationery and bundled letters.

I slipped a box of Dixon Ticonderogas into my jacket pocket and almost as an afterthought added two small notebooks – nice ones, with creamy pages and all-weather covers. The pencils rattled in my pocket as I went downstairs: a faint noise like the misgivings of my feeble conscience.

I left the house to get away from the funeral party milling around the garden and walked down the wooden boardwalk over the sand dunes towards the beach. The wind was blowing hard. The tips of the dune grass had bent over and inscribed hieroglyphs in the sand around them. I stepped onto the beach and sank in up to my ankles, so I took off my shoes and socks and walked down to the water barefoot. The sea was as green and sweet as peppermint mouthwash – and so cold it made the bones in my feet ache. I had the whole beach to myself – not unusual there even in summer. The only person I could see

was a man throwing a Frisbee for his dog to retrieve from the
tiny waves which burbled up the beach, and he was half a mile
away, beyond the jetty of black rocks that marked the end of
Patrick's patch of sand dunes. Much farther out, a fisherman
in a small boat with an outboard motor was checking lobster
pots. For all the strangeness of his life and death, Patrick
really hadn't had it too bad here, I was thinking.

But my father seemed to think otherwise. I could hear his
voice booming over the garden as I walked back up to the
house.

'I would never use the word "failure" of anyone,' he was
saying. 'I don't consider that to apply to him at all. He lacked
purpose. You know what he lacked? You really want to know
what he lacked? He lacked hunger.'

'Maybe you're right,' said Judith. 'It just makes me so sad
to think of him here on his own. I'd get so lonesome. Do you
think we let him down?'

'None of *us* let him down,' my father said.

I had my shoes in my hand. The spiky lawn was prickling
the soles of my bare feet. 'Post-mortem?' I said, cheerily.

A wary look came over my father's face, but he said nothing.

I caught the ferry back to the mainland that evening. I
almost regretted leaving when I looked behind us and saw the
lights of the harbour being eclipsed by the black edge of the
horizon. I felt like I was saying goodbye to it for ever. I
decided then that that was the reason I had come. That had
been the meaning of my climacteric. The last person in my
family that meant anything to me had died. There was no one
left for me in this country of a quarter of a billion people. I
was heading back to my poky flat on my own draughty island
and I would be staying there until my three-score years and
ten were up. So long, New World.

It suddenly got very cold. I went below to get out of the
wind and on one of the lower decks I bumped into Patrick's
Latvian roommate from law school, Edgar Huvas, who mistook

me for Vivian. I remembered him vaguely from his summer visits. He had a photographic memory and an obsession with women's necks, and looked like the Pillsbury doughboy. He had never been invited back after an incident in a clam bar where he tried to lick the waitress's neck as she leaned over to take his plate.

I offered him a lift to Providence, thinking I could use the company and that maybe he had anecdotes about Patrick's law-school days, but he fell asleep after ten minutes and only woke when I pulled up at the bus station. He shook my hand limply. 'Thanks, Vivian,' he said. I couldn't be bothered to correct him. He took the carrier bag containing the books he had just stolen from Patrick's library and ambled off to buy his ticket. I watched him leave. I thought about stopping in New Haven for a pizza, but in the end decided to see if I could catch an earlier flight to London, so I drove nonstop to Newark.

I was starving by the time we took off. I ate and enjoyed the in-flight meal: all of it – wrinkly roll, jaundiced salad, and trifle. I wondered if that was a sign of age. Once upon a time just the smell of aeroplane food had made me want to puke.

After the meal the cabin crew dimmed the lights for our three-hour parody of a good night's sleep. The rushing Atlantic wind outside the aircraft made me feel chilly so I got my jacket from the overhead rack and took out the clanking box of pencils and the pair of notebooks I had picked up about a thousand miles before.

Flicking through them, I saw that only one was completely blank. The other was about a third used. Patrick had started writing in the back of it. It began in bursts: notes at first, a word, a squiggle, a crossing-out, then sentences and whole paragraphs which ran through the book in reverse like pages of Arabic. It looked as though Patrick had intended to write a line or two and then been hijacked by an onrush of inspiration. About three pages in, it began to flow pretty much uninter-ruptedly. The angle of the handwriting altered where the velocity and pressure of the pen had increased – the way an animal running compresses its body for speed. Letters blurred together, words were skipped; some of the paragraphs sprouted thought balloons as though Patrick were marking places that he wanted to return to and amplify.

It was only a fragment: the beginning of a love story written in a pastiche of nineteenth-century prose, but beneath the formal pseudo-Victorian writing, I seemed to catch the inflections of a real voice – one that I hadn't heard for almost twenty years. 'More than fifty years have passed', it began, 'since the day I arrived in the capital by post-chaise, and watched the Thames, shirred like a matron's bustle, foaming into ribbons of lace beneath the arches of London Bridge.'

THREE

———

MORE THAN fifty years have passed since the day I arrived in the capital by post-chaise and watched the Thames, shirred like a matron's bustle, foaming into ribbons of lace beneath the arches of London Bridge. Old age, while dimming every useful faculty, has left the colours of that memory untouched. In the late afternoon light, the river shone as though gilded with the same aureate brush that seemed poised to draw the lineaments of my own future.

It was ten years after the Mutiny, the old East India Company had been wound up, and a new generation of gentlemen administrators were selected by competitive examinations to carry on its work. Some of them were bindlestiffs, slack-jawed second sons of country parsons who were doomed to wither like earthworms in the tropics. Others were cads of the old school: straitened Beau Brummel types, without the money to be malcontents. They oozed upwards in the service, their heads pomaded with smarm, their sharp elbows working like paddles on a riverboat. But a few young men were drawn by a sense of duty: a word which wasn't then pronounced as though it savoured of rotten cheese. They believed their vocation was to carry out the Queen's command, to secure the country's prosperity, to promote works of public utility among her dominions. Was it sanctimony? Or arrogance? Or wide-eyed hopefulness? Choose wisely and absolve me, reader. I was one of them.

The day following my arrival I walked through the garboil of West End streets to a clerk-infested antechamber on Whitehall. A certain Mr Ricketts came to fetch me before luncheon. As his head peeped around the door, one of his eyes was cast ceilingwards in a manner that might have signified a reflective mood in its owner, were the other not beadily roving up and down my person.

'Bad news for you, I'm afraid, young man,' he said, when I had taken my seat in his office.

'Bad news?'

'We had you down for a politico in the Rajputana, but rather a rum state of affairs have come to light in the district where you was to have been sent. Smoked out a circle of aspiring mutineers. Seems one of them broke cover about a week before it was supposed to happen. We stamped down hard on it, of course. Hanged some, spared others, blew the ringleaders out of cannons. But all in all, matters stand somewhat ticklish. It's not the place to break in new blood. We're of a mind that it would be best for you to hang fire. Cool your heels in London for a couple of months, while we sort out another posting. A young chap like yourself can't have any objections to that.'

All through this little peroration, his left eye was busily absorbed in the pattern on the ceiling while the right remained fixed upon me. It gave the impression that Mr Ricketts' mental processes were so valuable, he could only expend 50 per cent of them on anything in his immediate vicinity; the remaining capacity being reserved, presumably, for calculations on behalf of Her Majesty's government.

I told him that notwithstanding my eagerness to commence my service, I would bow to the wiser counsel of my superiors.

'Very good,' he murmured, and as a signal that the interview was at an end, his right eye snapped downwards onto the paper in front of him, while the left continued staring upwards, as though the reserved part of his cerebellum was devising further torments for the contumacious Hindoo regiments.

His counsel had provoked in me an opposite response to the one intended: it inflamed my enthusiasm to embark immediately. But since there was nothing to be done, I took rooms in Dover Street and passed four pleasant months in the capital.

It was during this time that I made the acquaintance of a young woman called Serena Eden. [*Patrick had tried and rejected several equally unlikely alternatives including Ethel Younghusband, Cissy Spanks and Dara Nightshade, but his final choice obviously pleased him − DM.*] O was ever human beauty so aptly named! In her name and in the deep, hurt ebony of her lustrous eyes she carried the very echo of lost paradise. Her name was beautiful, but less beautiful than she: she was a fawn, a nymph, an amaranth, a sacred flower.

She was an American from Louisiana and so dark-skinned that unkind speculation murmured of African forebears and a bend sinister in her family crest. It was envy. Her skin was the gold of the Scythians; gold that put gold to shame. And what shall I write of her eyes? Her black eyes, romany black, black of the rarest jade, the slow, inevitable black of death itself before which every man stands powerless.

Her father had sent her to London to complete her education − though it seems unlikely he had in mind the scandalous liaisons with older men, or the appetite for gambling, or the dozen other qualities uncharacteristic of her sex that made her the object of rumour in the circles in which we moved.

It was with some little apprehensiveness that I introduced myself to her during the interval of a comic operetta. I had been relieved of my virginity in a perfunctory encounter with a prostitute in a doorway off

Air Street during one of the long vacations, but my experience of women my own age and class was narrow.

Miss Eden's sloe-eyed glance initially reduced me to a nervous mumbling, but gradually my confidence asserted itself in sallies of wit. At the commencement of the second act, I pressed her hand and invited her to an exhibition of paintings by my unfortunate friend Doriment, who was then enjoying growing celebrity and showed no signs of the madness that was to unhinge him in his later years.

On the appointed day, I arrived early and spent twenty minutes pacing up and down on the pavement and adjusting my tie in the window of a wine merchant's facing the gallery. She alighted from her carriage without a chaperone and greeted me with a quip and a kiss.

I escorted her into the exhibition and followed her as though hovering on winged feet. Something fast and urgent swept me along with an exquisite motion.

I cannot remember one word that she and I said to each other, though we were never silent. A deeper communication was conducted with looks, the inclination of a head, the light pressure of her hand, and the air between us seemed to hum with invisible signification like the wires of a telegraph.

Or so I hoped. The counterpart to my elation was a profound doubt that she held my feelings in any but the lightest regard. She loves me; she loves me not: nothing was ever still, it was either budding or dying: the systole and diastole of some distant heart, filling with hope and then being emptied of it. It was divine; it was infernal.

I courted her for weeks. I knew she enjoyed my company, but all the time we sparred with and teased one another, I could not guess if her true feelings went any deeper. I was one of a number of young and not-so-young men, hopefully besieging her with their attentions. They would be camped in the drawing room of the family she lived with, which included a less well-favoured daughter of about Serena's age called Alice, and compete for the meagre privileges of opening a door for her, carrying her needlework, or reading to her from the newspaper.

Having made some initial progress with her at Doriment's exhibition, I became embroiled in this interminable siege along with her other suitors, each of whom seemed less concerned with advancing his own cause than ensuring that no one else had the opportunity to advance his.

It was while things stood at this impasse that I finally received a communication from Mr Ricketts. He gave me to understand that my eventual posting would not now be to the north of the country, but to one of the districts in the south. I forbore from pointing out the irony of this decision. Alongside two hundred other aspiring administrators, I had sat two weeks of examinations in a hall in Burlington House. (One of the invigilators later informed me, in confidence, that my marks were among the highest ever attained.) [*Patrick appears to have gone back to this section at a later date and deleted the word 'among' – DM.*] Alone of all the candidates, I had offered papers in Punjabi and Urdu. Now, by the wayward logic that I would find characteristic of my employment in the dominions, I was being despatched to the south of the subcontinent, where my painstakingly acquired languages would be as useful to me as Croat, or the secret tongue of Euskaadi.

Undaunted, I booked my passage, reacquainted myself with Sanskrit grammar and bought primers in Tamil, Telugu and Malayalam. I also amassed a small library for the crossing, comprising histories of the region, several volumes on native custom, and a general work on hydrology.

Accordingly, I spent less time in my futile courtship of Miss Eden and was more often to be found at home, studying (or rather, trying to study) my primers. Even then I found myself abstracted, unable to concentrate on anything but learning the endearments in my new languages that I lacked the courage to say in English. In my Telugu grammar, the use of the optative was explained by means of an idiomatic expression that compared a woman's breath to the scent of persimmons. I copied this out in the original and sent it to Serena with my kindest regards. At least it was a declaration of sorts, if not one she would be able to understand.

The next time I visited her for tea, there were two suitors and myself. I felt disinclined for the witty small talk that passed among that circle for conversation and directed most of my attentions towards Alice, who was a kindly young bluestocking with whom I was to conduct a correspondence two decades later while researching a – needless to say – unfinished monograph on the life cycle of the sand fly.

At the end of the afternoon, I rose to leave. Serena was playing cards with her two besiegers, who were undoubtedly glad to have seen me off. She had made no allusion to the note I had sent her, but as I said goodbye, she shot me a look so full of *something* that I can see her dark eyes now, as though they were imprinted upon my brain as on a daguerreotype. What she meant by that look, however, was as incomprehensible to me as my Telugu note must have been to her.

I had left the house and was walking down the glass-covered portico that led away from its front door when her low voice halted me. She called out my name.

I turned round: the vestigial wings on my ankles gave a flutter and raised me two inches above the pavement.

'Stop bothering me,' she said, dark fire flashing from her eyes.

'Bothering you?' My voice was the merest whisper. The wings on my heels had become a pair of rusty dumb-bells.

'I'm very impressionable,' she said, adding a reprise of the look she had offered me over the playing cards. 'Please don't trifle with me.' My feet had wings once more.

'I believe that if you had any inkling of my true feelings for you, you would not make that accusation,' I said.

'I hardly know you,' she murmured.

'That is little to be wondered at. The company here is not congenial to our deeper acquaintance. If you might be persuaded to meet me on more intimate terms . . . At my rooms, perhaps, for tea?'

'Yes,' she said, with a look that has no verbal equivalent in any language known to me, but which contained admixtures of love and

longing, and was sharpened by a sense that she was struggling to over-
bear the reluctant voice of her conscience.

She came to tea with me on the hottest afternoon of the hottest
summer of any I have known in a city I have since come to know well.
I had opened every window to its fullest extent and placed vases of iced
water around my rooms in a vain attempt to reduce the temperature.

The stiff fabric of my collar and cuffs restricted the flow of blood
through my body, causing my suppressed pulse to throb in my neck and
wrists. I felt the discomfort of the scold in the pillory, of the innkeeper
condemned to the stocks for watering his beer. My tongue clave to the
roof of my mouth. The china cup chattered in its saucer as I passed it to
her with a trembling hand. She steadied mine with hers, placed the cup
on an open dictionary, then led me to my bedroom. I was her first lover.

In all its technical aspects, the act was the same as my initiation in
that doorway in Air Street, but then two people may both be said to
have spent time in France when one has had rats for company in the
donjon of the Chateau d'Yf, while the other has been drinking
Sauternes with his feet in a stream at the edge of a field of lavender.

These were not the jejune ecstasies of pimpled youth. We led one
another to the winding heart of the eternal rose itself. O Mnemosyne,
paint for me once more the fine bone china of her skin that afternoon
with its film of perspiration; the wetness of her parted lips; the pungent
shag tobacco of her nether hair.

And then?

The time until my departure for India was ebbing like the tide that
would float my ship out of its harbour. I surrendered to this larger current. Out of fear? Perhaps. It was impossible for me to stay. I lacked the
passionate courage, I lacked the determination to please myself, I lacked
the knowledge of my own heart that would have made me a different
man and might have granted me a different fate.

In age, I have come to share the fatalism of the Mussulmans, to
believe, as they do, that the tortuous paths of each man's destiny have
been inscribed since Creation in the infinite Book of the Almighty. On

its secret pages are written the place of each man's birth, the travails of his life, the names of his enemies, the number of his children, the manner and the hour appointed for his death. Each year I pass in ignorance the future anniversary of my final day. I offer prayers to the infinite mercy of this Creator, who spares us the knowledge of our destinies, who, in denying us choice, takes upon Himself the authorship of our sins. *Inshallah*

That I would be the best scholar of my generation; that I would be distracted by indolence, that I would be parted from my lover, that I would never marry, never raise children – these were preordained, shards of a future that lay in wait for me, to be lifted from the dust year by year and fitted together like an Etruscan jar.

Serena and I made no plans; we did not discuss our future. We lived each moment together as though nothing could impinge on our happiness. And then on my last night in London, she met me at the dock. The yellow moon was snagged in the rigging of a tea-clipper.

'I would stay if you asked me,' I told her.

Her stiff bonnet shaded her face. 'I think you and I both know', she said coldly, 'that I'm not the kind of girl who *asks* for anything.'

When I said farewell, she showed no emotion, but promised to write to me.

The torturers of the Ottoman Caliphate pride themselves on prolonging a man's suffering by impaling him on a sword in such a way as to cause no mortal injury. I felt this pain then: as though a rapier had been run expertly through my innards. I stayed in my cabin and wept for two days.

I have to be truthful, some part of me was glad to be separated from her: the same part that exults in solitude and the smoky light of a solitary winter evening. It has always been easier to follow this unilateral instinct, and I can see now that the pattern of my life (I am writing this alone, in an empty house, in silence) owes everything to it.

I arrived in Bombay after a journey of six weeks to find letters from Serena that had preceded me on the outward voyage of a faster ship.

Her tone was warm but there was no mention of the intimacies we had enjoyed. She offered me her cordial regards.

I was poised on the edge of a strange continent, wondering inwardly whether to go on or go back. But as the weeks and miles had passed between us, the draw of my beloved had grown correspondingly weaker. At the very least, I reasoned, I must fulfil the minimum requirements of my contracted service.

I travelled by train to the eastern city of Madras to take up my post. It was a diagonal journey across the width of the subcontinent. I could see from the outset two Indias. The India I saw by day was full of the familiar reassurances of a life I knew well, but the India of dusk, of orange light settling across the flat plains behind the western ghats, the silhouettes of the spiky palmyras, was like another continent, vast and indifferent to our presence.

Those of my countrymen with whom I was stationed were uncongenial company. Belonging for the most part to the middle-ranking classes, they were willing to undergo the rigours of life in the tropics because the recompense was a pantomime of social advancement. They held dismal dinner parties where we sweltered in formal attire and ate approximations of our national dishes. Pig-sticking, whist and sleeping with prostitutes constituted the whole of their interest in their new surroundings. Sedulous in prosecuting the smallest details of their offices, they lacked the perspicacity to see the comedy of British rule in India. Ours was the folly of the cockerel who takes credit for sunrise; the vanity of the swimmer in the Thames who claims he controls the tides because they rise and fall as he does.

A map of India hung above my commode. I fell ill with malaria and in my fevered dreams confounded the shape of the country with the musky triangle of my forsworn lover.

FOUR

THE PASSAGE ENDED more suddenly than it had begun: a full stop after the last sentence and then nothing. I read it twice more on the flight, wondering who the unnamed 'I' was supposed to be. The character reminded me of a redoubtable Victorian explorer – a Burton, or a Livingstone – but he also resembled Patrick in various ways: the compulsive need for solitude, the self-advertising eggheadedness. He was an emotional retard too, which made me think of my father.

As prose, it wasn't my cup of tea. The high style leaves me cold – invocations to the muses and all that stagey dialogue. Was 'pungent shag tobacco of her nether hair' supposed to be a turn-on? It sounded like a description of the fur on a chimpanzee.

One small detail pleased me especially, though: that unfinished monograph. When I was at school I did a project on the life cycle of the house fly. I was flattered to think that this fact had somehow stuck in Patrick's brain. House fly, sand fly – it came to the same thing.

What struck me most about the story was Miss Eden. It seemed possible that she was a real person, a fancy-dress version of a woman Patrick had once been in love with. Her reply on the dock when the narrator makes his mealymouthed offer to stay and marry her – that sounded like something someone might have really said.

Compared with the little that was revealed about her – that she's beautiful, passionate, and brave enough to defy convention – the hero came off pretty badly. It's not clear why he's so wedded to the idea of leaving for India. Doesn't he see the risks Serena's taken for his sake? He won't stay unless she demands it, which is almost as odd and anachronistic as her making the first move in the seduction. There was something disingenuous about the narrator: this old chap who is haunted by a memory of a woman he says he wanted, but whom he gave up in favour of his job; a man who makes a foolish decision and can't admit it, who passes the buck on to the Almighty. There was something pathetic and very human, too, about his making a mistake and then disclaiming all responsibility for it.

Of course, it's possible that the narrator was going to come to his senses, jack in his job in India, and go back to the woman who loved him. But Patrick's narrator seemed to be one of those people who are in love with the idea of love. I wondered if he would have written about Miss Eden in the same way if they had been living together for ten years and the pungent shag tobacco of her nether hair was turning up on his face soap.

Overall, I didn't know what to make of it. Notes for a novel? A short story? A meaningless five-finger exercise? Or something else entirely?

Once when I was eight Patrick and I fell out over a game of Frisbee. My grandfather had given him a tin for cigarette butts that hung from a stake on the lawn. It was an ugly thing Grandpa had salvaged from the dump. My cousins had the idea of seeing who could knock it off with a Frisbee. No one could hit it and the game was losing its momentum when Patrick arrived, put fifty dollars in the tin and squatted behind the target like a catcher at home plate.

He would have been thirty-six, tall and dashing, every inch the successful writer. It had been a while since the *Peanut Gatherers*, but not yet an inexplicably long time. His hair was collar length, sort of late Beatles. He was tanned, solid, not yet balding, not yet jowly. He would have had owlish dark glasses, a T-shirt, black corduroys. Lydia was with him. The extravagant gesture with the money was probably intended to impress her.

We, the children, went insane with greed, flinging the Frisbee desperately at the tin from the line we had made with our shirts twenty or thirty yards away. The moment when I threw the Frisbee and knocked the butt-tin off the stake has a special exhibition space dedicated to it in my mental museum. I can enter it at will and poke around the related exhibits: the basketball boots I wore that summer, my brother's huge black swimming goggles that made him look like a pioneer aviator, the dried-up minnow from a pair my cousin kicked on to a sandbar and let me keep. But the mainstay of this gallery is a recording of the moment when the Frisbee struck the can with a *thunk!* From various angles, I can watch my cousins charge forward to ransack its contents while I, out of my wits with greed and overexcitement, fall sobbing to the grass. Patrick scoops up the money before anyone else can get to it and insists that he knocked off the butt-tin as he caught the Frisbee behind it. A replay of the action contradicts him: he is a foot away from the can as the Frisbee strikes it, again, and again, and again.

To appease me, Patrick constructed a paper chase that led to some wholly unimpressive bribe. But the paper chase itself was a revelation. We insisted he create more. Once, each clue yielded a fragment of a map, drawn in brown ink and aged with the soot of a candle flame. Others were based on pictures, or riddles. 'You've looked north, you've looked south, Now look for the clue in the genius's mouth' led memorably to a wad of paper that Patrick could barely conceal in his cheek for giggling.

Vivian and I even made paper chases for each other: ordeals of fifty clues that involved climbing trees and struggling through thickets of brambles. The pleasure was all in the anticipation. The treasure – candy, a book, a baseball glove – was discovered with a sense of deflation. My brother said he wished there was a paper chase where the reward was a paper chase. To me, that thought was nightmarish, as unacceptable as infinity or the endlessly repeating music of a fevered dream.

I couldn't persuade myself that what I had found in Patrick's notebook was meaningless. It seemed like a clue, if not one that would lead tidily to a Tootsie roll or a Three Musketeers bar. For a while, it fascinated me. I made various resolutions to find out more and went as far as ringing up the London Library until the inertia of my old routine drew me back in. The memory of Ionia grew very faint.

I doubt I would have thought about the story again, but two weeks after I got back, my father left a message on my answering machine asking me to call him. I was surprised. We had hardly exchanged a dozen words during my visit, which seemed to suit both of us, and I kept him waiting a few days on principle. When I finally rang him, he told me, in a more than usually resonant voice, that I was the chief beneficiary of Patrick's will.

FIVE

PATRICK HADN'T FORGOTTEN the rest of his family: on the contrary, his will had been drawn up with a thoroughness that made me think it was the final instrument of his anger against them. Patrick had the paranoiac's gift of investing everything with significance. His other legacies were small and sardonic: a pasta machine for an overweight sister (Judith); the complete works of Frederick Rolfe for an illiterate and vulgar niece (Tricia); a mechanical penny-bank for my father, whom Patrick had always considered covetous. He had amended the document constantly, according to his persecution mania, and whom he considered to be his current enemies.

It seemed improbable that he would choose me to be his chief beneficiary. I felt a little like that horse that Caligula appointed to the Senate. But there was a crazy logic to it, too.

In a way, I was the only person he could have chosen. The inheritance was mine by default. There was no one else.

The last thing in the world that Patrick wanted was for his family to benefit from his death. One way and another, he had fallen out with all of them, alienating them over the years with stinging letters or cold silences. He suffered from the worst kind of paranoia – the kind that has a firm basis in reality. Of course people talked about him behind his back. Of course people avoided him. Of course people were afraid of him – to have any dealings with him whatsoever was to risk coming into conflict with him. And the most trivial disputes could engender letters so offensive that the insults would be burned on to your consciousness for ever. 'You have all the attributes of a dog except fidelity,' he wrote to an ex-girlfriend. He once told my kindly Aunt Judith she was a two-hundred-pound puff adder.

I, in my dull job, neither rich nor poor, three thousand miles of ocean away, barely registered in his consciousness. I just hadn't had the opportunity to get on his wrong side. I flattered myself that he might have been inspired by some fond memories from fifteen or twenty years earlier, but I knew that most of the arguments in my favour had been negative ones: it wasn't who I was that mattered to Patrick, but who I wasn't. Leaving the estate to me was bound to antagonise the whole family.

The terms of the will were strange, I suppose, but it would have been stranger still for them to have been normal. I had only been granted a life estate in Patrick's house, its contents (apart from the things he'd left to his family), and the ten acres of lawn, marsh and sand dune that it perched on, along Ionia's eastern shore. It was a condition of the will that the contents of the house were not to be dispersed, and the building itself was to be maintained as it had been in his life. To accomplish this, Patrick had created a trust which would remain the real owner of all his possessions. The trustees would oversee the property, making sure I didn't do anything that would conflict with Patrick's wishes, and looking after the money invested for its maintenance. If they thought I was failing to meet the conditions set down by my uncle, they were to assume control of the property and hand it over to a charity that ran rest homes for old churchmen. If I died intestate (it did strike me as odd that my uncle had made contingency plans for my death as well as his own), the estate reverted to the same charity.

After the initial excitement of the bequest, it was disappointing to realise that it was all hedged about with conditions. It was very typical of my family: I couldn't see the gift for the strings. Patrick's money was all tied to the maintenance of the house – which I couldn't sell. Unless I went to live there, my life would change very little. My inheritance wasn't going to provide me with an income. The trustees would release money if tiles blew off the roof of the house on Ionia, but not a penny would be available for me to redecorate my flat in Clapham. So that was that. I could forget about the casinos of the Riviera, endowing lectureships, and acquiring a stable of polo ponies. In all my fantasies of sudden wealth, I had imagined that the principal feeling would be one of enormous freedom. But the news of the inheritance hadn't changed my life at all. My life was exactly the same. The only difference was that now I had an alternative: it came down to a straight choice – my life or Patrick's.

On one of my first night shifts after the phone call from my father, Wendy asked me to put together an item about a famine in Indonesia. I got the research department to send me over a whole screed of articles about the place.

At two o'clock in the morning, I was sitting in the tea bar reading about the Stone Age tribes who lived in the mountains of New Guinea. One of the articles was lamenting the decline of their culture, and saying that they simply weren't equipped for the brutal struggle that we accept as twentieth-century living. They were useless workers: after five minutes of digging a ditch, they would just get bored and go off for a smoke and a cup of tea. They wore penis sheaths and composed epic insult poems in blank verse. They conducted mock battles with one another. The apparent strangeness of their lives started me thinking about the conventions of my own tribe. What would an ethnographer say about me?

I defied nature by working at night. I made myself dyspeptic over fictional deadlines. I hoarded money. I was postponing life until I felt I'd earned enough to deserve it. I was very superstitious, believing my destiny to be controlled by a priestly class called Management. I lived alone.

I realised that although I felt bitter about life, I had experienced only a small corner of it. It was like rubbishing the whole of Indian cuisine on the evidence of the chicken tikka sandwich I'd just bought from the Headlines Tea Bar.

On the tube home, I could feel the decision to leave ripening inside me. The woman opposite me was sniffling from a cold and reading a voluminous guidebook to India. Then, somehow, a moth got into the train through one of the windows. It fluttered along the length of the carriage like a scrap of paper, unnoticed, except by me, and then exited through a window farther down the train into the blackness of the tunnel beyond.

I got home and switched on the television to see the morning news, half expecting my decision to be announced. My shoes had been bothering me on the journey home, so I slipped them off and tipped them out on the carpet, where each one left a tiny pile of golden sand.

SIX

MY IMMEDIATE FAMILY were reverse migrants – Americans who left the New World for the Old, and promptly became a kind of parody of Englishness. Americans like them created the idea of shopping-mall Europe: the belief that the continent is actually a collection of themed boutiques where you go to buy old furniture and stinky cheeses, and pick up an order of culture on the side.

I don't know how they chose our names. The family joke is that Damien March sounds like a private detective and Vivian March sounds like a hairdresser.

Dad became a born-again Englishman. He worked in London for a large corporate law firm, had shirts made at Savile Row, sent my brother and me to a boarding school, and drove a second-hand Bentley. At the same time, neither of my parents let go of America completely. My mother, a mid-westerner who grew up on a farm, was never completely happy in England, but my father had more complex reasons for remaining attached to his homeland.

In a way, Dad could only be properly English in America, because in England, his kind of Englishness barely existed. Perhaps there is somewhere in the British Isles where people have afternoon tea, bag grouse and talk in Lord Haw-Haw accents, but it wasn't in Wandsworth, SW18. Undoubtedly, my father wouldn't have been welcome in such a place; but this did not stop him from searching. Some weekends, he would take train journeys to destinations on the strength of the placename alone: Virginia Water and Strawberry Hill were two that seemed to promise the idyll he was after. But he never found it, and neither did his small group of expatriate friends who came over occasionally to smoke pipes and brag about their kids' schools.

America offered my father a kind of consolation. There, he was free to play cricket on the spiky grass of the house we rented near Provincetown each year; he could serve afternoon tea with cinnamon toast; and go up and down Scorton Creek in a punt he had had made in Maine and which he laboriously put in storage at the end of every summer. He was free to do these things without fear of ridicule. One of our neighbours on the Cape once said my father was 'as English as an English muffin'. This captures him exactly: so-called English muffins, as my father liked to point out, are unknown in England.

So, each summer for about fifteen years, we would all go back to America for six weeks. My father would take an enormous suitcase of work, which he would do in the mornings. Vivian and I would squabble, read, drink Hershey's chocolate milk and try to avoid the local children, who thought we were affected and stuck-up. Well, we were.

We didn't really fit in, and we weren't good at making friends, and it seemed more sensible to make a virtue out of our idiosyncrasies than to try to go against them. We had crew cuts (wiffles, they called them) when all the other boys had outgrown Tudor bowl cuts like Henry V's. They played Pong at Pucci Pizza; we went on mapping expeditions in the sand dunes at Truro, camping there for up to a week. I insisted on military discipline from Vivian, who was the only rank-and-file soldier in our army of two. By the end of seven days, we had sand in our food, our toothpaste, and our underwear; peeling sunburns; and a map that was redundant as soon as the ink had dried on it. The wind and the weather remould those sand dunes constantly.

My father encouraged this kind of behaviour. He took pride in our bizarre achievements. My brother learned the Latin names for all the local birds. Aged eleven, I lugged law textbooks to the family clambakes and told them I was going to be a barrister. I think our relatives thought all English people were like us.

Of course, all Vivian and I really wanted was cable television like everyone else had, and to be taken to the go-carts and the trampolines, but my father frowned on all that sort of thing, so we did too. We mocked our cousins behind their backs for their orthodontic braces, their annual fads, their Cabbage Patch dolls and baseball cards. And secretly we craved most of the vulgar things we turned up our noses at.

It was an odd life. On holiday in America we clung to our Englishness, and pretended to be upset when we visited Ionia and Uncle Patrick made fun of the Queen and said that all Englishmen carried handbags. In England, we boasted about America, and how many kinds of cereal there were and how many different television channels – even though we could get none of them on the black-and-white television at the rental house that had no outside aerial. But in neither country did we feel at home. It always makes me think of Aesop's fable about the war between the animals and the birds, in which the bat tried to pass himself off as a friend to each side, and ended up shunned by both.

My fondest memories of all those years are the few con-
nected with my uncle. Patrick, the Frisbee incident aside, was
a kind man and free of the self-lacerating regimes that Dad
imposed on himself. He ate ice cream, abhorred long walks,
watched television in bed in the afternoon, and put away heroic
quantities of fried dough at the Barnstable County Fair each
year. At least, that's how I remembered him. Of course he had
a darker side, but he never showed it to us. For me and
Vivian, he was the quintessential eccentric uncle: funny, prone
to strange enthusiasms, childless, childish. And he had the
capacity to bring out similar qualities in my father, who was
two years younger: the same age difference as between myself
and Vivian.

My mother died of ovarian cancer when I was six and a half,
an event which brought down the portcullis on my childhood.
She had been a healthy brake on my father's rampant
Anglophilia. Perhaps if she had lived I would have been an
American. She was less enthusiastic than my father about
living in Britain; she often complained about the weather, and
the rudeness of Londoners. She considered English plumbing
to be barely out of the age when the streets had open sewers
and the rich carried pomanders to protect their nostrils. When
my father reluctantly agreed to build her a house on a new
development in Sussex so we could leave London on the weekends, Mum insisted on having an American architect design it,
and even imported tile grout from America, because, she said,
it was more hard-wearing than the stuff English builders used.

There was barely a month between the diagnosis and her
death. I remember being taken to see her for the last time
when she was gravely ill in hospital. I sat on the side of her
bed and she said, 'Damien, your father is a very silly man.
Remember that, and love him anyway.'

My other vivid memory of her is of seeing her crying one
day by the kitchen window. When I asked her why, she said,
'There are some things little boys shouldn't know about.' I'm
still trying to figure out what she might have meant by that.

My father sold the house in Sussex soon after she died. He couldn't bear to stay there and be reminded of her. Anyway, I think a stately pile was more his cup of tea than a Sussex bungalow.

After Mum died, home became school and friends, and secondarily the detached house on the south London street where I grew up. But the visits to the States continued, and were a glimpse, every summer, into a glamorous parallel universe. We stepped off the plane in London at the end of each summer deaf from flying, and the accents of the immigration officials and cabbies grated, and going back to boarding school felt like beginning a stretch in Wandsworth Prison, which stood forbiddingly at the end of the Common and overlooked the garden centre and haunted my dreams. All the same, London was home.

There was little misery and no privation in our house. Perhaps there was a chilliness; perhaps Vivian and I suffered from the want of a mother. Well, we obviously did. But I can't say I noticed it then. Dad was a remote and rather austere figure – more so after my mother died – but he had enough money to pay for a succession of au pairs, whom we terrorised, and then to send us away to a school where we boarded even though it was barely five miles from home. Boarding school, with its unrelieved maleness, its emphasis on competition, and its intolerance of difference and sensitivity, was just an extension of my family life. I got teased about my father, who arrived for a parents' evening wearing plus-fours at a time when I was too small and insecure to laugh it off. But I toughened up, made friends and generally developed the false consciousness of adolescence that's quite as bad as the one your family foists on you.

A couple of teachers stand out from my schooldays. Herbert Chinn, who taught Classics, reportedly believed electricity was a fluid and put tape over the sockets each night, like that woman in the Thurber story, to prevent it leaking on to the carpet. Mr Hepplewhite, the physics master, announced to each class before he began the syllabus that he did not believe in molecules. He once spent an entire lesson showing us the correct way to fold a jacket. He wore silver sleeve holders and was obsessively tidy, but the backs of his shirts were full of holes. I stayed behind after one lesson and said: 'Mr Hepplewhite, if you don't believe in molecules, how do you explain everything?' He looked at me and said, 'Ah, March!' and then carried on with whatever he was doing. I wish I could say this bubble of benign madness protected him well into old age, but shockingly he was killed by a rent boy about five years after I left the school.

I was a mediocre student, although my father cherished the belief that both Vivian and I were highly talented. He had great hopes of our following him into the Law, which he managed to capitalise just by the way he said it. One of his fondest fantasies was to pretend that we had in fact already qualified as lawyers. It was flattering and touching, and I colluded in it when he discussed his business with us. 'I'd like to pick your legal brain on something, Damien,' he would say, and proceed to mystify me with juridical terminology, as though I were a forty-year-old lawyer, instead of a fourteen-year-old schoolboy struggling to achieve average marks in any of my subjects. 'I sure could use your mother's help on this one,' he would add sadly, although her understanding of corporate law had probably been only slightly more sophisticated than mine.

Looking back now, I think he was probably lonely, and thinking out loud, and trying to involve us in the only part of his life where he felt he had any competence. But that interpretation was beyond me then, and I felt ashamed of my father and almost protective towards him.

As a result, I had a secret life of vice which he was unaware of, involving cigarettes, drinking and futile excursions to West London to buy spliff. It all came painfully out into the open some time before my fifteenth birthday. One weekend, I was picked up by the police, drunk, at midnight, in Earl's Court station. The friend I was with had panicked and left me, passed out, on the platform. My father had to collect me from the police station in the middle of the night. I vaguely remember the dials of the dashboard doubling and quadrupling before my eyes.

The next day was one of the longest of my life. I was consumed with remorse, and even my tears had an alcoholic tang to them. My father didn't speak to me for two weeks. I don't think he had the first idea what to do, poor man.

Dad's solution to my waywardness was, even by his standards, spectacularly bad. He decided that he hadn't been setting enough of an example to me – that I needed to learn that hard work would bring results in my world as they did in his.

One weekend, I came home to find that Dad had started studying Latin with a tutor called Mr Sandford, an old boy of my school who can only have been about twenty-three and had a tiny blond moustache that looked like it should have been attached to a gerbil's arse. He insisted on addressing Vivian and me in Latin. If we bumped into him in the hall he would say: '*Salvete, pueri.*' And Vivian and I would always reply: 'All right, Mr Sandford,' like a pair of barrow boys.

I can only guess that Dad thought that the sight of him conjugating semi-deponent verbs would encourage me to work harder. He couldn't have been wronger. Around this time, I had to go back to the police station to receive a bollocking from one of the officers, who talked about 'boys with your opportunities' and the anxiety I was causing my father. He even brought up my mother's death; a manipulation that no one had been ruthless enough to try on me before. He made me feel that being middle class meant I had no right to be unhappy, so I assumed I wasn't.

In my opinion, this is a common fallacy. Middle-class people have paid for the relative safety of their lives by forfeiting the idea that their vicissitudes qualify as suffering. We are not supposed to be a wounded people. We are not cast in tragedies. We are cast in comedies and farces; we are found on running tracks with our silly blond wigs fluffed up by the wind beside us. There is no *Hamlet, Chartered Surveyor of Denmark*, no *Mr Lear*. A middle-class 'tragedy' is being run over wearing dirty underwear.

Real, raw life always seems to be somewhere else: in palaces or shantytowns, not among the clipped hedges of SW18. You can weep your heart out at the sight of the young princess's coffin being wheeled by on a gun carriage – even a pauper's grave is somehow full of pathos and terror. But I always had the impression that when middle-class people die, someone just slides us into a filing cabinet, and our silly bodies stink and decay and finally defeat a lifetime's attempts at hygiene.

But, let's face it, the human heart comes in a standard size. No one has a monopoly on misery. Obvious to you, perhaps; but the chief disaster of my life has been my inability to recognise when I was unhappy.

At some point, Dad really started to enjoy studying Latin. He was a much better student than I was. I wanted to be in a band, and get stoned and chase girls around west London. Dad was assiduous. He worked his way through the set texts, read up on Roman culture, and took Mr Sandford on a week's holiday to Pompeii, which I only avoided by deliberately giving myself food poisoning with a plateful of raw haddock.

My scholastic zeal waned in proportion as my father's waxed. And the upshot of all this was that, thanks to the intervention of Mr Sandford, Dad and I took Latin O-level together, in the gymnasium of my school; with Dad sitting at the desk in front of me: March, *pater*, and March, *filius*.

I remember the whole thing with an awful clarity. In two separate three-hour exams I watched my dad's head bowed over his desk and listened to his expensive fountain pen scratching away on the paper. In the final exam, he called the invigilator over to complain about an apparent misprint in the unseen translation, and the papers were taken away from us, and we had to wait forty-five minutes while it was established over the telephone that a misprint had indeed occurred and the erratum in question was chalked up on the blackboard.

The thing that etched it forever on my memory as a terrible

moment was the reaction of my fellow students, who treated me with a tender, kindly pity that hurt much more than any name I had been called in the preceding years.

Dad got an A in the exam and came second overall in the entire country. The boy who beat him was a nine-year-old prodigy from Scotland. I got an E.

The results were posted to us in America during the summer. Dad shot the cork from a magnum of champagne across the garden on the evening he heard the news. He commiserated with me, but to my eyes the arc of the cork seemed to inscribe the word 'parricide' in the night air. Or would have, had I learned enough Latin to know what it meant.

I did better in my other subjects, and tried to draw some comfort from the fact that the letter from the examination board which Mr Sandford forwarded to my dad, and which he exhibited casually on the dining table without seeming to draw attention to it, began: 'This remarkable young man . . .'; as though he were an inky-fingered schoolboy, instead of a middle-aged widower, with most of his life behind him.

'Dad's such a fucking horse's arse' was Vivian's reaction.

I toyed briefly with the idea of withdrawing from the economy of success and failure altogether, growing dreadlocks and going to live in a caravan. But instead, I changed schools, opting out of the private system and going to the local sixth-form college, where I discovered I wasn't as stupid as I'd thought. I went to university in Swansea, eventually, to do Soviet and East European Studies, which might have been some kind of Oedipal attack on my American heritage. I saw less and less of my father, who eventually gave up on London and moved to Italy, where he wrote law textbooks and was finally accepted as a bona fide Englishman. I spent two years after Swansea working in America, and came home to a job at the BBC, which seemed like the answer to all my prayers at the time, but over a number of years, it grew to remind me of my family, in the way that it seemed to be full of bright people competing for too little love and attention.

SEVEN

THERE IS A ROCK with a ledge worn into it at the end of the jetty that marks the boundary of the beach nearest to my uncle's house. When the sea is high, or rough, it's too dangerous to approach – a single wave could knock you senseless. But on a windless day, with the ocean as flat as the icing on a sponge cake, it is a perfect place to dive from. When my family was still on speaking terms with one another, we used to play here, in the summers when we visited Ionia.

The game we played was this: each of us had to jump off the rock and turn to catch a soccer ball before we crashed into the water. There were many variations: you could work in a spin or a somersault, or do it with two jumpers who had to pass the ball between them and then back to the thrower. It was the best game we had, and it was – not coincidentally – the only family game we played that lacked any sense of competition. We called it Bolder than Mandingo, because that was what you had to shout before you hit the water.

It was Patrick's idea to say it, and because of his Boston accent, and the obscurity of the phrase, and perhaps because of Patrick's obsession with hair loss (this was before the wig), Vivian and I thought we were saying 'Balder than Mandingo' as we leaped off the rock. But *Mandingo* was the title of a sixties novel about an interracial love affair, and 'bolder than *Mandingo*' a plaudit invented by some reviewer for another book.

Bolder than Mandingo became family shorthand for a leap into the unknown so I decided to write it on the invitations for the party I had before I left London for Ionia. Most of the guests thought it was a reference to a forgotten spaghetti Western, and my friend Stevo turned up in a bootlace tie.

My four-week notice period at the BBC had concluded the same day. It somehow reminded me of my last day at prep school, when I hung my tie on a lamppost on the way home in a moment of uncharacteristic spontaneity. Afterwards I dreamed about my dead mother telling me off and was racked by guilt and went back to retrieve it, the nylon stripes damp with rain. I probably still have the tie somewhere.

I was surprised how quickly the decision to leave my job had overtaken me. For a while, it had looked as though I was going to take a sabbatical, and leave a door open back into my old life at the BBC. But then I decided that after six months in Ionia, I would rather come back to London and start afresh than go back to a job I had grown to hate.

The possibility of change changed everything. The thought that I had no alternative was all that had kept me in my old life, and now that things could be different, they couldn't stay the same. I couldn't become a tribesman on Irian Jaya, or a Tatar horseman. But I could live as Patrick had lived. His will offered me that possibility. And his life seemed sufficiently different from mine to be the change I craved. By now, I felt too close to the idea of being free to contemplate anything else. It was that moment suspended between the rock and the ocean when you bunch your knees up and anticipate the cold shock of the water. It was too late to get back on the rock now. Bolder than Mandingo.

The rather complicated provisions of the inheritance had been simplified by the rumour network in the office. I had come into a fortune, the gossip went, so I was jetting off to start spending it. On my last day, one of the producers, a man called Derek Braddock, came up to me with a mock-quizzical expression on his face as I was clearing out my desk.

'Damien,' he said. 'Got a message for you, mate. Couldn't quite understand it.' He passed me one of the flimsy pieces of paper that we used for telephone messages. 'Bloke called Riley. Says he wants his life back.'

I looked at him for a moment. 'Life of Riley. Very good, Derek. You're wasted here.'

Derek chuckled like a moron. He had a pale and mumpy face – like a photograph of a Great War soldier. I thought: There's nothing more coercive than a bad joke.

Wendy had come up alongside him, with her hands behind her back. The dozen or so people in the office crowded around her while she made a short speech about what a pleasure it had been working with me and that I would always be welcomed back if the life of the idle rich ever got too much for me. It seemed churlish to contradict her, so I smiled and made a speech of my own about how much I'd enjoyed working there and how I'd be glad to see any of them on Ionia, if they didn't mind sleeping on the beach; just joking, they'd always be welcome.

One of the production assistants had gone out to buy sparkling wine in the lunch break and this was produced, along with a present and a card, amid much teasing about licence-payers' money and Producer Choice. The present was a book, a thoughtfully chosen anthology of writing about castaways which I made everyone sign. I felt a surge of affection for all of them, even Derek Braddock, whom I'd always found a pain. I thought to myself that even if work had replicated all the faults of my family, at least it had replicated some of its virtues too: the humour, the intelligence, the companionship. For the first time, I felt a sense of loss. For good or bad, the life I had made in London was something of my own, and I was leaving it behind. I was exchanging something real for something unreal. It suddenly seemed like a dangerous swap.

We went to the pub at five o'clock, a big, shabby crowd of us, looking conspicuously pale and also more awkward together outside the office. Derek Braddock bought an enormous round of drinks and clapped me on the back.

'You're a mystery man,' he said. 'Ten years I've known you and this is the first time we've had a drink together.'

'That's not true,' I told him. 'We had a drink after the US elections.' Secretly, I was rather flattered that Derek had spared my private life any thought at all.

'One drink in ten years! Oi, Wendy – he's a mystery man, isn't he?'

'I'm sure it was more than one drink,' I said.

'Damien is very . . . self-contained.' Wendy laughed. She looked much prettier outside work; her eyes were bright from drinking.

'You're making me self-conscious,' I said. 'Can't you wait until I've left to have this conversation?'

Derek paused before his pint of lager reached his lips. 'I've always wondered about your secret life,' he said.

'Secret life? I don't have one, Derek. I don't have a life. I go home to an empty flat.'

'What about that girlfriend of yours?'

I shook my head. 'Didn't work out.'

'Pity. She was a looker.' Derek took a sip of his drink and stared down at the floor, jingling the coins in his pocket with his spare hand. 'Well, then.'

I had never been able to dislike Derek properly since I had taken his notebook home one day instead of mine and found a brochure for a holiday home in Spain taped inside the front cover as though it was a talisman of another, better life. 'Wend your way along the road from Puerto Pollença, while the lights of the porch glimmer in the gloaming.' *Glimmer in the gloaming*: you knew that the copywriter who came up with that thought he was Gerard Manley Hopkins.

I gave the book back to him the next day without mentioning it, but I still felt he had shared a confidence with me, and I experienced a pang of guilt whenever I found myself thinking that he was an arsehole. I said, 'I'll miss you, Derek,' as a kind of penitence. Then he winked back at me as he swallowed his drink and squeezed my arm, and I felt marginally worse. I had an overpowering sense of all the small disappointments that wear you away over the years. I thought of work as a rhythm that marched Derek out of the house in the morning and back into his bed at night. And I remembered how quickly the employees in our department – men, particularly – died after retirement. Because that rhythm had gone, and it was too late for them to find another. Derek was about fifty-five; if he retired now, he would probably have two, three years at most, in which to wend his way back from Puerto Pollença in the gloaming. That was as much of the good life as his body would be able to take.

'Best of luck,' said Derek. 'It was nice knowing you – almost.'

I had to leave early because I had people arriving at nine. I felt miserable slipping away from my colleagues for the last time. Outside the pub it was raining, and I waited under its awning for a couple of minutes. I suppose the alcohol generated a false bonhomie, but looking back at them, flushed and laughing inside the pub, I felt strangely cut off from them. Derek was right; in the time I'd worked there, I hadn't got close to any of them. I think I just wasn't that good at making friends.

I had rented my flat through an agency on a six-month lease to a stockbroker called Platon Bakatin who strode around the place in his Gucci loafers, chatting in Russian on his mobile phone. He liked it, he said, but wanted me to redecorate and was sniffy about the furniture. I guessed that he wanted something more impressive than my worn-out sofa-bed and kilims. I thought of putting my stuff into storage, but it hardly seemed worth it, so I let a furniture dealer come round and take it all away for about seventy pounds. When he named his price I was initially reluctant. I remembered that Laura and I had bought one of the kilims on holiday in Turkey and I didn't want to part with it. Then I thought, Fuck it; and helped carry the furniture out to the van.

Repainted, the empty flat seemed like a stranger's when I got home to it. It was Platon's home now, I thought. His new sofa stood in the living room, still wrapped in plastic. There was an unfamiliar echo to my footsteps as I walked around the flat. All that was left of me were my clothes, a few crates of books, lamps, an old computer, my records, and me. And soon, all that would be gone. I felt like I was erasing my presence in the world.

It was odd how many people I ended up inviting to the party. The list of guests was a long one. There's a big discrepancy between the number of people you feel obliged to invite to a party, and the number of people you feel able to confide in when the sky falls on your head. At least there is in my case. Perhaps other people have a more healthy ratio between the two. I had invited a big crowd of craps who might or might not turn up. And I had invited my friends. More precisely, I had invited Stevo and Lloyd.

Stevo came early, full of effusiveness, and with half a bottle of vodka tucked into the pocket of his long smelly coat. He sat himself down on the crackling plastic sofa cover and started rolling a joint. He was crumbling bits of hash on to the tobacco when Lloyd arrived, straight from work, looking rumpled and tired, and collapsed on the seat next to him. 'Heather sends her apologies,' said Lloyd.

'What happened? Her broomstick break down again?' Stevo

spoke out of the corner of his mouth. He had his lips clamped around the joint while he frisked his pockets for the lighter that lay on the floor in front of him. 'By the way, Damien, mate, where are the honeys?'

'Did you say "honeys"?' Lloyd asked him, in a voice that managed to be both weary and incredulous.

'I most definitely did. Damien, where are they? You promised me pretty girls.'

I opened a bottle of sparkling wine. I had bought thirty-five, so there were just over ten for each of us. The evening had begun to take on the atmosphere of a doomed stag party. 'Get your laughing gear round that,' I said halfheartedly, handing them each a glass.

Stevo was not to be distracted from his theme. 'Seriously, Damien. Where are they?'

'What the fuck are you talking about, Stevo? Crisp, anyone?'

Lloyd took a bite of a crisp and said in a thoughtful and deliberate voice: 'I've come to the conclusion that you actually hate women.'

'Who, me?' I said.

'You probably do as well, but I was talking about Stevo.'

'Only the ones that won't shag me,' said Stevo, and he took an enormous inhalation of his joint. He let it out in little gasps and then offered Lloyd a puff.

Lloyd took the spliff but didn't put it to his lips. Instead, he passed it on to me. 'Here you go. Take some of Stevo's cold sores to your home in the New World.'

I turned up the music to drown out the two of them bickering and make it seem like there were more of us. I told myself that after two or three drinks, things wouldn't look so bad.

Lloyd lit a cigarette. 'What are you actually going to do when you get out there?'

I could tell Lloyd was doubtful about the wisdom of going. As we had all got older, caution had overwhelmed all his other characteristics. It was surprising if you had known him as long as

I had that this had emerged as his dominant trait, like the most
unlikely candidate in a thriller turning out to be the murderer.
But then two years ago, who would have thought Stevo would
become this raddled parody of a skirt-chasing hedonist?

'I don't know really. Read, paint . . .'

'I didn't know you could . . .'

'Paint? Not particularly well. That's not the point. It's just
a chance for a change. Things are going nowhere for me here.'

'I thought you enjoyed your job.'

'I don't know what gave you that idea.'

'Damien, is it okay if I use the phone?' said Stevo.

'Of course,' I said.

Lloyd sprawled back on the sofa and let out a defeated
sigh. He seemed to use his work as a narcotic. It drugged him
with exhaustion. He always looked tired, like a prisoner who
had been kept short of sleep and food to render him submis-
sive. It was as though Lloyd was afraid that if it were
contented and well rested, his body might make plans to escape
from him.

'Heather mentioned some kind of annuity,' said Lloyd.

'That's right. It's not much. It's tied to the upkeep of the
house.'

'Do you know what kind of trust it's held in?'

'No, I don't really. That's one of the reasons for going
over: I'll be able to find if there's any way I can rearrange the
provisions of the will.'

'Yeah, you ought to look into that.'

'Do you hear anything from Laura?' I asked.

'Heather talks to her now and again. I gather she's doing
well.'

There was a knock on the door which turned out to be Tina
from downstairs. She had lived there for over a year, but I had
avoided getting to know her on the very English principle that
it's better to have cool but cordial relations with your neighbours than try to make friends and discover you actually hate
each other. Since I was going away, I decided it was safe to

invite her to my party, but I hadn't really expected her to come. She was in her thirties and did something involving the Kurds which she had explained to me once when I was out trimming the hedge, but I'd forgotten.

She came in and I introduced her to Lloyd and Stevo. Her presence somehow exaggerated the atmosphere of oppressive maleness that we had managed to create between us. I gave her a drink and told her that more people would be along soon, but I didn't fully believe it myself.

Stevo's phone call conjured up a mob of people who spilled in at about half past ten. All of them were unknown to me; most of them were unknown to Stevo. By that time, some other guests had come, so the party didn't seem quite so bedraggled, or quite so male as it had at the beginning.

Once I had managed to stop nursing the party as though it were a sickly baby, it managed to thrive by itself and develop an unpleasant, vaguely rowdy personality that was all its own. Stevo's obnoxious friends commandeered the hi-fi. I went over to help out and a man with shiny silver trousers shook his head at me and said: 'This geezer's got crap records.'

Cravenly, I agreed with him and went into my kitchen to make a coffee.

Tina came in and I made her one too and bitched about Stevo's friends. We both agreed that the guy in silver trousers was an arse and I began to wish I'd made an effort to get to know her before my leaving party.

'So how are you settling in?' I said.

'Settling in?'

'To your flat.'

'Oh right.' A smile replaced her puzzled frown. 'I've been living there for two years, Damien.'

'Wow, two years. Time flies when you're doing night shifts. It doesn't seem so long since Mary was down there heating up soup on her Baby Belling.'

Stevo came into the room to find more alcohol. He was drunk and his contact lenses must have been irritating his

eyes because they looked big and wet like a spaniel's. Tina and
I both looked at him.

'Her Baby Belling?' she said.

'It was like a fifties time warp down there. Distempered
walls. No central heating. She came over from Estonia during
the war. It was funny actually. She used to leave jars on the
stairs outside her door for me to open. She had arthritis, so she
couldn't get the tops off. It was sauerkraut jars, Pepto Bismol
or toilet bleach. Do you think that tells some kind of story
about her digestive system?'

She laughed. You know you're getting closer to an English
person when you share a joke about bowels or toilets.

Buoyed up by her engaging laughter I went on: 'Her husband was Polish. He was a barber, she told me. Get this,
though: she said his business had been ruined by Beatlemania.
Because no one wanted to get their hair cut!'

'The estate agent said she went to an old people's home,'
said Tina.

'Oh no – she died in the flat. In fact, Stevo was with me
when they broke down the door.'

'Oh dear. I think I would rather not have known that.'

The room suddenly seemed so quiet, I thought I could hear
church clocks ticking over graveyards across south London. I
was trying to resurrect our conversation when Tina said: 'Your
brother is Vivian March, isn't he? I'm a big fan of his films.'

I was smiling politely and nodding and about to move on to
something else, but from behind us Stevo's voice said, slowly
and clearly: 'Oops.' And then. 'I didn't say anything.'

'Why *oops*?' said Tina, blushing. 'Do you not get along?'

'We had kind of a falling-out,' I said. 'It was a shame
because we used to be close.'

'I didn't know you did such a good *reasonable*,' said Stevo to
me pointedly. Tina looked very uncomfortable.

Stevo had a tendency of springing surprises like this: he
would call attention to some private matter when you were
with someone you barely knew, forcing you either to take

them into your confidence, or leave them feeling paranoid and excluded.

'Stevo's exaggerating,' I said. 'It's really no big deal.'

Stevo loitered around the kitchen until Tina said she'd better go. She shook my hand, thanked me for the party and left.

'Thanks for that, Stevo,' I said. 'We were getting on nicely until you arrived.'

'You mean, until you told her that the flat was built on the site of an Indian burial ground.' Stevo flashed me a smile of grey, wine-stained teeth.

People who didn't know Stevo thought he was tricky and self-seeking. I'm not sure. I would have thought that someone really tricky and self-seeking would appear to be a self-sacrificing *ingénu*. Stevo certainly seemed tricky, but maybe it was a protective display like the yellow and black stripes on a sting-less insect. I don't know. In those days, I suppose I was like Patrick, who believed that everyone was tricky and self-seeking. When I got to Ionia, I found a letter in his basement in which he'd written: 'Human beings have evolved to be assholes. *Homo simpaticus* is lying at the bottom of Olduvai Gorge with a flint handaxe in his rib cage.'

'Have a toke of this,' said Stevo, waving a conciliatory spliff in my face.

I hate pot, spliff, grass, whatever you call it. I could hardly wait to start smoking it when I was at school. Stevo and I would go buy it together in west London, and I think for a couple of years we smoked exclusively beef stock cubes and oregano. This prevented me from finding out how much I disliked the drug itself. Also, Vivian has always been a smoker and it took me a long time to accept that someone with so much of my DNA could have a fundamentally different reaction from me to a simple stimulant. So a very common experience for me would be this: I would be having a good time at a party or concert. Someone would pass round a joint as though it were as innocuous as a box of after-dinner mints.

I would take one, two, three ill-advised puffs and spend the
next two hours rooted to the spot, as though I'd been struck by
a curare-tipped blowgun dart. Anyway, these are the kinds of
things you find out about yourself, you learn to say no, and
you improve with age.

'Nice one,' I said, taking the joint from his fingers, and
inhaling greedily.

'Skunk,' said Stevo. 'You want to take it a bit easy with
that.'

I held the fumes in my chest and smiled at him. A stray
tendril of smoke curled into my eye and made it water.

'Thanks,' I said, and passed the joint back to Stevo and
rinsed my mouth out with wine.

'I just wanted to say, you know,' Stevo began, draping his
arm over my shoulder. 'We've had our ups and downs over the
years. You're a very difficult person, but you'll always be my
friend. I love you, mate. You're such a character.'

'Are you all right, Stevo?'

'Yeah – why do you ask?'

'You're being unusually generous.'

'I had one and a half Es off Fabrice in the pub – but that's
not why I said it.'

I began to feel light-headed and full of giggles – giggles that
pushed upwards from my stomach like bubbles in sparkling
wine. At the same time, I felt a familiar paranoia building up.
I was finding Stevo difficult to talk to and wasn't sure if it was
me, or him, or the drugs. I went out of the kitchen and sat
down on the sofa in the living room.

Lloyd had taken his shirt off and was dancing in the middle
of the room. This clownish, playful Lloyd made fewer and
fewer appearances, but it was always reassuring to see that his
body was still capable of usurping its gaolers. I smiled weakly
at him, but by now I was feeling too sick to move.

Someone came and sat next to me in the empty seat, so to
forestall conversation I put my arm over their shoulders and
patted them on the back, as if to suggest I was beyond the

reach of verbal communication. After a while, sitting upright
was too active a position. I didn't want to lie down in front of
everyone, so I went into my bedroom. I put one foot through
the bedclothes and on to the floor to keep the bed from revolv-
ing. That was the end of the party for me. I could hear shouts
and laughter coming from the sitting room, but I wasn't able
to get up and join in. I just lay there like a corpse at a wake.
At the end of the evening some of my friends came in to pay
their last respects. Stevo leaned over and ruffled my hair with
a sweaty hand. I acknowledged them all by feebly waggling my
fingers and groaning, then they filed silently out of my flat for
the last time.

EIGHT

THE HOUSE I HAD inherited had been built in the 1880s by a sea captain called Edward Nethers who made his money from whaling – the industry for which Ionia and the neighbouring islands became famous in the nineteenth century. Patrick had bought the house from one of Captain Nethers' granddaughters, who had grown too infirm to live there alone. She cried when she left it for the last time and gave my uncle a photo of her granddaddy, looking severe in Victorian side-whiskers. Patrick kept the photograph on the mantelpiece in the library – or the room Patrick had designated the library: it was hard to imagine Captain Nethers with his nose in any book but a hymnal or a tide table. Alongside it Patrick put the original title deed to the property and an aerial photograph of the house.

The house was neither old, by English standards, nor large, by American ones; but it was handsome and considered a good example of the island's architecture. Summer visitors would sometimes make the detour to look at it, occasionally coming up to the porch and asking Patrick's permission to take photographs. He was invariably courteous and would take them on a tour of the property before sending them away with brown paper bags of the hard little fruits that grew in his garden: apples, pears, peaches that were somehow tasty despite being very furry and juiceless.

It was a house that a child might draw, sketching out a crude oblong for the body, a triangle for the roof, regularly placed windows and a door in the middle. It was made of timber, two storeys high, with sides painted a blinding white, a steeply pitched roof and black wooden shutters on every window. One year, Vivian and I helped Patrick to paint the whole thing, using tall ladders to reach up to the eaves. It was an enormous job, and we had agreed to do it for what seemed like a huge fee: fifty dollars – between us. But it was a week's work and we finished each day exhausted and splattered with paint. Patrick always talked about covering the woodwork with vinyl siding, which would have spared him the trouble of having it painted, but he was too much of a purist to do it.

On the roof of the house, the Captain had built what is known in the region as a widow's walk. This was a form of balcony, like a crow's nest in a ship, that was reached through a hatch in the attic. From it, the island looked like an island, with the sea suddenly huge and menacing. Widows, I suppose, would patrol them hoping to catch a glimpse of a familiar sail on the horizon. Or muse on the immensity that had swallowed their husbands. Patrick used his mainly to check on his TV aerial, which would get blown down periodically in strong winds.

There were two other buildings on the property: a stable off to one side, and a summer kitchen on the seaward side of the house. I don't know if this was characteristic of the region or a unique example. Since the Nethers family wanted their house to remain cool in summer, the Captain had built a tiny one-room outbuilding to cook in during hot weather. Patrick almost never cooked anyway, so he barely needed one kitchen, let alone two. The summer kitchen contained a bed, a life mask of Keats, a fridge, a vintage jukebox and about thirty egg-weighers.

As I mentioned before, Patrick liked to collect things. A second fridge in the main house contained nothing but ice-cream scoops. The mechanical bank that he had left my father in his will came from a collection of about fifty. Patrick owned more than two hundred glass cup-plates; four complete sets of the works of Dickens; six filing cabinets full of 45s for the jukebox. And there were incipient collections everywhere of things that he was not consciously collecting but that had begun to propagate: blenders and tinned food; playing cards; piano rolls by the player piano; an alphabet of vitamin pills in the bathroom cabinet; lawnmowers and hand tools in the shed, which also contained a rusty cider-press and a trap for the deceased pony Spellvexit.

(An egg-weigher, as the name suggests, is a device used for weighing eggs.)

The main house had entrances front and back. The one that faced the street was shaded by an elaborate wooden awning and a stand of trees. The entrance on the seaward side faced the summer kitchen and looked down the slope to the marsh and the ocean beyond it. I remember this space as teeming with life on Patrick's birthday or during August barbecues. Patrick, or more likely one of his twentysomething girlfriends, would be tending the barbecue – an antique that had a metal chimney and looked as though it was for smelt-ing iron ore; Dad would be cajoling the rest of the family into a game of cricket; Vivian and I would be trying to persuade whoever was our age and female to come on a tour of the property. The sun would be high and bright; the sea glitter-ing beyond the marshes; and the grass so green, and so much trouble to cut, rolling under the apple trees, to the shady part of the garden.

'The grass,' said my Aunt Judith. 'It was always the grass. "I've got to go back and cut my grass." I think he used to lie awake at night and hear it growing.'

Judith had met me at Logan Airport. Stocky and tanned, she stood out in the crowd because of her make-up and dark glasses. She was in her late fifties, the middle child of five – the oldest after Patrick and my father but with none of their eccentricities. The first thing she did was give me a hug, enveloping me in her chunky arms and the smell of her perfume. 'Is that all you've got?' She pointed at my luggage. I told her I had just brought the essentials: egg-weighers, ice-cream scoops.

She laughed. 'Yuh. Cup-plates. Croquet mallets.'

On the way down, she started telling me that she had seen Patrick for the last time three Easters earlier. He had left early to cut the grass, she said.

'He just came to eat. He looked awful.' *Offal* was how she said it, which made it sound even more evocative. 'I mean, really awful. His hair!'

'Strictly speaking, it wasn't his,' I said.

She rolled her eyes. 'He had a plate piled this high with food.' She took her hands off the steering wheel to indicate a mound about six inches deep. 'He went back twice for more. I'd made some Swedish meatballs and offered him some. "Not for me," he said. He pointed at them. "Pure death." *Pure death!* "I'm dieting," he said.'

'Do you think he meant it or was he trying to be rude?'

She took her eyes off the road to look at me. 'You know what, Damien, maybe he was, but I don't care.' As a true Bostonian, she gave 'care' two full syllables: *ki-ya*. 'I would have done anything for him. He was my brother. He knew that I loved him. *I* can put my hand on my heart and say: My conscience is clear.' *Kli-ya*.

The subject of the will hovered in the air between us and
made the atmosphere in the car, despite the air-conditioning,
seem faintly oppressive.

'The will must have come as a surprise,' I said finally.

Judith turned towards me, pursed her lips, sighed and
pursed her lips again. 'I'll be honest. I was hurt. I don't want
you to think I'm jealous, because I'm happy for you. Really.
I'm hurt for my girls. Damien, they loved him. They loved
him so much. But he didn't just not think of them, he deliberately hurt them. He gave Tricia those stupid books. It was so
mean-spirited. They would have been happy with so little.'

Outside the car, the numbers on the exits were counting
down our approach to the bridge. I found myself saying: 'You
must come visit. I'd like people to look on it as a family
house.'

Judith startled me by saying, 'I know you do. And I know
that you and Patrick were close.'

I looked out of the window at the struts of Sagamore
Bridge, thinking that I knew neither of these things myself.

NINE

I FINALLY TOOK POSSESSION of my new home on a warm June evening slightly more than six weeks after my uncle's funeral. The ferry had been delayed because of rough weather. Aunt Judith left me at the dock to drive back to Boston.

It was dark by the time I arrived at the house. The taxi driver dropped me off at the side of the road, from where three steps led up to the swinging wooden sign that still said: PATRICK M. MARCH J.D. The driver offered to carry the suitcases all the way up to the door, but I told him not to bother. He climbed back into the car and set off towards Westwich. I could hear the clamour of his engine dying away in the darkness, until the only sounds were the crickets and the restful *boop* of the lighthouse ship miles out in the bay.

It was a mild evening and the moon was bright enough to

cast a faint shadow under the apple trees as I carried my bags
over to the veranda and searched on my hands and knees for
the envelope that was supposed to be waiting for me.

Mr Diaz, Patrick's lawyer, had told me he would leave a
set of keys under the porch. But there was no sign of them.
I cursed myself for not having thought to bring a torch. I had
a book of paper matches which flared brightly for a fraction
of a second before becoming too painful to hold. The pitch-
black crawl space under the porch had trapped a pocket of
the day's humid summer air. It was musty and smelled of
wood and paint. I had my chest flat on the ground and was
groping blindly around me, between striking matches, with
the awful presentiment that something was about to scuttle
across my neck. I gave up and crawled back out into the
moonlight.

I felt a diffuse sense of rage and regretted having come. At
that moment, Platon Bakatin was sleeping soundly on the
brand-new mattress I'd bought for his fat Russian arse. I walked
once around the house and once around the summer kitchen to
see if there was any way into either. There was none. The
storm windows had not been taken off since winter and the
doors were impregnable. I thought of smashing my way in, but
it seemed such a bad way to begin. And I had no way of reaching Mr Diaz without a phone.

The nearest houses were about a mile back the way I had
come, so I left my bags and started walking. If I waited any
longer, it would be too late to turn up on a stranger's doorstep
and ask to use their phone. I was reminded of the Japanese
tourist who had been shot dead when he knocked on a door to
ask directions in New Orleans.

Both sides of the road were lined with trees, whose branches
blotted out the moonlight. I felt disconnected from myself in
the darkness, as though I were swimming through warm ink.
I could hear the sounds of my feet on the tarmac, but my body
had become invisible, and I was momentarily startled by the
unearthly sound of my own whistling. Once I became aware of

it, I tried to shape it into a tune, but it sounded like something someone might whistle in a movie shortly before they get dragged into a bush and disembowelled by a man in a hockey mask. I thought how much futility and false levity is encompassed by the phrase 'whistling in the dark'.

After walking for about twenty minutes, I came to a shingled cottage set back from the intersection between the road that links Westwich and Pilgrim Point and the turnoff that leads to my uncle's house. I rapped loudly on the door, and rang the buzzer, my banging growing bolder and more insistent as I became more convinced that there was no one at home. I was ready to set off again when I saw the lights of a car approaching from the direction of Westwich and pulling into the driveway.

I shaded my eyes from the light and called out a greeting as the sound of the engine died away.

The middle-aged woman at the wheel switched off her headlights and got out of the car. I was so busy trying to look neighbourly and non-threatening that I barely noticed her two passengers.

'Hi,' I said again. 'Sorry to bother you like this. I'm Damien March. I'm staying up the road. I'm locked out of my house and I wondered if I could use your phone.'

The woman drew close to me. She was, I learned later, only about five years older than me, but the difference seemed greater, and not only because of the children. She was heavyset, with pale eyes and greying hair, and an expression that seemed to hover between humour and perplexity. She was studying me very hard.

'Sorry about this,' I continued, unnerved by her silence and talking loudly. 'Someone was supposed to leave the keys for me but there's been a cock-up.' 'Cock-up' was a deliberate Anglicism on my part. I was laying on the Brit stuff thick, as though my English accent was in itself proof that I was a gentleman and had no plans to rob them: a piece of romanticism I must have picked up from my father. But the woman said nothing, simply peering at my face as though she hoped to read my intentions there. It occurred to me that my accent, far from being reassuring, was just incomprehensible to her.

Suddenly she turned her head and looked at the boy beside her. A young woman in her late teens was eyeing me from a few paces behind him as intently as her mother had.

The boy asked me to repeat myself.

I was confused. I looked from one to another as I told them again that I was locked out and needed to use a phone.

The boy rested some groceries on his knee to free one of his hands and gestured to his mother. He shook his head as he mimed a hand fitting a key into a lock.

I pointed at my ear. 'You're deaf?' I said.

The woman nodded again, and then pointed first at herself and then at her daughter, who was unloading more groceries from the back of the station wagon and placing them on the driveway. It was only a small thing, but I was struck by the elegance and fluidity of her pointing, especially as she was a large, not particularly graceful-looking woman.

'I need to use the phone,' I said slowly, making a phone shape with the thumb and little finger of my right hand.

The woman smiled warmly and indicated that I should follow her into the house.

It seemed slightly odd to me that the family had a phone at all, but they did. It was coupled to a keyboard and had a screen for receiving typed messages.

Mr Diaz was effusively apologetic. He said that by 'porch' he had meant the tiny gingerbread entrance that faced the road – the opposite side to where I'd been searching. He offered to drive over and help me look for the keys, but I told him I was quite sure I'd be able to find them now. In that case, he said, he would drop by the following day to make sure I was safely in.

While we were talking, my neighbours were packing their shopping away into the cupboards around the kitchen. It was disorienting to be suddenly welcomed into the bustle of a family. The long, low-ceilinged room I was in was split into two sections by a breakfast bar. On one side was the kitchen, with its reassuring clutter, and on the other was a dining table and a hutch for crockery. The boy had gone into a room that gave off the main area. I could see the back of his head silhouetted by the flickering light of a television set. He had the volume turned up to just below the point where it would cause distortion.

The mother put a glass of iced tea in my hand, and went to speak to her son. I thought for a moment that she was going to ask him to turn down the sound. Instead, his head emerged from the doorway at a slight angle.

'Mom says you can stay and eat,' he said, as I hung up the phone. He had a milk moustache around his mouth.

His mother was frying some Italian sausages and the smell of them was making me salivate. I hadn't eaten properly since the flight and was tempted to stay, but I couldn't face an hour or so of polite incomprehension and improvised sign language.

I pointed at my watch and mimed a flying plane and then falling asleep on my own folded hands. Before I left, I wrote down my name and address on a piece of paper as a kind of introduction. The woman did the same. My new neighbours were Harriet Fernshaw and her children Nathan and Theresa.

While Nathan's hearing was unimpaired, Terry was as deaf as her mother. I could see mother and daughter framed in the kitchen window when I looked back from the driveway. It was eerie to watch them communicating wordlessly, flicking their hands in movements that resembled the gestures which accompany speech, but were speech in its entirety to them. A spoken language I might learn, but theirs seemed like a mystery that would exclude me for ever.

The keys were exactly where Mr Diaz had said they would be. I fitted them into the door with enormous, exhausted relief. I had anticipated getting into the house quite differently: ceremoniously taking possession of it, room by room. Instead, I was almost too tired to drag my luggage into the kitchen.

The house was stuffy and dusty from weeks of standing unoc-
cupied. My appetite had all but vanished, so I just drank a
glass of water from a tap in the kitchen and stumbled upstairs
to one of the guest bedrooms. I remember consciously decid-
ing not to go to bed in my uncle's old room because it didn't
seem right, but after that sleep overtook me so fast, it was like
being knocked down by a wave.

TEN

I WOKE UP SUDDENLY in a pitch-black bedroom with no idea of the time and a tinny ringing noise going off in my ears. My first thought was that I had overslept and would have to get dressed quickly to make it to work for my night shift. But the sound was not coming from my own room, and there was a smell in the air that reminded me I was in unfamiliar territory. I dragged myself out of bed and stumbled across the landing. The phosphorescence on the illuminated dial of my uncle's clock radio betrayed the source of the noise. The cheap fake plastic set had been playing an hour's worth of Golden Oldies to the empty house at 5 a.m. each morning since the day my uncle died. I snapped it off and sank on to Patrick's narrow single bed.

My uncle's room was the largest of all the bedrooms. The

summer Vivian and I painted the exterior, Patrick had done up his own room. He painted it a deep shade of blue he had concocted himself. He goaded the incredulous sales clerk at the hardware store in Westwich into adding squirt after squirt of red paint. The boy's hands had paused on the levers. 'More?' My uncle grabbed the lever himself and pumped red paint into the mixture in order to obtain the shade he wanted.

I felt slightly intrusive here among Patrick's most personal possessions. The Afghan rug with the Harvard motto that my grandmother had crocheted for him when he won his place at law school; the shelves of books; his woodcut of the crucifixion; the religious figurines; the icon above his bed that he'd smuggled out of Leningrad in a tea towel. It was probably worthless, but the story of its provenance made it seem priceless to me.

There was a stack of books reaching up almost to the top of the bedside table. I picked up the first volume – a trashy biography of Frank Sinatra. Beneath it was a book on Moroccan cookery.

I got out of bed and wandered through the rooms on the upper floor. The study seemed chilly. A window in front of the desk was half open. It didn't really strike me as odd at the time. I just assumed someone had left it open to air the study.

I sat down at the desk. The sea from the window was a leaden smear. The skull and the row of green files had gone, leaving a faint outline in the dust on the desk. I searched carefully through the drawers and found nothing, except a batch of fruity love letters in sprawling feminine handwriting. It seemed slightly indecent to read them, but I couldn't help glancing at a couple.

I was disappointed not to find any more of Patrick's writing, but consoled myself that something would turn up.

I lay on my bed not sleeping for the next hour. The windows on two sides of the room began to glow with clear seaside light. I began to think it was a lovely room to wake up in. Its wooden floor and walls were painted a pale lime green. There was a green ashtray in a cast-iron stand a few yards from the bed; a greenish commode by the window that Patrick had stripped of paint; a marble-topped stand which held a pitcher and bowl with a floral design; strange allegorical woodcuts on the walls. In another old-fashioned touch, the lumpy bed had bolsters instead of pillows.

But the prettiness of the room – like the house itself – was of a very fragile kind. It had been arranged for people to pass through fairly quickly, not for them to stay and make a life there. Anyone who stayed longer than a few minutes would begin to notice small mistakes and inconveniences. The orange anglepoise lamp on the dressing table was jarringly out of place; the bed sagged; the door on the commode was broken; in the bottom of the pitcher was a large dead spider, its legs shrivelled up round its body – it looked like a tiny grappling iron, left behind by a tiny prisoner.

And still, it was the inconsistencies and lapses of good taste that reminded me most of Patrick. Where he had tried to create an atmosphere of soothing Victorian calm, he had only managed to emphasise his eccentricities. In this room, some of the details were mysterious – why the lamp, which must have been brought from another room and forgotten? But together, the many indications of disuse spoke of a solitary life. I began to feel sorry for him. This was a guest bedroom, after all, that had never held any guests. It was like the roped-off bedrooms at Hampton Court; any sense of life beyond the furniture was wholly illusory.

I had managed to sleep all night on an empty stomach, but now that I was awake, my hunger was becoming impossible to ignore. I even had that extra sensitivity to smell that comes when you haven't eaten in a while. I noticed the mustiness in the air, and the way the slight dampness brought out the smell of the timber.

I went downstairs and attempted to make some breakfast. Now, anyone living alone begins to cut comers. You adapt to shortcomings you can't be bothered to fix. Sometimes, you

only notice when guests arrive and you have to explain the
bathroom door only closes if you pull it like so; that a certain
drawer won't shut unless you lift it when you slide it in; you
have to jiggle the handle of the toilet to get the cistern to fill.
But Patrick's house was only comparable for inconvenience
with living in a museum.

The fridge – which contained the collection of ice-cream
scoops – was purely ornamental. The cooker hadn't worked for
years and had a gloomy aura all its own – like a wrecked car in
a forest. The water wheezed and coughed its way out of the
taps. All the kitchen implements were of the oldest available
kind. Patrick must have either gone out for every meal, or
eaten canned food out of the tin.

There was an enormous pile of tinned food in the larder –
enough in fact to keep Patrick going through a nuclear
winter – but not much that I felt like eating for breakfast.
I saw tinned asparagus, tins of cherries, haggis (vegetarian and
non-vegetarian varieties), cassoulet, feijoada, along with a box of
wine gums that I remembered buying in Wandsworth for
Patrick's fortieth birthday. I found a bag of coffee beans in there
too, but not a grinder that I dared use. There were several
elegant-looking hand-operated ones, but they smelled of furniture
polish and had rusty or broken mechanisms. Knowing Patrick,
the one he actually used would be an ugly piece of 1960s junk
that he'd bought for fifty cents at a yard sale, but I couldn't see
anything that fitted this description. In the end, I settled for
Postum, of which there were three unopened jars, and added
instant coffee to my shopping list.

The picture on the tin of feijoada made it look not unlike
baked beans, so I decided to eat that. In the absence of a tin-
opener, I had to use a corkscrew to punch a hole in the can.
It took me about ten minutes to make an opening big enough
to pour out the contents, which turned out to be beans and
most of the distinguishing characteristics of a pig. By then I
was too hungry to care, and sat on the steps of the house with
my Postum, my pig's snout stew and a box of Ritz crackers,

wondering what unnatural instinct had made Patrick turn his own home into such an inhospitable place.

Twenty-eight years earlier, Vivian and I had followed our father up the steps on which I was sitting and been introduced to Patrick for the first time. He towered over us, a taller, swarthier version of my father, his eyes obscured by the sunglasses that he wore habitually, regardless of the weather.

It had been snowing that day. It was the Christmas after my mother died, and we were spending it in America. I suppose my father thought that celebrating it in our customary way in London would just underline her absence.

We were unprepared for the brutal weather. London had been unseasonally warm, but six inches of snow fell in Boston in the hour after we landed: great clouds of it seemed to swarm around the headlights of the other cars. The ferry was delayed for two hours. Vivian and I had no gloves or scarves, so my father bought us some at a drugstore in Hyannis. It was dark when the boat left the harbour; thick and swirling, the snow continued to pour out of the sky and silently extinguish itself in the boat's black wake. Snow lay along the eaves of our empty guesthouse in Westwich, where the cold cotton sheets looked and felt like snow. Vivian bunched up like an armadillo at the top of his bed to stay warm. I straightened my legs too quickly: it was like standing neckdeep in icy water. My teeth chattered until the bed warmed up. Outside the window, the snow had been scraped into piles; yellow under the streetlamps, they set off the blackness of the Atlantic night.

Early the next morning we drove to Patrick's. My father struggled with the ignition of the rented car as Vivian and I shivered on its cold vinyl seats. It had started to snow again – tiny flakes of it this time, like salt. By the time we got to Patrick's house, the path he had cleared across the porch had been dusted over again. His house seemed to disappear into the sky behind it, camouflaged like the black and white of ermine.

My father banged on the door and flapped his arms to keep warm. 'Cold, huh?'

Patrick appeared. The whole of his nose was swathed in white bandages. Much later, my father explained that he had had an operation to straighten a deviated septum. Along with the dark glasses, the bandages made him look like the Invisible Man. He was easily the most frightening person I'd ever seen in my life.

'What's that in your hair?' he asked.

I said nothing. I was speechless with terror. Vivian was looking at me, his face blotchy white and pink from the cold, swathed in his drugstore hat and muffler.

Patrick bent down and produced a Reese's peanut butter cup from the air behind my left ear. I burst into tears.

Patrick was mortified. 'I didn't mean to scare you. It was just a trick.' He unwrapped the chocolate. 'Look, it's candy!'

'It's the bandage,' said my father. 'He's frightened of it.'

Patrick touched it. 'This? Does it look terrible?'

'It's not so bad,' said my father. Something about my father's deep voice and the way frozen vapour came out of his mouth made me think of smoke pouring from a censer in church.

Vivian quacked: 'Your nose looks like a big white doorknob.'

My father took my hand and we followed them over the threshold, me grizzling slightly, not so much from fear as from the feeling that I had disgraced myself with my tears.

The house must have been very different then. There would have been much less in it. It seems a trite thing to observe, but Patrick only began collecting things in earnest when he'd given up on human beings. In those days, the eccentricities that eventually made the kitchen useless were so far from conquering it that Patrick was able to cook Christmas dinner for five. The fifth person was Patrick's girlfriend Lydia. She was frail-looking with a bun of blond hair. She called him Paddy and cracked open walnuts with the heel of her clog.

Together she and Patrick had cut down a tree which they had decorated with ribbons, and candy canes, and Christmas biscuits that were as hard as plywood.

It was a subdued occasion. We ate much of the dinner in silence. I was too young to understand fully, but I think I sensed it was a reconciliation of some sort between Patrick and my father.

My father insisted on going for a walk on the beach after lunch before we opened our presents. Patrick and Lydia sat drinking whisky by the fire.

The sea was grey and foamy, churning up the beach. Even the sand dunes had a grey, damp look, like heaps of aggregate at a building site.

'I don't want you to be disappointed if you don't like what Patrick gives you,' my father explained. 'He doesn't understand small children very well.'

'But why not, Dad? Why doesn't he?' said Vivian.

Something foul and fishy had been deposited by the sea high up on the beach and half covered with sand. We were poking at it with sticks.

'I want you both to behave very well,' my father said, 'so that when you leave Patrick will think to himself: What nice children!, I think I'd like to have some of those myself.'

It was a sensible warning. Patrick gave Vivian and me Harvard sweatshirts that were about eight sizes too big. If I still had mine, I would still be waiting to grow into it. But I heeded my father's words and said nothing. Vivian couldn't conceal his disappointment. 'It's a wearing present,' he said. 'I hate wearing presents.'

'I love mine,' I said smugly. 'Dad, Vivian said he doesn't like his sweatshirt.'

My father had given Patrick a miner's helmet with a Davey lamp attached to it. Patrick put it on and mugged at Lydia, mocking the gift.

'Dad, Uncle Patrick doesn't like the hat!' Vivian was thrilled.

'Give it back, then,' said my father. 'You asshole!' He was smiling. It was the first time I had ever heard him swear. They pretended to wrestle over the hat.

'Dad, you said —'

'Come on, give it a rest, Damien,' my father said. 'Lighten up.'

I think my lip must have trembled. I was being a tiresome goody-goody, but I was too close to my last fit of tears for me to take the comment in good spirit, and Patrick could see this.

'Damien's right,' he said. 'A gentleman should never swear or fart.'

'I stand corrected,' my father said.

'Look at the parrot!' screeched Patrick's parrot.

Later on, Patrick showed off his toys to us. The board games, some of which he had designed himself, were too grown-up to arouse our interest. But I was captivated by a clockwork train and somehow got it into my head that Patrick had given it to me. My father quickly disabused me of this idea. He pointed out that I didn't have room in my suitcase. I said I would leave my clothes behind.

'It's Patrick's train,' my father insisted. 'And it will remain Patrick's train.' Patrick was sheepishly silent. Something he had said had sparked off the whole scene.

I threw a tantrum and was exiled to the summer kitchen until it was time to leave.

The rental car wouldn't start, so Patrick drove us back to Westwich in his car – a white Triumph convertible with an eight-track tape player and an exhaust loud enough to announce the Last Judgement. He played Latin American pipe music at the highest possible volume to compete with the borborygmus of the engine.

I don't remember much else about the trip. I was mortified not to keep the train, but in its place I had the inkling of something else: the distinct feeling that I was Patrick's favourite; a feeling that was as small and steady as a pilot light – a feeling that I had begun to recall since I got the news of his death.

ELEVEN

MR DIAZ, PATRICK'S LAWYER, stopped by at about eight o'clock. Seeing him, I almost did a double take – he was boss-eyed: exactly as Mr Ricketts was in Patrick's fragmentary story. In every other way, however, he couldn't have been more different from a desiccated imperial administrator. He was a courteous man of around forty with olive skin. His jet-black hair was greying at the temples. The distinctive long vowels of his Boston accent sat oddly, I thought, with his suavely Mediterranean appearance. He refused my offer of a cup of Postum with humour. 'Promised my wife I wouldn't touch that stuff. I'll take a glass of water, though.'

He apologised again for the mix-up over the key. 'I sent one of my paralegals,' he said. 'It was the first time she'd been out to the house.'

I told him it wasn't his fault.

'I brought you these,' he said, handing me the keys to Patrick's car. 'We brought it back from the high school and disconnected the battery. You shouldn't have a problem getting it started. If you do, try scraping out the inside of the leads.'

He sipped his water slowly and looked out over the lawn towards the ocean with his one good eye. 'Nice spot. How long are you planning to stay out here?'

'At least the summer, possibly longer.' It was the answer I'd been giving for months, but after one night and breakfast in my new home, it seemed like foolishness. Practical and well dressed, Mr Diaz was a physical reproach to the vagueness of my plans. I missed all the familiar indignities of work and life in London.

'Mind if I look around?' said Mr Diaz.

'By all means.' I opened the door for him.

As any visitor would be, he was struck by the mechanical banks arrayed on the shelf around the wall of the kitchen. 'So these are the famous banks.'

'Famous?'

'Your uncle itemised them in the inventory. He gave each one a name.'

There must have been fifty of the little machines. Several were in dubious taste: there was a ginger-haired Irishman who snuffled coins off the snout of a pig; a dicky-bowed black waiter who swallowed his penny off his own pink palm and rolled his eyes gratefully.

'I guess he just wanted to be thorough.' Mr Diaz seemed to smile to himself. 'He was quite a character.'

Quite a character. It made Patrick sound endearingly strange, as though he was odd by choice, instead of the victim of his own compulsions. Among the vitamins in the bathroom was a whole pharmacy of antidepressants. Paranoid, lonely, chronically depressed: he was quite a character all right.

I gave Mr Diaz a quick tour. The house charmed him, as it charmed everyone, even though it was becoming obvious to me that living in it was going to be difficult. I was beginning to feel odd about my whole project, and to think that the principal intention behind my uncle's will had been to found a museum in memory of him and make me its curator. And with Platon in my flat for at least six months, I couldn't just get back on the plane and go home. Bolder than Mandingo, indeed.

Mr Diaz's asymmetrical gaze was scanning the spines of the books in the library. It reminded me again of Mr Ricketts and I asked him if he knew what had happened to the files that had been on Patrick's desk.

'Box files,' he said thoughtfully, rounding out the vowels in a jocular imitation of my accent. 'I'll have to ask at the office. Weren't they on the inventory I sent you?'

I told him I had seen nothing since I had heard the news from my father.

'I sent one to your address in London. I'll get you another.' He said I would have to come into his office in Westwich anyway to sign some of the paperwork relating to the will.

'I meant to ask you something about that,' I said. 'Under the terms of the will, I understand I'm supposed to maintain the house as it was during Patrick's lifetime. Now, I get that in principle. But in practice, can I alter things to make it more habitable? For instance, it needs a new fridge . . .'

'Well, I'm afraid this is one of those "How long is a piece of string?" questions,' said Mr Diaz. 'I don't see getting a new refrigerator as problematical, or moving a painting from one wall to another. Let's say, for the sake of argument, that you wanted to put in a new bathroom. You'd have to persuade the trustees that it doesn't conflict with the letter or the spirit of your uncle's directions. Any alterations to the fabric of the house would have to be approved by the trustees.'

'What if I want to sell the house?' I said, trying to make it sound as hypothetical as possible.

'Out of the question. But in the example of the bathroom . . . I mean, we have a certain latitude in the way we interpret the document. I would have no objections, nor do I think would Rosie Queenan, the trustee appointed by the bank. The only trustee who might object is Mr Blair, the guy from the churchmen's fund, but I doubt it.'

I wanted to ridicule his careful, legalistic replies. Did the prohibition against altering things mean that I couldn't throw away the jars of vitamin pills that cluttered the bathroom floor? What about the spider in the water jug, was it protected by the will?

I must have looked anxious, because Mr Diaz felt he had to reassure me. 'I wouldn't worry too much about it. I'm here to advise you. Let me do the worrying. You enjoy your break,' he said.

He meant to be encouraging, but I was disheartened by the implicit assumption that no one would come to the house for longer than a holiday.

We went back to the kitchen and Mr Diaz took his glass of water off the sideboard and drank it in one go, with his hand pressed against his stomach. He smacked his lips. The gesture signalled the end of his visit. 'You've got your own well, haven't you,' he said, dabbing at his moustache with a hand-kerchief. 'I always prefer the taste of well water.'

I opened the screen door for him. It slapped shut behind us. The sun had burned off the early morning haze and it was getting hot. We set off across the lawn towards Mr Diaz's car, which was parked in the driveway, about a hundred yards away. He said I should make an appointment to come see him about the paperwork. 'Get yourself settled in first, then give me a call,' he said.

I stooped to pick up a handful of dead twigs from the lawn as we walked: they were like a speck of fluff on a huge baize billiard table. 'There's no phone,' I said, 'but I think I can call from my neighbours'.'

'The Fernshaws?'

'That's right.'

'Real Ionians,' he said. 'Not wetbacks like me.' He smiled, his teeth ivory in the sunlight under his clipped moustache.

'They're deaf,' I said.

'Sure are. Used to be a lot of deaf people on the islands.'

'I didn't know that.'

'Not so many of them now, but in the old days, I mean it's a rural thing: small gene pool – lot of double yolkers.'

'Inbreeding.'

'That's right. The islanders even evolved their own kind of sign language. My wife knows some actually. She's a real islander.'

'She's not deaf though?'

'Who?'

'Your wife.'

'Oh no. Everyone spoke sign language back then – everyone was related to someone who was deaf so it was the easiest thing for everybody.'

We reached Mr Diaz's car. He shook my hand and got in, then rolled down the window. 'I was sorry I couldn't be at the funeral,' he said. 'My wife had to go into the hospital and I drove up to Boston to be with her.'

'Nothing serious, I hope.'

'It looks like she's out of the woods now, but she'll be taking it easy over the summer just to be sure. She was real sorry about Patrick, too. He wasn't the most easygoing guy in the world, but he was a kind man.'

While not the whole truth, it was as accurate a eulogy as anything that had been said at the funeral.

'His death came right out of the blue,' he added.

'Yeah, it was a shock to me, too,' I said, but I thought it was probably better not to explain why.

TWELVE

PATRICK'S CAR WAS PARKED inside the shed. It didn't look much like it had twenty-eight years before, but then neither did I. The bodywork was pitted with rust and a dent in the door on the passenger side had been mended with a piece of plywood. It wasn't a car you would want to pick up a date in. And that was sad. Every summer, Patrick told us the same stories about the dating rituals of his teenage years. They were stories like Homeric myth with their own catchphrases and epithets, and they had undergone much embellishment over the years. They were peopled with bizarre characters: the Bubble brothers, Mrs Thornquist, one-eyed Captain Spadger, Tackaberry Mackadoo; and they covered the years of Patrick's youth, as an altar boy, as a student, as a high-school basketball star, a life-guard at Revere Beach. It was a life that I envisaged taking

place in Technicolor; a life a hundred times more exciting than
the life I led.

Mr Sandford – he of the gerbil's-arse moustache – once told
my father that the function of epics is to embody the cardinal
virtues of their society and their historical moment. In the
Aeneid, I gather it's filial piety; in the *Iliad*, it's martial valour;
in 1950s America as described by my Uncle Patrick, the most
important qualities a young man could possess were the right
car and a duck's-arse hairstyle.

Patrick went into more detail about how he used Vitalis to
sculpt his hair before a date than Homer did about the armour
of the Trojan heroes. He really didn't care whether it was of
interest to us. He was in a state of what recovering alcoholics
call euphoric recall: he wasn't here, he was there, in the
America of Eisenhower and Elvis and tailfinned cars, shaping
and preening before the bathroom mirror; almost believing
that his bald head was covered with lustrous black locks.

So, for Patrick to have allowed his car to fall into a state of
such disrepair was a bit like Siegfried selling the ring of the
Nibelungen for two dollars at a yard sale.

To make matters worse, whoever had returned it from the
other side of the island hadn't bothered to disconnect the battery or even remove the towel from the passenger seat, which,
presumably, Patrick had taken down to the running track to
dry himself after the run which killed him.

The space behind the two front seats was so small that it
seemed improbable that Vivian and I had ever fitted inside it,
but we had. The two of us had been squashed in there as we
drove back to Westwich that first Christmas.

When we got back to London at the beginning of January
we had begun to correspond with Patrick. The two of us
wrote long letters on my father's yellow legal pads, and Patrick
sent us drawings and silly poems back. I copied out the story
of David and Goliath from a book I got from the library and
told Patrick I had written it.

The following summer my father rented the house near

Provincetown that became an annual fixture for the next ten
years. We saw more of Patrick and Lydia, but to my recollection my father and Patrick never spent a night under the same
roof. It was as though there was a tacit understanding that
there were limits to their renewed friendship. If we stayed on
Ionia, it was at a guest house in Westwich; and when Patrick
stayed on the Cape, it was usually at a place in Provincetown.
The only exception was the summer when we painted Patrick's
house. Vivian and I camped on Patrick's lawn. As self-
conscious adolescents, we didn't feel comfortable sharing a bed.

But given these limits, I remember those summers as the
happiest of my life. When I think of the word 'childhood', the
first, most pleasant associations that spring to mind are the
gold summer light on the beach outside Patrick's house; the
smell of candy-floss at the Barnstable County Fair; the tingle
of a mild sunburn; my father and uncle squabbling over the
barbecue; the cold, cold water of the Atlantic Ocean. These
were my real inheritance. A happy enough childhood is the
capital that supports you during your adult life.

About two years after that first Christmas, Lydia left Patrick
for another man. My father told us we should remember
Patrick in our prayers because he wasn't well. I suppose this
was his way of saying Patrick had had a nervous breakdown.
Lydia's departure marked the beginning of the closeness
between Patrick and my father that lasted until I was about
sixteen. They were both in effect now widowers, and I think
they must have found the symmetry reassuring.

The idea of Patrick's being jilted by Lydia got mixed up in
my mind with a book I was reading at the time. The memory
of his big white doorknob was still very fresh, and I've never
quite shaken off the idea that my uncle was in fact the Dong
with a Luminous Nose, abandoned by his Jumbly Girl, and
searching for her by night over the Gromboolian Plain.

The battery in the Triumph was almost completely dead, so I
found a charger in the shed and set it going.

Patrick's car had played another role in the history of my family. The need for spare parts from England – they were unobtainable on Ionia – had been a link between Patrick and my father. I don't know if it prevented them from falling out sooner than they did, but we stopped shopping for wine gums and wiper blades just before my sixteenth birthday. And it's from then that I date the break-up of my fissiparous family.

If brothers can't get on, my father once said to me and Vivian after we'd quarrelled, what hope is there for anyone? Of course, it doesn't follow. Brothers – sisters I'm not qualified to speak about – are brought up to want the same things. Hence the emulousness, hence the contention.

And who was Dad to preach? For the last twenty years of Patrick's life, he and my father did not speak. My father claimed it was Patrick's fault. Patrick claimed it was my father's fault. Who knew? I never got to the bottom of it, and I felt that to attribute blame to one side or the other just perpetuated the split. In any case, it seemed obvious that a quarrel as permanent as theirs didn't arise from a single cause, any more than a man banging in a tent peg over a seismic fault causes an earthquake.

I got a clean towel from the house and walked across the marsh and down the powdery sand dunes to the beach. I was finally glad for not being in London. The sea was as clear and green as it had been that day in May. Another month of sun had warmed it slightly, but when I jumped off the jetty, the cold water squeezed my skull like a metal band. After a few moments it eased a little, and I struck out, swimming over a patch of long seaweed, like a stand of pine trees under water. I turned on my back and the sea closed over my ears. I wondered if this was what it might be like to be deaf: was it silence, or the close gurglings of your own blood, or some other sound which, never having heard another, you could never put a name to?

Even on a still day, the sound of the sea was everywhere on

Ionia, but the Fernshaws and the other deaf Ionians dwelled in
a place where sound was absent. Their island was a place of
light and movement: the quick glittering of the ocean, the
changing clouds, the vast blue sky. Perhaps their pleasure in
these was all the greater as a kind of compensation. I thought
of the surprising grace of Mrs Fernshaw's pointing fingers, and
the fluidity that seemed out of keeping with her age and size.

The battery would take about twelve hours to charge, which
was too long to wait for a cup of coffee, so I dug out an old
bicycle which had not much wrong with it apart from flat tyres
and brakes that rubbed slightly. I managed to get it more or
less roadworthy and then set off for the Colonial Market.

Once I had started cycling, I had a moment of enthusiasm
for my new home. The sun was right overhead, and I could
smell the tarmac baking in the heat. Butterflies winked their
colours at me from the long grass by the side of the road. By
the junction of the main road to Westwich, where a bridge
forded the creek that drained the marshes, a child had set up
an iced-tea and lemonade stall with a hand-lettered sign. I was
encouraged to stop by the thought that Patrick would have
stopped: he unfailingly supported children who sold lemonade,
yard sales and anyone selling vegetables from a shack with a
sign saying, 'Home-grown produce'.

The hub of the bicycle ticked as I rode one of the pedals to
a standstill. I saw that the boy was Mrs Fernshaw's son,
Nathan. Boxes of saltwater taffy were stacked under the table
to stop them melting in the heat.

'How's business?' I asked him.

'I only just got here,' he said.

After the turnoff to Patrick's, the road we were on continued
along the edge of the island to the War Bonnet Cliffs –
supposedly named by the first English settlers after the headgear
of the indigenous people they displaced from the island. Patrick
used to say that the original inhabitants of Ionia were a pacific,
agrarian people whom the English had softened up with
whisky and imported diseases and then bilked out of their land.

I doubt this story, and not just for patriotic reasons. The settlers were Puritans and more likely to hand out Bibles than firewater. But it is true that the War Bonnet Cliffs got their name long after the last full-blooded Ionian Indian had succumbed to cirrhosis – or old age – on the mainland. The cliffs were the island's most famous beauty spot, and the farthest point from the dock at Westwich.

I'd only been to the cliffs once, and I remembered them as a big disappointment. My father had insisted on cycling the entire forty-mile round-trip on rented three-speed bicycles. I was twelve. We barely had time to down a soft drink before turning the bikes around and pedalling back. Patrick had wisely refused to contemplate the outing.

The cliffs had been much less garishly coloured than they were in the souvenir photographs. In fact, the high point of the day was the incredulous reaction of the man in the rental shop when we got back to Westwich and told him where we'd been: 'War Bonnet? On bikes?'

Visitors to War Bonnet went on rented scooters and in air-conditioned buses like the one that was now pulling up on the verge and discharging a gaggle of tourists.

They streamed past me towards Nathan Fernshaw's stand, snapping his photo and buying up boxes of saltwater taffy as fast as he could stack them on the table. It struck me that his resemblance to a child in a Norman Rockwell painting was not accidental, but shrewd marketing. Somehow, Nathan had grasped that he was really a vendor of nostalgia, as bogus in his way as the people at Plimoth Plantation who wore buckled shoes, churned butter, and pretended to talk in Elizabethan English. It was a reminder of another anomaly: while Ionia and the Cape were my New World, for many Americans they had more in common with the Old.

The driver was last off the bus. He gave the boy a wink. 'Hiya, Nathan. How's your mother.'

'She's good.'

'Let me have some of that tea.'

The road which had been empty a moment ago was alive with people. The driver stood apart from them, slurping his iced tea from a polystyrene cup. He was in his forties, florid-faced, with a crew cut that looked like it came out of an old L. L. Bean catalogue. He saw me looking at him. 'How you doing,' he said, without giving it the intonation of a question.

'I'm Nathan's neighbour,' I said.

'Oh – you're the English guy from the Captain's house.'

I must have looked surprised because he threw his head back and laughed. 'You know what island people are like.' He made a gossiping beak with his thumb and forefinger.

'I only arrived yesterday.'

'Here for the summer?'

'We'll see. I may stay through the fall.'

'Oh, fall's beautiful here. Well, I'd better round up my people.'

When I cycled back that way an hour later the road was empty again. The midday sun was beginning to bear down on the island, wringing a little heat haze out of its seams, like whey from cheese.

Nathan Fernshaw was packing up his things, moving slowly in the heat. He didn't look up. The *tsk-tsk-tsk* sound of the headphones he was wearing seemed to follow me along the road for more than a quarter of a mile. I kept hearing the same noise at intervals for the rest of the afternoon, which puzzled me, until I realized it was the whine of insects from the marsh.

THIRTEEN

TIME PASSED SLOWLY on Ionia. Without the incident of office
life and the distractions of other people, the days seemed
empty. I didn't exactly miss my job, but I realised that it had
been my strongest connection to the world. Even when I had
hated it, it had given me a feeling of being involved in a flux
of events – wars, peace talks, elections, natural disasters – that
I took to be the life of the planet. Following them, if only
remotely, from the newsroom had been a way of navigating
through time: it gave a form to something that was otherwise
infinite and blank. For a while in Ionia I felt as though I'd
fallen off the map.

I made myself as busy as I could. I set myself the task of
painting a series of views from the widow's walk – one in each
direction – and I bought paints at an art supply shop in

Westwich as soon as I could get the car to start. My first attempts were poor but I told myself not to worry; the gift shops on Ionia were full of bad local art. And the weather was good for seven days straight from the moment I set up the easel. I wore long sleeves and a sun hat to protect myself and took a pitcher of iced tea up to the roof. As I painted each morning, I could hear the ice cubes cracking in the jug, and the smell of the acrylic paint grew more intense as it warmed up in the sunshine.

Bit by bit, I began to establish a routine that made me feel less adrift. I bought a shortwave radio to keep in touch with the world beyond the island. I thought of my colleagues in the television newsroom hustling to produce the bulletins. For a while I wrote down the headlines in a notebook, as a way of marking off the passing days. But it made me feel like a prisoner scratching lines on the walls of a cell, so I stopped.

The wind always changed direction in the midafternoon and then picked up, making the wood of my eyrie creak. That was my signal to go downstairs, have a martini and cook myself spaghetti on the two electric rings I'd bought from the hardware store. Each evening, I read in Patrick's library until my eyes began to close over the pages. I found that I slept better and I dreamed more – or remembered more of my dreams, anyway, which seemed healthy.

I spent almost two days searching the house for something that would explain the fragment of writing I had read on the plane. There was nothing, not a trace, although in a filing cabinet in the basement I found manuscripts of Patrick's novels along with carbon copies of correspondence.

In one folder I found a letter on Harvard stationery inviting a priest – let's call him Father Xavier – to give a talk to the Harvard Theological Society. The letter was fulsome; it praised the priest's work, his publications. It even hinted that he would be paid generously for the lecture. Father Xavier's response was not included, but from the next letter it was obvious that he had taken the bait. Patrick's second letter was a derisive attack, written on the same stationery, in which he called the priest an 'intellectual stick figure'. 'When we need a jug-eared ass-kisser to address the society, rest assured you will be our first port of call.'

There were some unspeakable letters to my father; a crazy letter to Nancy Reagan in the White House in which Patrick called her 'a one-titted witch'. In another letter – apparently in response to a request for an interview from a prospective biographer – Patrick bragged about having a wealthy patron to support him in a libel action and stopped just short of an outright threat to break the recipient's fingers.

Some of them were funny, but too often you felt that Patrick's attack was out of control. It was shocking to feel the force of his hatred, even second-hand. What made them so potent was that the venom was allied with an acute sensitivity to people's weaknesses. He knew where to stick the knife and how to twist it. Even when his attacks went wide of the mark, there was something so concentrated, so spectacularly ruthless in his efforts to offend, that the effect was still unsettling. Everything was thrown at the attackee: crimes, sins, birthmarks, poor grades, big ears, bad debts, flat feet, buck teeth, homely relatives. You sensed Patrick thought somehow that he was always on the side of the angels; somehow, he was the one victimised and misunderstood and therefore justified in whatever he flung back at his tormentors. I couldn't face reading more of them. They were an unworthy epitaph: his brilliance, his humour, his erudition, his empathy – all subjugated to the desire to wound. And I knew – because I had known him – that they weren't the whole story.

Patrick and I had been working in his garden once. An apple tree had fallen down in a storm. Its silvery trunk was blistered with lichen the colour of oxidised copper – a very soft green. We dragged the sawn-off branches up the garden. 'Jeez, you're a strong sonofabitch,' he said. This made me brim with pride – particularly as I was thirteen and undersized for my age, with arms and legs like pipe cleaners.

When we were finished we picked cherry tomatoes from the small vegetable garden on the lawn. They had a very herby and intense flavour. We sat outside the summer kitchen eating them from a colander. 'Do you ever give the finger to God?' he asked me.

'Not really,' I said, wondering what my father would make of this blasphemy.

'You don't ever want to throw up the window, flip Him the finger and say, "Eat me!"?'

I shook my head. He looked mildly surprised as he popped a handful of tomatoes into his mouth.

Another time we went rowing together off Pilgrim Point. We had rowed out about a mile and half on to the black water of the open ocean when the current seemed to alter. It began in one corner of the sea in front of us – a little patch of waves dancing up from the flat water – then it spread, until it was all around us.

'Know what I think, Skipper?' said Patrick, as a wave slopped in over the side of the boat.

'That we should get out of here?' I said.

The rowboat had two sets of oars and we pulled like madmen for the safer waters of the point. Patrick explained that the trick was to keep the waves abaft us and not to take them beam on, or we would capsize. Even at that moment, when we were both fearing for our lives, I liked the sound of those unfamiliar words: 'abaft', 'beam on', 'capsize'.

When we got to shore, Patrick made me promise not to tell my father what had happened. I was a little proud of myself: there was a bond between us – first of shared fear, and now a secret.

I didn't know which was stranger: to be remembering so much about Patrick, or to have forgotten so much in the first place. My uncle had been indispensable – whatever his faults, his love and curiosity had softened some of the austerity of my childhood. He was a spokesman for the importance of small things, enthusiasms, hobbies, games, puzzles, jokes, words, hot fudge, cream cakes, fried dough – all helpful talismans in a cold and draughty world that seemed to belong on the whole to people like my father.

I wasn't the only person who felt like this – it's why people over and over again were prepared to forgive him when he acted out of a child's untempered indignation and wrote them one of those letters, or told them to their face that they were a pain in the ass, or berated them for some peccadillo.

I often dreamed about Patrick – not surprising when you think that the whole house vibrated with his presence. I encountered it everywhere. It was apparent in the look of the house, the possessions with all their associations – any visitor would have noticed that. But living there gave me a more pervasive sense of him. Over time, his preoccupations became my preoccupations: I fretted over the low water pressure in the shower; I worried about cutting the grass; I kept milk and drinks cold in a box-cooler that Patrick had left under the kitchen table. The house bore the impress of Patrick's personality so strongly that by fitting myself into it, I began to resemble him.

I didn't notice it at first; the feeling stole up on me. Then one afternoon I was queuing in the post office to send some letters back to London and I caught a glimpse of myself in the mirror above the counter. Because it was a nuisance to drive into the town to do laundry I had got in the habit of supplementing my clothes with Patrick's – I borrowed a shirt or two, a pea jacket to wear on cool evenings, an old pair of trousers for wearing when I painted or cut the grass. I was shocked by the reflection partly because it was out of step with the image I had of myself: my hair had grown and was unkempt from my fingering it at the easel; I was unshaven and my clothes looked ragged. But I was also shocked that I looked so much like Patrick. And I thought I detected a watchfulness behind the postmistress's breezy efficiency.

That afternoon I drove up to the running track behind the high school. It wasn't just morbid curiosity. I wanted a clue. Perhaps the scene of his death would provide it.

Heat haze shimmered above the edges of the running track so that it looked as though it were cooking on an enormous griddle. The school's sports grounds had been carved out of a scrubby pine forest that was making halfhearted efforts to regain territory. Long strands of creeper reached almost to the one-hundred-metre start line – the straight bit of track that was joined on to the circuit like the tail of the letter Q. Poison ivy was growing thickly among the grass, some of it green, some of it brazen or bright red. Come September it would all be chased back to the woods, but for now it was permitted a temporary reconquest.

The main building of the high school wasn't old – a geometrical castle of pink bricks – but the extremes of temperature had weathered the track. On summer evenings it was a popular place to run, but it was relatively early and though I could hear the hollow thwack of tennis balls from the court on the other side of the softball pitch, the running track was empty.

Standing at the chain-link fence for balance, I stretched my calf muscles, then set off towards the start line and jogged slowly round. A catbird squawked in the pines around the track. I tried to imagine myself into Patrick's pristine size-twelve running shoes.

Spring is a dangerous season for old men – you don't have to be a poet to figure that out. Something in their blood starts bubbling at the approach of summer. It's the time of year, after all, when life calls on the living to get up and at it. And who wants to admit he's past the age when life called to him and meant it? Do anything but face that truth.

Mad with spring breezes, my Uncle Patrick had taken up jogging at the age of sixty-three.

Sixty-three. That's a number to conjure with. Patrick always said that people's numerical imaginations were very jaded. Between two and ninety-nine there's not much to hold their attention. What he called zero and I call nought is mystical, inviolate, virginity. Number one is golden, primacy – the American obsession: One hundred is a century, tantalizingly outside the span of human life. *The days of our life are three score and ten.*

Jogging lends itself to mathematical speculation. There's the beat of your shoes on the asphalt, measuring out four hundred metres with each lap. Each one is a quarter of a mile. Each time you pass the start, it's a lap gone. From here, it's only a small sideways step from maths to metaphysics: every birthday is a year gone. Every summer gone means another winter. And your whole life goes, seven years at a time, as invisibly and relentlessly as the hour hand. Seven, fourteen, twenty-one, twenty-eight, thirty-five, and so on: the scheduled climacterics, the times allotted by nature for retrospection and despair. Patrick was at sixty-three – the ninth lap of ten; thirty-five, which I was at the time, is the fifth.

I suppose that, pounding round the shimmering asphalt, Patrick was pursuing his youth. His heart was in the chase, but not up to it. He must have been miles away: remembering the summers he spent as a lifeguard along the North Shore; or the gleaming pompadour that he whipped up with Vitalis for the high-school prom; or some other memory that was too important to share with anyone, something that he kept back for himself as a bulwark against despair. A kiss, perhaps; or a poem; something he told no one. I wondered what he remembered as his congested heart gave out on the back straight; I wondered if it was an answer to the question that was bothering me: *Who was Patrick March?*

FOURTEEN

PATRICK MARCH WAS A WRITER but that's not the first thing that
I remember about him. The first thing that I remember about
Patrick's life is that he wet the bed as a child. I say 'remember', but this fact surfaces without any effort on my part. At
boarding school, I suffered from enuresis too – an improbably
tidy term for a constellation of humiliation, discomfort, rubber
sheets and special talks with the housemaster. You can imagine how understanding thirteen-year-old boys are about
someone who can't help pissing in his own bed. And I grew up
in more enlightened times than Patrick. His own uncle, a
priest – who like other Catholic priests was considered an
authority on children and marriage on account of having no
personal experience of either – was delegated to talk to him
about it. 'You're killing your mother!' was, according to Judith,

his memorable first approach. Then: 'When you're married, are you going to piss on your wife?'

Patrick's bedwetting, like mine, cleared up on its own, but it was always looked on as something shameful. Tricia, the niece who inherited the collected Frederick Rolfe, once tried to humiliate him by alluding to it. The three of us were standing on the deck of my father's rented house in Provincetown. Tricia was in her early teens, and a broth of hormones, orthodontic engineering, big hair and pullulating skin. Patrick had been teasing her about her boyfriends.

'I know something about *you*,' she said.

'What? Come on, what?' Patrick dared her, his voice rising an octave on the final question.

'I could say something about you, but I'm not gonna.'

'Come on.'

She narrowed her eyes and hissed at him: 'Wed-betting!'

Wed-betting. Her unintentional spoonerism dissipated the tension and gave Patrick a let-out.

'I've never bet on a wed in my life,' he said.

As the oldest son, Patrick had borne the weight of his family's expectations. He had carried this burden invisibly – in high school he was handsome, popular, athletic and outgoing. Then, at seventeen, he went to a Franciscan seminary to train for the priesthood – a choice that seemed less of a non sequitur in those days. Patrick used to describe arriving on the first day and choosing a box of cornflakes from a variety pack for his supper. It stuck in my mind because it seemed like the last thing in the world trainee priests would eat. What's more, there were no bowls. The seminarians would lay the cartons flat, tear off the front panel, pour the milk in and eat the cereal straight out of the box.

He left the seminary after two years, went to the state university at Amherst and then got a job teaching English in a missionary school in Western Samoa. He was happy there for a couple of years, but when the principal left, Patrick fell out

with his replacement and came home. He won a place at
Harvard Law School in the same year as my father, but left
after two semesters. The 'J.D.' after his name on the signpost
was wishful thinking.

Aged twenty-five he seemed to be settling into a pattern of
false starts. He had acquired a range of almost wholly useless
abilities – basic conversational Latin from the seminary, good
Samoan, a degree in English Literature – and a new prickliness
about what he felt was his inability to live up to his potential.
Meanwhile, my father was lapping him, winning plaudits from
his professors and showing a single-mindedness that must have
seemed like a reproach to Patrick.

My grandmother was so anxious about him that she agreed
gladly when he proposed going to art school in New York. To
a second-generation Italian American like her, it can only have
seemed a slightly less criminal waste of money than dropping
a suitcase of dollar bills into the Charles River.

Patrick drifted through art school. He took himself off the
Fine Arts course after a couple of semesters and studied
instead for a degree in commercial art – another name for
graphic design, I think. Previous experience had stiffened his
resolve to finish and he stuck it out to the end, but then had
difficulty finding work. He toyed with the idea of a doctorate.
'More education?' was his mother's incredulous reaction. My
grandfather said nothing: it was his nature to be as stoic and
uncommunicative as Plymouth Rock itself. By this time, my
grandparents' ambitions had devolved entirely on to my father.
By the time Patrick finished art school, my father had been
practising law in London for almost two years and his wife was
expecting their second child.

Patrick spent a miserable summer working night shifts with
a team of construction workers, building a tunnel to carry a
road through downtown Boston. In the fall, he found a job
teaching art at a private girls' school in Rhode Island. He got
paid enough to live on, had rooms on the campus and enough
free time to paint and write.

He taught his lessons in a perfunctory way and saved his energy for the evenings when he would write in longhand at the kitchen table of his tiny one-room apartment. He used the same long yellow legal pads my father used for his work.

The first draft of *Peanut Gatherers* was finished in less than three months. It's a remarkable fact – all the more so when you consider that Patrick struggled to finish anything else for the rest of his career. He was borne along by alternating spells of fear and enthusiasm. He once compared writing to a walk that began as a gentle downhill stroll in sunshine and quickly became an uphill struggle against worsening weather and diminishing light. What kept him going, I think, was the fear of adding another failure to the train he felt he dragged along behind him.

It is a novel about an innocent abroad, drawing heavily from Patrick's own experiences as a teacher in Western Samoa. He took advantage of the increasingly liberal sexual climate of the time to write frankly (and titillatingly) about the customs of the island and the adventures of its protagonist, Horace: the apparently innocent title is a punning allusion to a Samoan sexual custom.

Peanut Gatherers is a great book. It's written in a breezy style that's quite uncharacteristic of Patrick and is full of mischievous humour. There's a funny section about two witch-doctors who conduct a necromantic mind duel from their respective huts over the ownership of a Boston Red Sox baseball cap. In my favourite episode, a missionary from Utah gets Horace to help him translate the Book of Mormon into Samoan. Horace sabotages the translation, filling it with swearwords and nonsensical idioms. There's a brilliant set-piece where the missionary reads the translated book to a church full of incredulous locals. ('My manly element is as kinked as a taro root. I allow eunuchs to pleasure my rectum with green bananas. May ringworm visit my mother's descendants unto the fifth generation.') His services become the most popular events on the island. At each one, members of the congregation cry and wet themselves from laughter and the missionary thinks they're being visited by the Holy Ghost.

The book was quickly accepted by a Boston publishing house. It didn't sell particularly well, but by one of those twists of good fortune which had so far been absent from Patrick's life story, the rights were bought outright by a Hollywood studio for a fairly considerable sum. Patrick was given a lot of money to write the screenplay, and then when he and the executives found themselves at loggerheads, he was given even more not to write it.

Peanut Gatherers opened in 1966 as one of the last big-budget Technicolor musicals just as old Hollywood was about to be swept by a new avant-garde. It bombed at the box office but was nominated for two technical Oscars – set design and make-up.

Patrick had long before dissociated himself from the movie. His experience of Hollywood soured him and brought out an ugly – and uncharacteristic – streak of anti-Semitism. One of his pet projects was a list he kept of important figures in the film business and their original, Jewish, surnames.

His subsequent books were either unreadable or unpublishable: a libellous *roman-à-clef* about Hollywood; a novel about Button Gwynett – one of the signatories to the Declaration of Independence; a stream-of-consciousness novel about a left-handed hero that would be written in mirror-writing.

With many of these ideas, it was almost as though he was avenging himself on the approachability of the novel that had brought him his first success. As he got older, and none of his books gained an audience, he found himself in the perplexing position of being haunted by his own ghost, the ghost of a successful young novelist.

He did write children's stories and publish books of poetry privately. But what literary reputation he enjoyed was damaged by the whole scandal over *Amazon Basin*.

Amazon Basin was – even by Patrick's standards – a strange book. It purported to be a straight account of a journey through the Brazilian rain forest, but almost as soon as it was published a few careful readers had written to point out that the whole middle section had been lifted, unchanged, from a 1920s travelogue called *I Married a Headhunter* by a woman named Edna Beveridge.

This is odd for two reasons. Firstly, the plagiarised section of Patrick's book is easily the worst thing in it. The beginning and end of *Amazon Basin* together form a wonderful long essay about the nature of travel writing itself. The opening chapter ('The Fiction of Solitude') argues that all travelling is really a version of a more profound interior journey; that we are all, always, 'travelling' in this way; and that an unknown country is just a screen on which the traveller encounters his own fantasies. Patrick's version of this idea was a very extreme one. He insisted that all travel writing was actually fiction. Since the true subject of every journey is the consciousness of the traveller, he wrote, patently untrue tales of sea monsters and flying islands are actually more valid than 'accurate' accounts of places and customs. The conscious fabricator is more aware of his real theme than the traveller who mistakes his perceptions for objective reality. It's a dense and peculiar piece of writing which draws on phenomenology, medieval travel writing, the Vinland sagas, fake maps, budget guidebooks, the works of T. E. Lawrence and Sir Richard Burton and the logbooks of Donald Crowhurst – the yachtsman who went crazy during a solo circumnavigation of the world.

'The Fiction of Solitude' convinced at least one person that all travel was really unnecessary. Having written the chapter, Patrick didn't bother leaving Massachusetts to write about Brazil. He just slapped someone else's travel book into the middle of his own, as though his only concern was fulfilling his contractual obligations to his publisher.

The second strange thing is that *I Married a Headhunter is* not even a book about Brazil, it's a book about the dayaks of Borneo.

Amazon Basin was eventually withdrawn. It has a certain cachet with collectors.

Subsequent projected volumes included a Comparative Dictionary of Onomatopoeia – Vivian said it would be *Finnegans Wake* without the laughs; a novel about a woman who runs a marathon within two hours – the action was to be set within the time frame of the marathon with flashbacks; and a book that was actually a kaleidoscope, its pages to be sheets of textured and coloured glass that could be shuffled to produce different optical effects.

Thinking about the windfall that had altered Patrick's life, I couldn't help comparing it to the one that had altered mine. Luck – whether apparently good or bad – has a way of reversing itself in its consequences; and then repeating the trick. I wouldn't say that it was completely bad for Patrick, but the independence he got in this unanticipated and unlooked-for way exacerbated a dangerous part of his character. Money had released Patrick from any dependency, but it meant that he had been able to give up living, in the way that most people understand the word. He'd locked himself away; had become as autochthonous as a heartbeat or a self-winding watch. But why? 'He lacked hunger' was what my father had said. It seemed improbable to me.

These were the bare outlines of my uncle's life as I knew them. I was aware of gaps and missing years; episodes that blurred into one another; contradictions of time and place. What I knew, I knew imperfectly, and I was sometimes confronted with objects that showed the limits of my knowledge.

One evening, looking for a book to read, I found an album of photographs on one of the shelves in the library. They were of Patrick and my father some time in the 1950s. I knew instantly they had been taken in London, in winter or early spring. It was something about the colours. A rainy London day has a very specific palette. And the two brothers had the wintry, grey faces of early morning commuters. I turned the page, idly wondering who had taken the pictures, and saw two or three more, all in the same location (Wandsworth or Streatham Common?). These were all permutations of three people: Patrick, my father and my mother – looking improbably blonde and pretty. There were perhaps ten pictures of them, and the last two showed all three of them standing together. They were smiling awkwardly in the first – at whoever had been corralled into taking the picture – the second had been taken immediately after, and already the pose of the first had begun to dissolve, my father had turned away from the camera, my mother's eyes were closed as she laughed and brushed her hair out of her face. Patrick's hand was on her shoulder, and he looked absently across the frame.

The fact that Patrick had visited London came as a revelation. I didn't recall his ever mentioning it. I knew he had travelled in Europe – the rest of the photos were snaps of various European capitals, and blurry ones that looked like they had been taken out of a train window (Poland? Russia?) – and I suppose that would make a visit to London inevitable, but neither he nor my father had ever said anything about it.

It was only a glimpse into a single afternoon of three lives, but it implied that the dimensions of my ignorance were vast.

For a few days, I got so caught up thinking about the past that I stopped paying attention to the present. When I came back to myself, it was with the dawning realisation that coming to Ionia had led me to a dead end. It wasn't a flash of insight – a conversion – but something more slow-growing and deeply rooted: I couldn't stay. Sooner rather than later, I knew I would have to move forward and that meant leaving the island. What I didn't – couldn't – foresee was that going forward would just lead me more circuitously into the past.

FIFTEEN

AT THE BEGINNING, when I wasn't painting, I found myself odd jobs to do: I rooted around in the shed, planted vegetables and put up a bird feeder in Patrick's Japanese maple tree. I harvested pears and peaches from my orchard and delivered some in a brown paper-bag to the Fernshaws with a note thanking them for their help on the day of my arrival. There was no one at home, so I left the bag on the steps of their house. I occasionally passed Nathan selling lemonade on the empty highway as I drove back and forth to the Colonial Market for milk and newspapers.

I made a point of stopping every time. He was unfailingly rude, which I began to enjoy in a strange way. It became one of the reliable features of my routine. I always pretended not to notice, and chatted happily to him when I pulled up to buy his lemonade. He never took off his headphones, but served me with the music leaking out of them into the sunshine.

My proprietorial zest for my new home soon waned. I found living in the house even more uncomfortable than I had anticipated. To stay there with time on your hands was to get sucked into the unwinnable war against entropy that Patrick had been waging halfheartedly for years. For every one thing I fixed, two more seemed to break. Or, the quest for the right tool would take me to another part of the house where I would uncover worse damp, more dangerous wiring, or an impassable mountain of crockery that had been stacked up because the cabinet it was intended for needed fixing.

If I was careful, the situation wouldn't get any worse, but improvements were pretty much out of the question. House and owner had found themselves in a kind of stalemate between order and chaos and things had stayed that way for years. There might have been occasional skirmishes (grass-cutting, cleaning windows, taking trash to the dump), but no significant exchanges of territory.

Even though I intended to leave before the summer was up, I wanted to postpone my departure at least until I'd finished my first painting. It was also a way of deferring making a decision. I knew I needed time to figure out what to do next. If I went back to London, I would have nowhere to live until Mr Bakatin's lease expired.

As a result, there wasn't much incentive to work quickly. But I didn't fully share Patrick's talent for procrastination, and one Friday lunchtime in early August, I finished my picture. I hung it up in the summer kitchen; hammering the nail in gave me an illicit thrill. What would Mr Blair of the churchmen's fund have to say about that? I wondered.

But standing back to look at the completed painting, I felt deflated. It could have been any stretch of coastal Massachusetts. It lacked the sense of menace that I felt up on the widow's walk, where the disparity between the size of the ocean and the size of the island suddenly became clear.

I gave myself the rest of the day off – which meant a day away from the house. Getting out of the house was a little like coming off a nuclear submarine. Leaving my clothes at the laundromat in the local mini-mall, I was struck by its spaciousness and efficiency. Opening the washing machine, I half expected to be confronted by a collection of baseball cards, or a crate of empty jelly jars. Two weeks in Patrick's house would have made a minimalist out of anyone. I wanted to spend an afternoon in an air-conditioned shopping mall, surrounded by clean glass and the smell of new sneakers.

The sky was clouding over as I drove into Westwich. The road curved past a handful of shingled houses, and for a couple of miles it was shaded with trees. These, and the stone walls that divided up the cleared land into fields, made me think of the Kent countryside – where many of the island's first settlers had come from. There were still some orchards, but little of the countryside was agricultural. Some of the smaller houses had boats or lobster traps outside them, but the real income of the island came from tourists.

The islanders bitched about them – they drove too slowly or they drove too fast; they had too much money; they spoiled the views with obscenely large holiday homes – but there was no future on the island without them. Still, when motorists fought over parking spaces and rights of way, '*I'll* still be here in September' was sometimes used as a battle cry.

The traffic was backed up on the main road into Westwich. The bridge into the harbour had been raised to let an enormous yacht pass under it. Its sails were raised, but it was travelling under the power of its engines, and the canvas flapped uselessly in the light breeze. The people on deck were the bluebloods of Ionia's visitors. Theirs was an exclusive lifestyle that centred on the marina and a handful of waterfront properties in fashionable parts of the island. There was a circuit of elite cocktail parties that sometimes counted the President among their guests. Ionians were openly proud that they hosted such grand visitors. It always baffled me that

those people came at all. It must be something puritanical in
the American character that finds a kind of rugged virtue in
the chilly water and craggy beaches of Ionia. It's nobody's
image of a holiday island. From the ferry, the original houses
with their tiny seafront windows look as if they're narrowing
their eyes against the wind.

The ferry from Falmouth had arrived about half an hour
earlier. Squadrons of tourists had just rented mopeds from the
shops that lined the quay. They looked insectile in their cheap
helmets, buzzing around on tiny hornet engines. Six times a
day in summer, the ferry from Falmouth disgorged its load of
passengers. Many of them made it no farther than Westwich
itself. They were content to stroll around the town, visit the
Toy Museum, and eat a plateful of fried seafood.

There were big lines outside Grandma Wobbly's Taffy
Pantry, but I had the shopping mall pretty much to myself. I
browsed around the bookstore and then went for lunch at a
place called the North End Pizzeria. Pixellated giants played
baseball on a projection screen in the corner. Outside it was
beginning to rain lightly. With the sun extinguished and the
streets empty, the town seemed to be practising for the out-of-
season — the notoriously bleak winters and acres of dull time
between Labor Day and Memorial Day that the islanders
boasted of having to themselves.

I bumped into Terry and Nathan Fernshaw outside a hi-fi
shop in the mall. They'd just finished lunch themselves and
Nathan had disappeared to go to the toilet. Terry was standing by herself gazing at the stereo equipment. I didn't
recognise her — she was wearing a robin's-egg blue cashmere
sweater, sparkling new white jeans and a pair of clogs. The
effect was stunning, but a little odd. It seemed old-fashioned
for a woman barely out of her teens.

When she noticed me she gave me a wave and smile. I
realised she was thanking me for the apples I had taken round
to her house.

I thought she looked beautiful. Standing there, smiling back at her, but unable to talk to her, I felt a pang of homesickness like a cold finger on my heart.

Nathan appeared from the toilet. He was wearing baggy hip-hop-style pants and an LL Cool J T-shirt.

We all drank chocolate milk under an enormous skylight that relayed the spattering of the rain. I couldn't be sure how much Terry understood of what I said. She never spoke herself, although she occasionally made a noise that was her approximation of 'No, Nathan!' when she felt her brother was getting out of hand.

'My mom doesn't let me drink chocolate milk at home,' Nathan confided. 'It makes me hyper.'

I realised Terry was accustomed to a hearing person's inability to understand her language. She was patient with my incomprehension and, like her mother, skilful at using simple gestures to communicate. Nathan was our interpreter of last resort.

The two of them had been shopping, Terry explained. She needed some things for when she went back to school in the autumn. She was in her final year at Gallaudet, a university for the deaf in Washington, DC. She rolled her eyes when I admitted I hadn't heard of it.

'Ask your sister if she's heard of Swansea,' I said to Nathan.

'Swansea?' He finger-spelled it to his sister. She looked baffled.

'It's where I went to school,' I said.

Her face said: Where?

'Wales. It's beautiful.' I mimed big mountains. 'It's three thousand miles over there.' I pointed through the back door of the drugstore.

'I want to go to Indonesia,' said Nathan. He was speaking and signing simultaneously. 'I want to see the Komodo dragons.' He performed an extravagant mime which concluded with him writhing on the floor. 'They can swallow a whole goat.'

Terry was trying not to laugh. She warned her brother to take it easy. He was standing on his chair and lurching around with the frenzied energy of a dog who has just been let out of a car. I felt slightly envious that chocolate milk didn't have this effect on me.

'I'm thinking of seeing a film,' I said. 'I don't know what's on, but you're both welcome to come.'

Terry looked doubtful. It hadn't occurred to me until I said it that she wouldn't be able to follow any of the dialogue. The gaucheness of my suggestion was overshadowed by Nathan's reaction. He accepted my invitation by shouting, 'Yeah!' and standing up so quickly that he knocked his chocolate milk on to his sister. It spilled on to her lap. She was on her feet, scraping vainly with a napkin at a dark blotch that had spread down the front of her jeans. She was patently furious, both with Nathan and me. She flashed me a look that seemed to say: 'You bought him the chocolate milk!'

I went to get some sturdier paper towels from the men's room. As I stood holding the door ajar with my foot, snatching fistfuls of the green towels from the dispenser, I could see Terry upbraiding Nathan in sign. He kept looking away abjectly.

The towels made no difference. Terry went to the ladies' room to try again with soap and water. I wanted to say, 'It doesn't look so bad,' but it would have been a lie. The pristine effect was ruined: it looked like someone had poured a bottle of ink on a swan. The colour and location of the stain couldn't have been more unfortunate. She walked slightly pigeon-toed to the toilet.

'Your sister's really cut up about those pants,' I said.

'She's really mad,' said Nathan. 'She's supposed to be meeting Michael.'

'Who's Michael?'

'Her boyfriend.' Nathan slurped the last half-inch of his milk.

Terry came back from the toilet. The ugly stain wouldn't shift. I could see how badly she wanted to look good for her boyfriend.

'What time does the ferry get in?' I asked her.

Terry pointed at her watch and held up one finger.

'Why don't you go back home and change?' I suggested. 'Nathan and I will go to the movie and I'll drop him off at your house afterwards.'

Terry considered it for a nanosecond. If she had any misgivings about entrusting her twelve-year-old brother to the care of a virtual stranger, they were quickly put in perspective by the stain. She gave him a perfunctory kiss and practically ran to her car, her wooden soles clattering on the tiles of the mall.

Most of the films had already started. We were left with a choice of two: an animated version of the *Mahabharata* that took place underwater, or a stalk-and-slash called *Cross My Heart and Hope to Die*. I would have been happy to skip it altogether, but Nathan was keen on the horror film.

'It's supposed to be wicked scary,' he said.

The auditorium was less than a third full. Nathan and I appropriated a whole row and put the popcorn on a spare seat between us.

'So did you ever see the Queen?' said Nathan.

'I've had her over for cups of tea once or twice.'

'Have not.'

'Have too.'

I felt very conscious of my responsibilities in loco parentis. I don't think I would leave my child in the care of a man I'd only met two or three times. Laura and I once overheard part of a conversation between two black mums in Battersea Park. 'Black people might be muggers,' one of them said to the other, 'but white people fuck their kids.'

The movie was an absolute dog and I drifted off to sleep about halfway through. The plot contained some or all of the following elements: an Indian burial ground, a girls' boarding school, an unpopular fat student, heartless prefects, a Ouija board and a portal to another dimension, along with a high frequency of bloody murders and sexual shenanigans.

Towards the end of the film, I looked despairingly across at

Nathan as the script yanked another worn garment out of the cupboard of horror ready-to-wears. The coldest hearted and best looking of the fat girl's tormentors was necking with the young janitor in a row-boat, unaware of the music that announced the imminent approach of the ghostly knife-man.

Nathan's face was itself a horror cliché. His mouth was slightly open and his eyes wide with fear. I could hear a faint rustling noise as he ground kernels of popcorn reflexively in his hand.

Twenty years earlier I had come to the same cinema with Patrick, Vivian and my father. It had been another overcast day. I had nagged my father to take us to see a 3-D Western called *Comin' at Ya*. We were given special spectacles to watch the film and Patrick, who wore glasses anyway, had to figure out a way of wearing the two pairs together.

The movie was outstandingly bad, but my strongest memory of that afternoon is looking over to see Patrick with the 3-D glasses fixed crookedly under his own spectacles and shaking his head in resigned disbelief. My father claimed he had dropped his own glasses in the popcorn and had obscured half the screen with a buttery thumbprint.

After the cinema, the four of us had gone to play mini-golf. Vivian somehow managed a hole in one on his last shot and was awarded a free round by the man in the booth.

They were innocuous memories. It was impossible to square them with Patrick's crazy letters – one to my father had ended 'Watch out, short man' – or with the writing in the notebook. Either I had been wrong to see the fragment as a clue, or it was just too dense for me to unravel.

'That was awesome' was Nathan's verdict on the movie. 'Were you scared when the girl looked in that mirror and saw the face of the demon?'

'Not really,' I said – honestly, since I'd been asleep at that point.

'Me neither,' said Nathan.

It was almost five by the time the film ended, but it seemed later. Thunderclouds had taken over the sky, and the rain, which had been desultory as we sat with Terry under the skylight, crowded my windscreen faster than the wipers could clear it. The drops threatened to tear through the car's ancient plastic roof.

'Cool car,' said Nathan.

We drove back under the raging canopies of trees. At the intersection with the road to Patrick's house, a man was standing with his thumb out for a lift. He was wearing a black bin-liner as an improvised mac. For a moment my headlights illuminated his pale, unshaven face and the dark arch of his loosely open mouth. I saw him for less than a second, but it was enough for me to remember him later and recall myself thinking: He's got a long wait.

SIXTEEN

NATHAN AND I RAN the few yards from my car to the Fernshaws' porch but still got drilled with big cold bullets of rain. Mrs Fernshaw opened the door just as another clap of thunder struck. It was odd to see it register in her face. I wondered what it must feel like to her.

Mike Winks, Terry's boyfriend, was ensconced in a chair at the dining table. He turned out to be a paunchy academic in a moth-eaten cardigan – or at least I remember him in a moth-eaten cardigan, but I can't be sure I didn't make it up afterwards because it was an article of clothing that would have suited him so well. He was a couple of years older than me. His pale, saggy face suggested a constitution that had consumed too much caffeine, smoked too many cigarettes and spent too many hours in a dusty carrel up in the book stacks.

The three of them had been chatting. Terry, whose white jeans had been magically renewed, sat beside him, resting her hand on his knee, and looking at him with evident adoration.

'Aha, Nathan! Remember me?' he said, getting up and holding out his hand. His voice was pleasantly hoarse. 'Imagine: If a man who shakes hands up and down meets a man who shakes hands side to side, what will happen?'

Nathan looked perplexed but he extended his hand all the same. As they shook, their clasped hands went round and round in circles.

Mrs Fernshaw was baking macaroni. This time, when she invited me to stay to dinner I accepted immediately. I felt heavy-hearted at the thought of going back to my empty house. The Fernshaws' tiny home seemed full of life and companionably cosy. Winks was brandishing a bottle of red wine and pouring it into tumblers. Even the light from the television in the other room seemed to crackle round the walls like flames from a hearth.

'This is nice,' I said. I didn't speak much during the meal, which was conducted two-thirds in sign. Winks joked and teased. He was easygoing and likeable. Even when he was just talking to me he had the odd mannerism of signing his words as he spoke. He wasn't dashing, but there was something reassuring about his presence. He had that odd American gift – or is it a kind of insensitivity? – of talking all the time and still seeming able to form a distinct and favourable impression of your personality.

Mrs Fernshaw – Winks called her Harriet – chased us out of the kitchen while she and Terry cleared up. The rain had stopped. Nathan was back in front of the television. I went out to the porch with Winks while he had a smoke. We kept the lights off to discourage the biting insects, and the darkness gave our conversation some of the intimacy of the confessional.

'I met them doing research for my thesis about five years ago,' he said. 'It was me who encouraged Terry to go to

Gallaudet. Now she's planning to go to med school. They're quite a find. We used to think the indigenous sign communities of the islands were extinct. We had an idea that some of the signs got adopted into ASL along with a lot of French. But what we've got here is a living link with the nineteenth-century deaf islanders, possibly even further back than that, maybe to seventeenth-century England. But that's not a conjecture that a respectable academic would want to stake his tenure on.'

'Is that your plan?'

'I made it this year. I should say *we* made it. We've been together about a year. People had researched the deaf community on the island before but they kept missing the Fernshaws. I've got a hunch it was something to do with the old man. They don't talk about him much, but I gather he was pretty much of an asshole.'

'Where is he now?'

'He died when Nathan was a baby. He was a fisherman. Hell of a tough guy by all accounts. Freak accident. Man works his whole life at sea and then drowns about twenty feet from shore. They don't like to talk about it. It was a shame. That whole thing – sign, fishing – it's all going. It's all gone, practically. This place is turning into Long Island. Used to be it was far enough away to keep it special. But nothing's far any more.'

'No,' I agreed, but I was thinking how far we seemed in that darkness from any life I knew properly. 'How many people still use the language?'

'This is it. A speech community of three. Maybe the world's rarest living language. That's what made the work so special.'

'I know someone else who says his wife knows it.'

'Who?'

'Mr Diaz, he's a lawyer in Westwich.'

The tip of his cigarette glowed brightly as he inhaled. 'Well, I've checked out everyone who has ancestors on the island. Diaz is obviously not an island name. You know her maiden name?'

'Nope.'

'Thing is, she may know some signs, but that's not the same thing as speaking the language. I can get us two beers in Tijuana, but that doesn't mean I speak Spanish. People here like to say that everybody here spoke sign language. I don't think it's true. Everyone knew a couple of signs, knew enough to lip-speak so they could be understood. In LA, a lot of people can tell their maid to "*limpia el baña*". It hardly counts as speaking the lingo, does it?'

'My uncle had a couple of manuals of the language in his library,' I said, to change the subject. With academics, you sometimes stumble on to some innocuous topic that turns out to be the pet rock they've been stroking for twenty years. Once Laura mentioned we'd just been to see *Hamlet* to an academic at a dinner party and we got three-quarters of an hour of *ur-texts*, Bad Quartos and printer's errors.

'Really? Why'd he have those?'

'Local interest, I suppose.' I realised that Winks assumed my uncle was English. 'He was from Boston. He lived on the island.' Mentioning Patrick made me remember the house, like a pile of a homework that I had left undone. The wicker rocker creaked as I stood up.

'In the old Captain's house?'

'That's right.'

'Funky-looking old place.'

'Well, you should drop round some time.' I had begun to get ready to leave.

'We'll do that. Nice meeting you, Damien.'

'Likewise.'

To their obvious pleasure, I thanked Terry and Mrs Fernshaw with a sign that Winks had shown me, then I went into the television room to say goodbye to Nathan.

'See you, mate,' I said.

'See you. Thanks for taking me to the movie.' He didn't look round from the TV, but I felt so embarrassingly moved by his spontaneous gratitude that I didn't know where to put

myself for a second. I stood there long enough for him to turn
to me with a puzzled expression, as if to say: Still here?

'I'm off then,' I said redundantly.

Winks stopped me by the kitchen table. He had his arm
round Mrs Fernshaw. 'Harriet says she remembers your
uncle,' he said. 'It was your uncle, right?'

'Patrick, yes.'

Mrs Fernshaw made a quick movement, drawing her hand
over her face and pointing at me, nodding all the time, in a
gesture that can only have meant: Yes, your face is familiar. I
felt she wanted to say something more about him and I waited
for a moment on the step. She hesitated, then smiled and
turned away.

As I got into my car for the short drive home I was thinking to myself that the real risk in spending time with other
people was that you might find you liked it. That was the dangerous outcome Patrick had ended up protecting himself
against.

The grass on my lawn seemed to have grown during the
afternoon. The blades were loaded with rain and brushed
water on to my feet and the bottoms of my trousers. I tried to
avoid getting my shoes soaked by picking a path along a slight
ridge in the roll of the lawn where the grass was shorter and
less like a brush full of wallpaper paste. I was so absorbed in
finding my way in the dim light that I had virtually reached
the porch before I noticed that my front door had disappeared.

The gap that remained was perfectly neat, but there was a
suggestion of violence in its absence – like a missing tooth, or
an empty sleeve pinned to the front of a veteran's jacket. It was
only when I got closer that I realised the door had been taken
clean off its hinges and laid flat inside the entrance.

SEVENTEEN

I CALLED THE POLICE from the Fernshaws' house and waited there for the patrol car to arrive. I had thought of going in by myself, but my natural timidity and a reasonable fear that whoever had knocked the door in might still be inside soon put an end to that plan. I had been thinking about the bit in *Cross My Heart and Hope to Die* when the caretaker of the school gets out of bed in his pyjamas to check a door banging in the attic and ends up impaled on a flagpole.

Officers Santorelli and Topper from the local force followed me back up the road in their car and we investigated the house together.

'When did you become aware that your property had been burglarised?' said Officer Santorelli.

'An hour, half an hour ago. Whenever I called.' I was

distracted by the figure of Officer Topper, who was creeping through the kitchen with his long-handled torch held in that odd overhand grip that seems to be an obligatory part of police procedure, along with resting your thumbs in your belt loops and having a swaggering-buttocked waddle. I switched on the main light and he gave a slight start which he tried to conceal.

'Apart from the damage to the front door, have you noticed any damage or items missing?' said Officer Santorelli.

'Hey hey, what's this?' said Officer Topper, playing his torch over the vitamin pills in the bathroom. 'Looks like some-one's been after your pharmaceuticals.'

'No, that was like that,' I said. 'There's no room in the cup-board.'

'Entry was gained via that. I'd guess egress was made via the same route,' said Santorelli, pointing at the front door. He made 'route' rhyme with 'grout'. 'I'm going to take a look upstairs. Wait down here and see if you can find anything missing.'

The house looked much as I had left it – or, more accu-rately, as Patrick had left it. The burglar had opened some of the cupboards in the library, but didn't seem to have made it as far as the second storey of the house. The hard part was fig-uring out what, if anything, he had taken. It took a peculiar kind of mental effort to look at everything that Patrick had gathered under that one roof and try to determine what wasn't there. It was hard to imagine which, if any, objects would appeal to a burglar. It didn't seem likely that someone would have bothered making off with an ice-cream scoop, or a set of hub-caps decorated with the Coca-Cola insignia.

'British?' said Officer Topper shyly.

'Excuse me?' I said.

'You're British.'

'That's right.'

Officer Topper looked pleased with himself. 'I thought I detected an accent. What part are you from?'

'Wandsworth,' I said. 'But my family's originally from the States.'

He nodded knowingly. 'My own family hail from up Norfolk way. The Thetford Toppers. The name Topper comes from "de Pearce". My ancestors fought alongside Richard the Lionheart in the Holy Land. That there's my crest.' He held out a ring as big as a knuckleduster so that I could peer at his coat of arms. 'A serpent couchant on a ground of gules,' he said.

'De Pearce – I think I've heard tell of their deeds,' I said. 'Will you and your colleague be dusting the house for prints?'

'Unfortunately we're seeing a lot of these seasonal break-ins,' said Officer Santorelli when he returned. I explained about the derelict I had seen in the rainstorm. Santorelli made notes and then told me I would be contacted by a counsellor who specialised in helping the victims of crime.

I walked the policemen back to their squad car and then tried to go to sleep under the life mask of Keats in the summer kitchen. Although I felt indifferent about any losses, I had misgivings about sleeping in the house until the door had been strengthened and put back on its hinges. There was the unpleasant possibility that whoever had broken in might return to find something he had missed the first time. The summer kitchen had a sturdy wooden door with a porthole. It looked like something you would find on the wheel-house of a tea-clipper and felt solid enough to withstand a typhoon.

I was scared, of course, because of the burglary, but I also felt disappointed and angry. I turned on to my side in a futile effort to get comfortable in that narrow bed. I felt the weight of the possessions in the main house exerting a gravitational pull on me. I was a swimmer unable to free himself from the vortex of a sinking ship.

Irrationally, the break-in seemed to confirm all my misgivings about living in the house. This life wasn't what I had imagined, I thought ruefully. I had turned out to be the beneficiary of a dusty, fusty, overcrowded, high-maintenance, accident-prone wooden shack of a building. The house was a tar baby.

EIGHTEEN

THERE WAS WORSE NEWS to come. The burglary had delayed any possibility of my leaving by at least two weeks.

A cursory inspection of the house in the morning showed no obvious evidence of theft or damage, apart from the broken door. But after a frantic hunt for money to pay the locksmith, it became apparent to me that the burglar had made off with the black leather pouch that contained virtually all my cash, my credit cards and chequebook, both my passports, and my plane ticket back to London.

The locksmith was sympathetic; I was mortified. We had to drive in convoy to Westwich where I borrowed the money to pay him from Mr Diaz.

The previous day's rain seemed to have purged the air of humidity. It was bright and dry, and the sea sparkled lazily all

the way out to the horizon. It was a beautiful place, no doubt
about that. The horn blast of the outgoing ferry split the air
with an enormous *moo*. At the beginning of the summer I had
welcomed the idea of spending months on Ionia. Now, two
obligatory weeks there felt like a prison sentence.

'What else did you lose?' said Mr Diaz, when the locksmith
had been paid off. His assistant brought us crullers and strong
filter coffee. The office was furnished with a chunky reproduction Victorian desk and armchairs upholstered in generic
law-office leather.

I told him I had no idea. 'Nothing is obviously *not* there. I
mean, nothing that was there is obviously missing. But you've
been to the house – the difficulty is knowing where everything
is . . . was. I could really use the inventory you mentioned.'

'I am *so* sorry.' Mr Diaz slapped his hand theatrically on his
forehead. 'I promised to get one to you and it completely
slipped my mind. Let me get one copied for you now.'

Mr Diaz joked with his secretary for my benefit as he
passed on his instructions to her over the intercom. 'First we
lock him out of his house, then we forget to send him his
inventory. He must be wondering how I stay in business.'

The burglary involved me in several days of boring hassle
with insurers, passport offices and the airline which had only
two high points. One was using Mr Diaz's office as a base for
making phone calls and receiving faxes. I found myself enjoying being in an office again and flirted with a pretty paralegal
called Stephanie, who unfortunately turned out to have a serious boyfriend. The other was my first-ever identity parade.

Officers Topper and Santorelli waited with me behind the
one-way mirror while the suspects were marched in.

My guy – Bill Kelly – could hardly have been more conspicuous if he'd had three arms. He was the only one in the
line-up who looked like he had spent the night in a bush. He
had an uneven skull like a bumpy old potato – I heard later it
was caused by an industrial accident – and I recognised the
slack, unshaven face that I'd seen poking out of the bin-bag.

Leaving the police station, I was hopeful that I might find out what Kelly had done with my plane ticket and passports at least, but he remained adamant that he was not responsible for the break-in. He claimed he had been sleeping on the beach when he had been woken up by the rain. He wasn't sure where he got the trash-bag sou'wester he had been wearing when I saw him, but eventually 'remembered' seeing a new-model Japanese four-by-four parked in my driveway.

'Right,' I said to Officer Santorelli. 'In other words, the car that belonged to the real burglar.'

'He says he took nothing from the house.'

'But you don't think he's telling the truth?'

'I'm not paid to have opinions, I'm paid to catch bad guys,' said the policeman. I was beginning to miss Officer Topper and his signet ring. Officer Santorelli was a pencil-thin Italian American whose meagre physique somehow suited his offi-cious, cheese-paring manner. He went on: 'There have been cases – I'm not saying this is one of them – where collectibles are stolen to order. This kind of crime on the island has just exploded in the last couple of years. I guess the only way of knowing for sure is to go through the inventory and check it's all there.'

I was so furious I could barely bring myself to speak to the trauma counsellor who came round to visit me – and turned out to be Officer Topper. 'We're a small force,' he admitted. 'We need to multitask.'

'I'm very keen to get my property back,' I said. 'I would be inclined not to press charges against Mr Kelly if he just told me where I could find my passports and plane ticket. This whole . . . debacle' – if in doubt with an authority figure it's always good to slip in some ten-dollar words – 'comes at a very unpropitious time for me.'

Officer Topper nodded sadly and told me that the first stage in overcoming any form of loss is learning to accept it.

After half an hour of this nonsense, he tried to engage me in another genealogical discussion but I couldn't bring myself to humour him. People trace their genealogy to find out who they are, but as you climb up a family tree, the branches multiply exponentially. You don't arrive anywhere, you dissolve into atoms, into primordial soup. Ten generations back, we all have one thousand direct ancestors and that number continues to double as you go further and further into the past. Who knew how many generations there were between Officer Topper and the Siege of Acre? He might have had a million ancestors alive at that time. There was a chance he was related to My Lord de Pearse, but there was an equal chance that he was related to some poxy old falafel seller in the Saracen army, or a one-eyed washerwoman who gave hand jobs to the Norman cavalry. We've all got kings, peasants, blackguards, bishops and salt-of-the-earth village blacksmiths in our ancestry.

But fixating on some probably spurious ancestors was no more ridiculous than what Patrick had done. Out of all the objects in the world, Patrick had chosen a handful with some arbitrary association to himself and designated them to be his legacy. Keeping it all together was so important that he'd made arrangements for its survival beyond his own life into the Patrick-less world that came after him.

I began to wish that Bill Kelly had just taken the whole lot and saved me from my role in perpetuating a dead man's foolishness.

NINETEEN

IF THE POLICE BELIEVED that the likeliest villains were a gang of well-organised crooks who wanted to get their hands on my uncle's cup-plate collection, it wasn't my business to contradict them. In fact, it seemed more sensible to go along with their theory and inflate my insurance claim accordingly. I wasn't hopeful that I would see much of the money myself, but I figured I might get some, and besides, the idea of selling or hiding some of Patrick's beloved possessions satisfied an irrational desire for revenge on the house and its contents. At the back of my mind, I think I knew that I was behaving like someone who kicks a table leg after he's barked his shin on it. All the same, I was determined to find some things in the house worth stealing.

Patrick had word-processed the inventory on his computer,

a machine so obsolete it used floppy disks that looked as if they belonged in the jukebox. The printer was no less antique. It typed the text through a ribbon in a feeble, crabbed font that I remembered from letters he'd sent me at school. The document itself was two hundred and fifty pages long. I imagined Patrick revising it lovingly over long winter months, adding to it, elaborating his descriptions of the objects. Its tony prose read like the brochure of the auction house where I'd worked during my summer holidays: 'twin-handled chamber pot in Sèvres porcelain, hand-painted with rosettes of acanthus leaves'; 'four blown-glass decanters mounted in buffalo-hide tantalus, monogrammed in gold lettering, TWO'.

More than half of the pages dealt with his book and record collections, but I decided that in the interest of realism, I'd set these sections aside at first. The thief I had in mind was an opportunist with no special knowledge of the house. It would strain credibility for him to be sifting through the filing cabinets of 45s in the hope of unearthing a rare piece of vinyl. Similarly, I knew various books were definitely missing from the library – having seen Edgar Huvas making off with them at the Greyhound station in Providence – but a bibliophile burglar was an unlikely apparition. My thief – and I was beginning to feel as if I knew him quite well – was more of a magpie. He would have sneaked in, grabbed the shiniest, most valuable-looking things he could find and made off with them.

The difficulty was that even the most optimistic or desperate burglar would have looked around Patrick's kitchen with a sinking heart. I imagined the beam of his flashlight flickering over the penny-banks. He might have rummaged through the drawers over the sink looking for some cash. All he would have found were 'five lace-trimmed tea towels in Derbyshire needlepoint'. Maybe he'd snatched the painting from above the kitchen table – 'contemporary landscape in Primitive style by Martha Calhoun of Dennis, Mass. Painted in 1983 and signed by the artist' – only to realise it was a picture of the house he was burgling. The burglar who tried to fence that might as well include an arrow showing where he'd got in.

I opened the inventory at random and stabbed at the page: 'Alpine wineskin with hand-carved wooden stopper' – hopeless.

Another stab: 'authentic Gurkha kukri with notched blade. Cased in original leather scabbard.' I remembered the knife – it looked like something for peeling potatoes. Then: 'hand-painted satirical Russian matryoshka dolls'. I turned over half a dozen pages impatiently. This was more like it: 'pair of early nineteenth-century English duelling pistols with chased silver handles'. Without thinking what I was doing, I put a tick by it on the list.

Was that smart? I reversed the pencil and rubbed out the mark. I started to feel slightly guilty about the whole exercise.

A bang on my door made me jump. I looked up to see Nathan Fernshaw shading his eyes and peering through the kitchen window.

'What's up, Nathan?' I said, overcompensating for my nervousness by being overfriendly.

'My mom said you might need a hand.'

'That was thoughtful,' I said. I was trying to remember how I'd last behaved when I'd had nothing to hide. 'You know what, it would be a big help if you could cut the grass – I'll pay you.'

I took him down to the shed and showed him how to drive the mower. 'Take your time,' I said. 'If anything gets caught in the blades, do *not* try to free it, come and get me. I don't want you jeopardising your future as a concert pianist.'

He was excited by the chance to drive the mower by himself. I told him to go slowly: I would pay him by the hour. This small act of patronage made me feel better about my criminal activities. I also thought he might alert me if Officers Topper and Santorelli turned up unexpectedly.

For the next two days Nathan mowed and I went through the inventory, ticking off the items that would have appealed to a sharp-eyed thief. As the fictional burglar enriched his swag bag hourly and I, his accomplice, rummaged around the house aiding and abetting him, it became clearer that Bill Kelly had taken almost nothing apart from my money and travel documents. All the most precious objects remained untouched. Nothing had gone from the cabinets in the library or the packing cases in the cellar. I worked slowly, accumulating a stash of items which I hid in a sea chest in the attic. I erred on the side of caution, but still ended up with a fairly valuable-looking haul, including some nice silver pieces and jewellery. The pistols were less glamorous than the description in the inventory would have led you to believe. They were stubbier, less ornate, rusty and a little greasy. I cocked one and aimed at the wall. The hammer tripped with a satisfying click. The other was faulty and wouldn't work at all.

I found myself often distracted by the things that I unearthed: photos of Patrick, a dozen different kinds of Chinese cricket cages, a Victorian toy theatre with a painted proscenium. Meanwhile, the lawnmower buzzed just out of conscious awareness.

On the second day, I heard the mower stop. It was around eleven-thirty in the morning. I was in the library, sorting through a drawer of cuff-links – the light was better in there.

Peering out of the window, I saw Nathan, still sitting on the mower, talking to a blonde woman in a frock and pointing towards the house.

I put the drawer back upstairs in Patrick's bedroom and came back down when I heard knocking. I could see the woman's shadow outlined on the mesh of the screen door. She was shading her eyes with her hand and trying to peer in.

The lawnmower started up again as I stepped out on to the porch. My first look at the woman was enough to disabuse me of the idea that she was a police officer. She was wearing too much make-up, and was too expensively and impractically dressed in a frock and a pair of heels. She had big sunglasses on, and crazy hair in blond corkscrews which were loosely tied back. She was nervous, I thought, but greeted me with an enthusiasm that bordered on the ferocious. 'Well, hi! You must be Damien.'

I was taken aback. Something in her manner made me think of a little girl, but she was certainly over fifty.

'Miranda Delamitri,' she said, giving me her hand. 'I was a friend of Patrick's.' She lifted her sunglasses with her free hand, exposing plenty of blue eye-shadow, and smiled at me. She had great teeth and the time-defying youthfulness of a well-loved vintage car.

'I've heard so much about you,' she said. She didn't let go of my hand.

'You're a friend of Patrick's?' I said, feeling a little uncomfortable.

'Uh-huh.' She was looking me up and down. 'You know, you remind me of him so much.'

'It's probably the clothes,' I said. 'They're his.'

She gave a little yelp of pleasure. 'Oh! That shirt was a gift from me! I'm so glad you're wearing it.'

I'd found it in Patrick's closet. Its quality had set it apart from all of the others. By now, Mrs Delamitri had stepped over the threshold into the kitchen. 'Oh my,' she said plaintively. 'And everything's just the same.' She seemed overcome for a moment. 'I'm sorry. It's been a while since I was here. This is rather painful.'

I offered to get her some Kleenex but she pulled out an expensive handkerchief of her own and dabbed at the corner of her eye mournfully.

'Would you like to be alone?' I said.

'I'm fine,' she said. 'Just give me a minute.' She took a couple of deep breaths. 'They say you should just let it out, don't they?'

'Let what out?'

'The grief. The pain.' She blew her nose silently. 'How are you coping, Damien?'

'I'm coping,' I said, with a stab of guilt as I thought of the sea chest full of valuables in the attic. 'One day at a time, you know. Remembering the good things.'

'And there are so many good things,' she said with passion. 'That's right. What are the good things that you remember?'

A voice in my head said: *pair of early nineteenth-century English duelling pistols with chased silver handles.*

'His humour. His kindness. What about you?'

Mrs Delamitri took another deep breath. There was a slight catch in her voice as she said: 'His mind.'

Through the window behind Mrs Delamitri's head, I could see Nathan raking apples from under the apple tree as I'd asked. If they were left where they lay, they could clog up the blades of the mower.

Mrs Delamitri wandered into the dining room. 'I've always loved this one,' she said, gazing at a framed Mughal fan painted with a semi-erotic scene of a woman entertaining her moustachioed lover in a garden.

'You're welcome to take it,' I said. As odd as she was, Mrs Delamitri's grief about Patrick's death exceeded anything that had been expressed by his own family.

She looked at me with amazement. 'I could never do that. He wanted it all to stay together.' She seemed overcome again. 'I – oh my. Do you mind if I sit down?'

I got her a glass of water from the kitchen. Since she seemed disinclined to take off her sunglasses, I switched on the light.

'Patrick and I were close,' she said. 'I just wasn't able to come to the funeral. I hoped he'd understand.' She dabbed her eyes again. 'You're probably wondering what on earth this crazy woman is doing in your house.'

'Just slightly,' I said as a joke, but she looked puzzled, so I put my arm on her shoulder to reassure her.

Her sob turned into a chuckle. 'So like Patrick,' she said wistfully, holding on to my sleeve as if it were a holy relic, and gazing at me through the big moons of her glasses.

'Don't be silly,' I said. 'I'm glad you've come. Please excuse the air of chaos. I got burgled earlier this week.'

'How awful,' she said.

'It's more of an inconvenience. The police picked up the guy who did it, but he's insisted he didn't take anything. It's all a big pain in the arse.'

We sat and talked in the library for about half an hour. In spite of her oddness, I couldn't help liking her. She had met Patrick at a writing class he had taught during the summers in Westwich, she said. He'd had a reputation as a gifted teacher. All of this was news to me. She said he'd also commuted to the mainland to teach at a prison outside Boston, where he was popular with the inmates. Although she didn't say so, I had the impression that Mrs Delamitri's relationship with my uncle had eventually transcended literature, but I was trying not to think about the two of them in bed together.

'What was he up to?' I asked her.

'I think he was doing a little painting, more writing.'

'Any idea what? Not the dreaded dictionary?'

'I don't know,' she said. 'He wouldn't talk about it.'

The screen door creaked open and then slapped shut. Nathan Fernshaw called out from the kitchen, 'I'm going home for lunch.' His head poked round the door of the library 'I'll finish the lawn when I get back. Hello, Mrs Delamitri.'

'Hi, Nathan. How's your sister?'

'She's good.'

'You two know each other?' I said.

'Oh, sure,' said Mrs Delamitri. 'We're old friends, aren't we, Nathan?'

Nathan's bicycle was parked beside the front porch, so I unlocked the front door to let him out. Mrs Delamitri was looking more composed when I got back. She'd tethered up her crispy blond hair and applied a lick of lipstick.

'One of the reasons I came, Damien, is that I have some things of yours. Patrick left them with me, but I'm sure he wanted you to have them.'

'Thank you,' I said. This seemed very odd to me, it wasn't like Patrick to let anything out of his sight.

We went out to her sporty, powder-blue convertible and she opened the trunk. In it were eight green box files of the kind that had disappeared from Patrick's study.

'Any idea what's in them?' I asked, trying to sound breezy, though I felt puzzled and suddenly suspicious.

'I'm not sure,' she said. 'Letters, I think.'

Carrying the boxes back to the house, I was dry-mouthed with anticipation. I wanted to open them, but not in front of this nutty woman. I was torn between my eagerness to see what was in them and a fear that the contents would disappoint me. I was sure they were the files that had disappeared from Patrick's desk.

We stacked them in the library.

'Well, thank you very much, Mrs Delamitri.' This definitely seemed like the right place to end her visit. 'I hope this didn't take you too much out of your way.'

'Oh no, I'm staying with one of my girlfriends up at War Bonnet.' She took a long, valedictory look over the bookshelves. 'I've just had a crazy idea,' she said suddenly. 'Why don't you let me buy you lunch?'

I hesitated. I was trying to cook up an excuse to stay behind and look at the files in privacy, but I couldn't think of a good reason to refuse.

'Please. It would mean a lot to me.'

'That would be nice,' I said, half hoping I sounded lukewarm enough to make her rescind the invitation. I didn't.

We drove to a fancy upscale place on the other side of the island. It was in a beautiful position, set back from a cliff top. The maître d' treated Mrs Delamitri with an un-American deference. This, and the fact that she seemed to have booked a table, made me think there was something more calculated about our excursion than she let on. But since she was buying me lunch, it seemed a bit rude to accuse her of boosting my uncle's papers.

I said I preferred to eat outside, and the waiter showed us to a table with a fantastic view of the sea. Mrs Delamitri pressed me to order whatever I wanted and chose an expensive white Burgundy from the wine list. I had to restrain myself from glugging it down. I told her the flavour reminded me of English strawberries.

'Life's too short to drink cheap wine, Damien,' she said. 'Now tell me about you.'

I explained as much as I thought was tactful about coming to Ionia and how I felt that, all in all, it would be good to get back to England. I told her I'd been marooned for a while by the burglary.

'That's such a shame,' she said.

She was skilful at turning the conversation away from herself, and appeared so genuinely interested in everything I had to say that I started to worry I was talking too much. I gathered she visited her friend on Ionia a couple of times a summer. But about herself, and her life in Boston, she wouldn't be drawn.

We drank that whole bottle of wine and most of a second. She pressed me to have dessert and ordered me a glass of sweet French wine to drink with it. It tasted of nuts and cream and God knows what else, and must have cost roughly what I spent on food in a week. She just seemed pleased that I was enjoying myself. During a pause after the dessert, I had a moment of inspiration. 'Did you ever come here with Patrick?' I said.

She looked down at her hand. Her painted nails were tracing lines along the tablecloth. She seemed to be struggling with a couple of contradictory impulses.

'I have a confession to make,' she said, touching her sunglasses nervously. 'Patrick and I were . . .' Her voice dropped as she added, almost in parentheses, 'There's no easy way to say this, Damien.' She made an impatient little gesture with her fingers. '. . . More than good friends.'

'The thought had crossed my mind.'

'I'm married, Damien.'

I nodded and tried to look soberly non-judgemental.

She went on. 'I did something rather silly. I wrote Patrick a number of letters. They were just . . . letters. Maybe a little bit explicit. Whatever. Within the context of our relationship, it seemed entirely appropriate. It's just . . .' She rolled her glass between her palms. 'My husband's a decent man.'

Phrases were coming back to me from the bundle of letters I had found in the drawer, in particular something rather outlandish Patrick's correspondent had suggested doing with a colander.

'Mrs Delamitri, you're welcome to have them back. I don't want your letters. I can't say I know where they'll be, but I'll be happy to return them.' I had that drunkard's expansive confidence that everyone's problems are soluble.

'Actually, that's not the problem I have. I already got them back. I . . . panicked slightly. I mean, I had no idea who was going to come and live at the house. I hope you understand. I truly felt I had no alternative.'

I couldn't tell if she was sweating slightly, or if her make-up was melting in the sunshine.

'Alternative to what?'

She rummaged in her handbag. I had the feeling that she was going to pull out a gun and shoot me. Instead, she produced her handkerchief, which she pressed against her temple. It smelled faintly of cologne. 'The sun's awfully strong.' She took another sip of wine and her rings clinked against the glass. I had the cruel thought that, however young she managed to keep her face, the backs of her hands still looked like the skin on a roast chicken.

'I had someone break into the house and take them,' she said. 'I hope you're not mad at me.'

'Mad at you?' The truth was I didn't know what I felt about it. 'Why? If you'd asked, I would have given you your letters.'

'I know you would've. Now that I've met you, I'm just so sorry about everything. But you must see that not everybody is as nice as you are. I had a lot to lose.'

'So Mr Delamitri has no idea about you and my uncle?'

'Mr O'Brien,' she said. 'Delamitri is my maiden name. And no, he doesn't.'

I said nothing. I was befuddled.

'I came to apologise,' said Mrs Delamitri. 'These things can be very upsetting. Believe me, I know. The last thing in the world I wanted was for you to feel unsafe in your home. I hope this will put your mind at rest.'

'So what did you do? You just looked under "Burglar" in the Yellow Pages and someone broke down my door?'

'It's not quite that simple, but if you have money, most things can be arranged.'

'What if I'd interrupted these guys?'

'These men are professionals, Damien. They wouldn't have harmed you in any way.'

'Well, while they were getting your letters, they also took the opportunity to steal my money, and passports, and my air ticket out of here.' I was counting out my losses loudly on my fingers and she tried to silence me with a discreet *Shush*. 'Did you pay them to do that or was it freelance work?'

'That was unavoidable. Tug – one of the . . .'

'Thieves?' I suggested.

'He said we had to make it look like a random break-in. It took them almost an hour to find anything a random burglar would be interested in.'

'Well, I'm relieved he's happy.'

She took my hand. 'Please don't be angry with me.'

I wanted to tell her that her simpering little-girl routine might have worked on Patrick, but she was old enough to be my mother. I sulked for a while, enjoying the view and going over the sequence of events in my brain. Mrs Delamitri fiddled with her handbag. 'Here,' she said. When I looked over at her, there was a cheque for five thousand dollars folded in half by my wineglass.

'I can't accept that,' I told her.

'Damien, don't be proud. I want to make amends. You

have every right to be angry with me. I don't want anyone else
to be the victim of my selfishness.'

As the afternoon had gone on, I noticed Mrs Delamitri's
accent meandering between Boston's North End and somewhere in the Cotswolds. The idea that Mr O'Brien and I were
victims of her selfishness seemed part of the same aspirational
self-deception: that she was the star-crossed lover of a famous
writer.

'Believe me,' she added tartly, 'I spent quite a bit more than
that having your house broken into.'

'You know what's strange, though,' I said. 'I could have
sworn those files were on Patrick's desk when I went to the
house after the funeral.'

She looked very sneaky for a moment. 'How many times in
your life have you done something really foolish, Damien?'

'Probably not as often as I ought to,' I said.

'You have to put yourself in my position. I was distraught.
I was in a hurting place.'

'You were composed enough to organise a fairly efficient
burglary.'

'Not the first time.'

'The first time?'

'Janine and I came with a ladder. It was her idea. I'm – I'm
not blaming her. I'm just saying I'm not proud of what I've
done.'

'You burgled the house *twice*?'

'I had no idea where the letters were. We took the boxes
because they were the first thing we could find. Then Janine
decided she wanted the skull.'

'She just took a shine to it?'

'I told her to leave it behind. It was Patrick's. All I wanted
was what belonged to me. But Janine's like that. She's creative.'
Mrs Delamitri made it sound like a medical condition – like dia-
betes. 'Once she gets an idea in her head, she just runs with it.
Well, we argued about it. I told her it would be terrible feng
shui – I mean, it's basically the head of a dead person. Can you

imagine? Then I was sure I heard someone coming. We rushed
out. Janine took the skull and sprained her ankle on the way
down. I had to carry her to the car. I *warned* her about the skull.'

I had a mental image of Janine and Mrs Delamitri struggling
up and down the ladder in shoulder pads and high-heel shoes.
Or possibly, Mrs Delamitri would have bought a special outfit
for cat burglary – a one-piece black number with a matching
mask by Donna Karan.

When the waiter brought the bill over, Mrs Delamitri
slipped him a credit card made out of some rare metal – tita-
nium or zinc or something.

'But the letters weren't in the boxes, so you had to hire professionals to do the job properly,' I said.

'I'm sorry, Damien.'

'What *had* you stolen, the first time?'

'I really don't know. I mean – I have an idea that there's
some bills and stuff. This probably sounds silly after everything I said, but I wanted to respect his privacy.'

Far out to sea, a three-masted yacht was under sail and
carving a chevron into the deep blue water.

'What will you do now?' she asked.

'Go back and have a swim,' I said.

'I meant more generally.'

'I'm not sure,' I said, and for the first time, my uncertainty
seemed like a virtue. I knew that I would leave the island as
soon as the cheque cleared. I wanted to go somewhere where
I could have a life of my own, but where or what that might
be, I couldn't say.

She talked about Patrick on the drive back. 'I saw him last year
about this time.'

'Did you stay at the house?'

'Yes,' she said, 'but I didn't spend the night with him. Not
in the same bed. He had terrible dreams. I used to hear him
crying out and I'd want to go to him. But I always stopped
myself.'

'Was he on medication?'

'Two or three kinds. For the depression and the mood swings. He could just about keep it together living the way he did.'

'Yeah, seeing people in homoeopathically small doses.'

'I loved him, you know,' she said. 'But there was always this feeling that he'd done something awful. I kind of felt bad for thinking it about him . . .'

We talked about funny things Patrick had said or done. I recounted Patrick's description of the fungus on the saucepan of soup that had been sitting on Edgar Huvas's stove for three days. 'It looked like an echidna!' 'What's an echidna?' I had asked. 'It's a species of anteater. Green, and hairy, and, I might add, inedible.'

Mrs Delamitri pressed a button and the top of the car folded up in a slow, creaky way like an old woman settling into a chair. I closed my eyes against the sudden sunlight and drifted off into a pleasant alcoholic reverie.

The clocks in the house were striking five in a dishevelled chorus of bongs and plinks. Nathan had gone home and left a note inside the front door saying he would be back to finish off in the morning.

I grabbed a couple of towels and we went down to the beach. I swam lazily in the cold water, while Mrs Delamitri took off her shoes and paddled along the shoreline.

Afterwards, we sat on the towels and I smoked one of her cigarettes.

'Thank you,' I said.

'For what?'

'For lunch, for the money. For bothering to tell me the truth.'

'Oh . . . Don't mention it.' She smiled, but I thought she looked a little sad.

'You can see the Vineyard sometimes from here on a clear day,' I said. 'Look.'

She dusted the sand off her hands and stood up. The sky to the west was beginning to turn a lobster pink. 'Where?'

I came up behind her and put my hands on her shoulders; she softened slightly into my touch. 'Over there, I don't think you can see it today.'

I put my arms round her waist and pressed my face into her crispy, dry hair.

'Patrick hated this beach,' she said, in a whisper. 'He complained about the flies and the stones.'

Her back arched slightly towards me, her hip pressed into my crotch. She stayed there for a moment and then gently disengaged herself.

'Miranda,' I said.

'I'd love to, Damien,' she said, 'but I think it would be a little weird.'

TWENTY

MRS DELAMITRI KISSED ME on the mouth when she left. She honked her horn as she backed out of the driveway, and I waved at her as Patrick must have done many times from the bank of lawn beside the road. Then I went back to the house and had another drink.

I hadn't been drunk since coming to the island. I think I had some idea that it would set a dangerous precedent for someone living alone. It had been part of Patrick's weird stability that he rarely drank – although I had a distant recollection of him drinking whisky and listening to opera on a rainy afternoon while following the libretto.

But I was already drunk – and I was already leaving – so I poured myself a whisky, leavened it with a couple of drops of water from the tap, and turned on the jukebox in the summer kitchen.

The sunset was fading out of the sky, and the evening that
drew on seemed to hum with possibility. It was the wine, but
it wasn't just the wine. All I wanted was to be back among the
living – anywhere – in Vientiane, Cardiff or Cuzco. And I
didn't care what I did. Even going back to work in London
held no terrors; at least it was a life.

Now that I was able to leave the house behind, I realised
that the solitude had been a purgative. My old life had died
with Patrick. And the dusty, isolated, frugal legacy he had left
me actually affirmed its opposite. I felt grateful to Patrick. I
was Scrooge, waking up on Christmas morning after the third
visitation, having finally grasped the message that the dead
bring to all the living – that there's still time. Patrick was my
Ghost of Christmas Future. I felt grateful to him for being my
unwitting angel.

I lay down on the grass and looked at the sky, and by a
strange reversal, it seemed to be below me, like an ocean of
stars, fading away in its depths to blackness. Around me, the
island seemed to be breathing in time with the sea. Then I
realised it was my own breath, respiring as the waves broke
and withdrew.

Going back into the house to refill my glass for the second
or third time, I remembered the box files. They were stacked
where we had left them in the library. I carried four of them
up to my bedroom to open them.

The first one contained letters, but there were fewer than I
had expected. I threw them into the air – a sheaf of yellow
pages covered with round, childish handwriting spilled over
the floor.

Because I'd seen his handwriting so recently, I got it into
my head that the author of the letters was Nathan Fernshaw,
and I wondered why he had written to Patrick in such detail.
I picked up a couple of leaves from the floor. The first lines I
read had the felicitous spelling mistakes of a young child: 'my
friend raymond was unconshase'; a second page was written by
a self-conscious adolescent wiseacre: 'Dear Patrick, I just

wanted to write a letter that doesn't begin, "How are you?" –
oops – it managed to sneak in anyway . . .' A third page was
somewhere in between:

'it is the end of my holiday and it is halloween. we are going
for a midnight walk with dad and we will bring our scooters
and vivian's go cart we hope we are thought to be ghosts and
suspicions are arosed about ghosts walking across the common
but we will no who they were but if real ghosts did walk across
the common brrr.'

And now there was a flash of recognition – or flashes that
froze instants of the distant past. My widowed father pushing
Vivian along a path on Wandsworth Common. The great
orange lights of Trinity Road pushing back the blackness. A
'midnight' walk that took place at 8 p.m. The first anniversary
of my mother's death. I knew instantly what would be at the
foot of this page, and the previous page, and every other page
in the box. *Love Damien.*

I opened the other box files, thinking I might find more of
my own letters, or Vivian's, or letters from my father. One box
contained yellowing royalty statements for *Peanut Gatherers.*
The others held a miscellany of unconnected papers: receipts,
invoices for some gardening work, an old copy of *Boston* mag-
azine with an article about Patrick's writing classes for the
prisoners, and a coffee-stained manual for the computer in the
dining room.

I gathered my own letters into a thin sheaf and lay in bed
poring over them. They were embarrassing reading, as only
your own letters can be. I had sent my uncle an exhaustive
explanation of the rules of conkers with diagrams; various
thank-you letters; two pieces of correspondence written from
boarding school in consecutive late Octobers full of nostalgia
for summer barbecues and Bolder than Mandingo. By a weird
symmetry, the mild Ionian night that I said I missed in my letters hung thickly over the window of my bedroom, where I
lay, more than twenty years later, reading my own handwriting. I felt able to recognise, at that moment, what my teenage

self, cooped up in the oppressive male atmosphere of a boys' boarding school, couldn't or wouldn't remember: that those summers had been full of *longueurs*, that we had had no friends, that there was a loneliness intrinsic to time spent with my family. And I remembered too that each holiday contained a moment of recognition when I realised I ached with boredom and solitude, and that Stevo was having a better time working in his dad's sportswear shop in Kentish Town.

I had to go back downstairs to get the other boxes. It was past midnight. It had begun to rain and clouds had extinguished the starlight. Inside the house, the darkness was so deep it seemed to have a texture – the restless, electric quality you find on the inside of your eyelids.

The first box was empty, and my disappointment deepened when I found the second also contained nothing. I wondered if Mrs Delamitri had been telling the truth when she said she had respected Patrick's privacy. The third held a collection of auction catalogues. But in the fourth, concealed under several sheets of blank paper, was a typescript with the same quirky lettering as the inventory.

I pulled back the wire trap that held the typescript flat in the bottom of the box. There were close to a hundred pages, loosely fastened through a hole in the top left-hand corner by a piece of cord with a metal stay at each end. The first page was blank, the second was a title page. A single row of capital letters across the middle of it read:

THE CONFESSIONS OF MYCROFT HOLMES

TWENTY-ONE

THE NAME ALONE was like a spark igniting a gunpowder trail of associations in my brain. Mycroft is Sherlock's older brother. That's a fact – a fictional fact, in the sense that Arthur Conan Doyle invented him, rather than Patrick. Mycroft is mentioned in only a handful of Doyle's stories and there's something troubling about his absence.

Nothing really explains Mycroft. He's superfluous to the stories. That's what's so interesting about him. He's not created for a reason, he doesn't have a function in the plot. He's there because he's there, vivid and unnecessary – like all the best things. He's extra, the imagination's tip to the reader.

And as fictional characters go, there is less of him than most. After all, what is a character in a book? Four facts, a speech impediment, boss-eyes, a fluffy moustache from a box of costumes. Mycroft is empty. But it's a pregnant emptiness. And Patrick had seen something moving there, something that reminded him of himself.

Doyle portrays Mycroft as an indolent genius, with more natural aptitude than his younger brother, but without the drive to achieve anything with it. The first time he meets Watson (in 'The Greek Interpreter') he astonishes him by out-deducing Sherlock. In 'The Bruce Partington Plans', we learn that Mycroft plays a significant role in the British government of the time. Sherlock calls him 'the most indispensable man in the country'. The only other things about Mycroft that are certain are that he is very fat, and a member of the Diogenes Club, where conversation is forbidden.

Sherlock Holmes trivia was one of Patrick's minor enthusiasms. Vivian and I didn't share it to the extent of actually reading the stories, but we were able to participate in Patrick's quizzes because, like his anecdotes and riddles, the questions were the same every year: 'What was the curious incident of the dog in the night-time?' (The dog didn't bark, that was the curious incident); 'In which story does Holmes say, "Elementary, my dear Watson"?' (He never says it); and, of course, 'What is the name of Sherlock's smarter older brother?'

Patrick had mentioned Mycroft in one other place. In a footnote to *Amazon Basin* (the unplagiarised section) he calls him one of literature's three most intriguing absences. The other two are Yorick – the fool who's dead before *Hamlet* begins – and camels from the Koran. Patrick maintained that if God had indeed written the Koran, He would have remembered to put in the camels.

Patrick's typescript began where Doyle had left off. It consisted of three stories which delved into the absent personality of Mycroft. Even before I got down to reading them, I was virtually certain that Mycroft was the unnamed hero of the fragment that had puzzled me on the plane. The stories would confirm it. They were written in the same antique style. Serena Eden was not mentioned again, but Doriment was – the mad painter – and in an aside in the final story, Mycroft referred to his time in India.

As impatient as I was to read them, I was conscious of my obligations to Patrick. Before beginning, I made some tea to sober me up. I found a comfortable chair in the library. I moved a standard lamp to give me the right degree of light: the yellow bulb spawned a twin in the rainswept window behind it.

The first completed story, 'The Fairy Feller's Master Stroke', found Mycroft back in London. He's trying to help rehabilitate the crazy painter Richard Doriment, who has been put in an insane asylum after murdering his father. Mycroft petitions the governors of the asylum to allow Doriment to exhibit his work. However, when Mycroft finally succeeds, the weird new paintings confirm the judgement that Doriment is completely bonkers. Among the VIPs invited to the exhibition are Sherlock and Watson. They and Mycroft find themselves standing baffled in front of a portrait of a bizarre-looking mythical beast which is in the process of ingesting a human corpse. This is how the story ends:

> The doctor paused before the canvas. His gaze fixed on the organs of the fanged beast, which appeared visible through an opening on the crown of its head.
>
> 'The beast's tubes must serve some purpose!' cried the doctor.
>
> My brother looked at me in bafflement.
>
> 'Alimentary, my dear Watson,' I said.

The last line makes me think of one of those replica guns that fire a flag saying BANG! Patrick seems to have based Doriment on the mad Victorian painter Richard Dadd.

In the second story, 'The Duellist', Mycroft goes to visit the painter Horace Vernet in Paris. Vernet (1789–1863) was a real French painter whom Doyle claimed was Sherlock's maternal uncle. Horace needs to get some money for a purpose that is never made clear and takes Mycroft with him to the apartment of an old Russian émigré by the name of d'Anthès. The description of d'Anthès, who is attended by an elderly lady called Yelena Gravanova, was one of the funniest things I had read in the stories so far. Patrick/Mycroft describes 'the great bully-bag of his testicles bulging out of his trousers', and the old man 'wheezing through interminable descriptions of his salad days at the Russian court, name-dropping lists of the titled ladies he had bedded'. Mycroft and Horace leave the apartment and the story concludes with the following exchange.

'What an unbearable fraud with his hideous Countess Gruffanuff!' I said, finally free to reveal the extent of my revulsion.

'He may be loathsome, but his notoriety is, I assure you, genuine, and rests on a very singular claim indeed,' said my uncle.

'Which is?'

'The Baron d'Anthès killed Pushkin.'

D'Anthès, a real historical figure, died in Paris in 1895 without ever having expressed remorse for killing Russia's greatest poet in a duel. I don't think this fact improves the story, but it authenticates it as one of Patrick's. D'Anthès was a man in the same mould as the other antiheroes who peopled our summer quizzes: John Wilkes Booth, Charles Manson, Reginald Christie, David Berkowitz. Something in Patrick's internal world drew him towards vivid examples of human cruelty.

Reading these two stories at two o'clock in the morning on a leather armchair in Patrick's library, I felt sorry for my uncle. It was a sad thought: Patrick, isolated and embittered, directing all his energies into pastiching Victorian prose. I remembered that haunting line in the notebook: '(I am writing this alone, in an empty house, in silence).' It made me think of a rock climber, doing a tricky solo ascent which no one will see or remember. After the long wind-ups, the endings were a bit facile, but I liked the stories. They were funny, and as Mrs Delamitri might have said, 'so Patrick!'

And I wondered if Patrick realised how revelatory his writing was. Mycroft was clearly a fantasy Patrick had about himself. But there was more to the character than simple wish-fulfilment. Mycroft had a dark side, absent from Doyle's originals, but worked up in Patrick's version of him. He was almost a tragic figure. He was a kind of Atlas – carrying the world inside his brain instead of on his shoulders – though it was no less a burden to him there. He was paralysed by his knowledge; it oppressed him. His corpulence was symptomatic of this: like the overspill of his stuffed cranium. If only he could know less . . .

The third story was separated from the others by a couple of blank pages. It was quite different from the previous ones. There was no sense that the narrator was trying to set up another surprise ending. In fact, the darkness and guilt that were hinted at in the other stories grew more explicit. The narrative drew nearer to Mycroft's empty centre and sought to explain what it found there. Beneath the costumes and the grease-paint, I glimpsed real people, people I actually knew. I heard Patrick's voice speaking to me through Mycroft. And as I surrendered to the story, I had the odd feeling that I was entering my uncle's dream life.

TWENTY-TWO

___

The Death of Abel Mundy

BY PATRICK MARCH

Gods, judge me not as a god,
but as a man
whom the ocean has broken

WHOLE DAYS together I dwell among ghosts.

I saw Abel Mundy in a dream again last night, drowned and dripping, with dead eyes, and river water running from the folds of his drenched clothes. His cold fingers burned like whipcord where I shook my wrist free from his grip.

I pleaded with him. 'Abel Mundy,' I said, 'let an old man rest.'

His voice uttered from somewhere inside him as softly as his last breath. 'Where was your pity?' he hissed at me, in an awful parody of my words to him. 'Where was your pity?'

I REMEMBERED this morning the name of the man who gave me instruction in boxing during my early years in the city: R.M. Fernshaw. When I close my eyes, I seem to see the brass plate that was fastened to the door of his gymnasium in Golden Square; and when I open them, I can read the inscription on it, reflected at me in the dull gold nib of my pen:

R.M. FERNSHAW, LATE 2ND LIFE GUARDS,
EXPERT IN PUGILISTICAL AND FISTIC SCIENCES:
GIVES INSTRUCTION DAILY IN
FENCING, SINGLESTICK, SABRE, BOXING,
MILITARY DRILL,
CLUB AND DUMB-BELL EXERCISES &C.

And beneath it were posted the hours of admission.

It was a habit with me to take exercise here at least once each week: vigorous endeavour being the only proven tonic against my melancholia and the tendency to corpulence which ultimately triumphed over all my countervailing intentions.

It was one of Dick Fernshaw's less likely contentions that a person's griefs are buried in the fat which exertion dissolves. On this plan, Fernshaw himself must have been the most sanguine man on the planet. There was not an ounce of fat on his spare frame. In the words I once heard him use admiringly of an aspirant boxer: there was more fat on a butcher's apron.

In those days, I was spare and quick myself, lacking the heft to deliver a resounding blow, but strong and fast enough to give a good account of myself against most opponents. Of course, this was gentleman's boxing: the Prize Ring had been extinct for more than ten years, and the young men who came to Fernshaw's gymnasium fought with the mufflers on.

Fernshaw often talked of his Prize Ring days, though I calculated that he hadn't had above two bareknuckle fights in his career (to his credit, he won them both). He always maintained that a man who had boxed only wearing gloves would never be more than an amateur, but he disapproved strongly of brawling. He insisted on discipline in the ring, and would berate both boxers if a bout threatened to degenerate into 'a rough unmeaning unscientific scramble'.

I well remember Dick Fernshaw, not less than sixty years old, interposing his spry frame when sparring threatened to become too warm. The bobbing fringe of red hair ringed his pate like a hedge round a ploughed field. 'Never forget: in the midst of impetuosity remember coolness, my lads,' he would say. 'Be manly; seek no undue advantage. Science and pluck give advantage enough. Pluck! Science!' Then, after a pause to restore calm, he would have them go at it again.

It was at Fernshaw's school of arms in the autumn of 18— that I first met Abel Mundy. He was older than most of us, forty, florid-faced, with a distinctly military deportment. I knew at once that he had seen service in India, and surmised from the oakum and tar on his boots – and the ink on his cuffs – that he was now employed as a shipping clerk at one of the warehouses on the river.

It was some time before I could verify my hypotheses. Mundy was a quiet, some would say brooding man, of a formidable intensity, great physical strength, but few words. That first day, he was matched with another heavyweight, Dickinson, a solicitor and Blue, for light sparring after the dumb-bell exercises. Dickinson was a more than capable boxer, and the two men finished amicably enough, but Mundy gave him a rough time of it. Fernshaw, without being partisan, urged Dickinson to counter when he was having the worst of it on the ropes. 'Come on, lad. Don't let him hang you. He's older than I am.'

That day was memorable for more than just the arrival of Abel Mundy. Fernshaw had been dropping hints to me for some time about his intention of distilling the wisdom he had gained cultivating the physical sciences in a book. It was a harmless enough ambition, and I confess I egged him on to it, because I found his cherished convictions amusing. He held, for example, as many do, that Onanism drained fluid from the brain and weakened the nervous system. He counselled the wearing of undergarments fashioned from a single strip of cloth folded around the nether parts in Hindoo style. He drank neat vinegar to strengthen his digestion. He – and I would not believe this, had I not seen it myself – he preserved the parings after he had dressed his nails and ate them, in the belief that it restored vital energies. All this, and a good deal of no doubt sensible information concerning boxing and physical culture, was to be collected in Fernshaw's volume. It was almost too much to hope that all of his wrong-headed snippets of wisdom would be gathered in one place for the edification and amusement of the general public, and many of Fernshaw's students looked forward to its publication for reasons quite other than the ones he supposed.

After our exercise was over, and Fernshaw was preparing the hall for one of his private pupils, I happened to mention the subject of the book to him, in the hope of teasing more foolishness out of him.

'Ah – Mr Holmes,' said he. 'I'm glad you mentioned this to me. I was discussing the slim volume, or pamphlet – as you know, I'm not ambitious concerning its size, but merely concerned to preserve, as it were, some of the axioms of pugilistical science – I was discussing it, as I say, with my wife, and it was her contention – where she thinks of these things I don't know – that a favourable commendation from someone highly esteemed might further its cause. I thought naturally of you . . .'

'My dear fellow,' I began, 'I'd be flattered.'

'And wondered if you might show it to your brother.'

'My brother?'

'Seeing that he is in an illustrious and some might say unique position, I thought a recommendation from him would carry the most weight. Naturally, I don't want to put him to any trouble, but it would be rendering me a service. If he could see his way to penning a few lines as a form of introduction to the work . . . Well, that's as much as anyone could want.'

'Certainly,' I said. 'Let me know when you have the finished draft and I'll bring it to his attention.'

'Much obliged to you, Mr Holmes. May I offer you in return a word of advice about your choice of undergarments?'

'The deuce of the thing is I'm already late for a rather important engagement. I'm afraid it will have to wait until next Thursday.'

'Until then, sir. Keep your guard up! Pluck, Holmes. Science!'

The last few words pursued me from the basement of the house and out into the warm twilight of Golden Square, while Abel Mundy looked on silently from one of the benches smoking a cheroot.

The truth of it was, I had no engagement, but I had found myself rather taken aback by Fernshaw's request. As much as I thought his projected book a foolish undertaking, I couldn't help but feel hurt that it was the commendation of my brother that he sought, rather than mine.

I lodged at that time in a set of rooms on Dover Street, where I had a bright drawing room that served me also as a studio. That evening, I remember, I did not return there immediately, but went from Fernshaw's gymnasium to visit a young lady in Shepherd's Market who worked as an artist's model but who also submitted herself to the sexual attentions of wealthy men. After the knock-back of Fernshaw's request, I wanted to restore my self-esteem with a vigorous rogering.

[NOTE by Damien March: The next two pages are just sub-Victorian pornography of the *Pearl* variety, but less effectively done. Since this section doesn't further the plot of the story or do my late uncle much credit I've left it out.]

ABEL MUNDY came regularly to Fernshaw's gymnasium and was soon among the group – which did not include myself – who contested amateur prizes at tournaments. Despite his relatively advanced years, he invariably won and earned something of a reputation for his strength and ringcraft.

It was an unspoken rule among the men who trained with Dick Fernshaw that the subject of our occupations was never mentioned. In a city where too much store was set by a man's work, his income, his place of residence, it was refreshing to consort with fellow humans on terms simply human.

It was another year before I deepened my acquaintance with Abel Mundy in circumstances that would have repercussions for both of us.

AN ERRAND had taken me far out of my usual haunts, east of London Bridge to the wharves on the south bank of the river. The scents of a hundred nations mingled here: spices, sugar, exotic banana-fruits from the West Indies, tea from the East, chocolate beans from Java and Sumatra, and bolts of Calico were stacked in the warehouses that fronted the busy Thames.

It was past five, and the flood of commerce had slowed to a trickle. A few clerks lingered over their account books, but ships lately in waited until the morning to be unloaded. A lamplighter was working his way along Tooley Street, confounding the darkness with a twinkling yellow flame.

Some distance away, a man emerged from a doorway, glanced upwards to ascertain the clemency of the weather, pulled his greatcoat around him, adjusted the hat on his head, and made his way along the pavement with a broad-backed, hunched-over walk that gave me his identity as certainly as his face did, lowered and concentrating as if examining the paving stones for fallen pennies.

'Abel Mundy,' I said, and on hearing his name he started upwards with a hunted expression and peered at me through the darkness.

'Who the devil . . . ?' he began to say.

'Mycroft Holmes.' I extended my hand to him. 'We box at Fernshaw's together. I never expected to encounter a friend so far east. You work here, I presume?'

The explanation of our acquaintance and my use of the word 'friend' appeared to set him at his ease.

'Well,' he said, gruffly, 'I'd wager long odds against this encounter. What brings you here?'

'A combination of business, bad luck and curiosity,' I said, thinking that this was a tactful way of explaining that I was visiting the unfortunate Richard Doriment, an artist of my acquaintance who was incarcerated in a lunatic asylum not far from the docks.

'Ah,' said he, 'the three most powerful forces in a man's life.'

'You forget two more powerful,' I said: 'God and woman.'

'Yes,' he said, with an odd look. 'There is *that*.'

We fell in together and crossed London Bridge, engaging in pleasant enough conversation, until our ways parted at the Monument: his to the east, mine westwards to my lodgings.

'You've come this far,' he said. 'Do me the honour of having your supper with me at my house.'

I must admit that even then there was something about Mundy that struck me as not altogether canny. There was a submerged malevolence, a quiet kind of anger that I found all the more unsettling for its being hidden. Still, I assented, because the pull of curiosity had always got the better part of me than the push of fear. I also had a sense that the invitation was made more for the sake of form than from a real desire to share his repast with me.

As we walked together to a house near Fenchurch Street, Mundy confirmed my suspicions, apologising in advance for the frugality of his table, and hinting that I might in fact be happier to have my supper at one of the ordinaries near his home. This only strengthened my desire to see where he lived. I told him to set his mind at rest, saying that I only ever took a cold supper in the evening myself, or sometimes a little thin soup. We drew nearer to our destination – a house of average size, none too smart from the outside, in which the Mundys occupied the upper two storeys – when he turned to me again, stopping altogether this time.

'Holmes,' said he, drawing his large hand down his face from his cheekbones to the tip of his chin, 'the other thing you should know is that my wife and children are deaf–mutes. We converse in gestures.'

It was hard for me to know exactly how to respond to this. 'Deaf from birth?' I said.

'Deaf from birth,' said he, cleaning his shoes on the cast-iron scraper inside his gate.

'Deafness is a terrible affliction,' I said.

'It is,' he said; and then with a glint of pride: 'But I consider myself lucky not to be one of those husbands who must suffer a wife's constant prating, chattering, idleness! I have what all men want and few have: utter obedience. You're not married yourself, Mr Holmes?'

I told him I was not.

'You'll want a wife for three things, Mr Holmes,' he said. 'Fucking, cooking and bearing children. Given those three things are of sufficient quality, the absence of speech will not, I assure you, appear to be a heavy burden.'

I was glad it was dark here, because the coarseness of his expression brought the blood to my face. We had by this time ascended the creaky interior staircase of the Mundys' home. On entering their house I was struck by two things. The first was the heat of the fire. It was not a cold day, but the coals were piled high in the grate and burning merrily. The heat of the room was such that even far from the fire, I was uncomfortably hot in my jacket. 'Time in the tropics thins a man's blood, Holmes,' Mundy said. 'Were the fire any smaller I would be freezing to death.'

The second thing that struck me was the pungent aroma of exotic spices. This was not fully explained until we took our seats at the supper table.

The two floors which the Mundys had to themselves were furnished comfortably, but not lavishly. We sat until the meal was ready in the overheated drawing room, where the air was made more oppressive by the fumes of Mundy's cheroots. He offered one to me which I declined.

Finally, Mrs Mundy bid us to table. It was my first sight of her, and I was surprised to see that she was as dark as a lascar, with ebony hair and skin the colour of horse chestnuts. She was a handsome woman, of some elegance, thin; silent, of course – and in all things so attentive and deferential to her husband that I felt uncomfortable on her behalf, recalling his harsh words as we stood on the threshold of his house: 'Fucking, cooking and bearing children.'

The two Mundy children were of a colour somewhere in between that of their parents, as though the hue had been formed by the admixture of her skin to his. The younger, a boy, was three years of age; the elder, a girl of thirteen or so. Mundy did not bother introducing me to any of his family, and communicated only sporadically with his wife in gestures that sent her scurrying from the table for a dish of pickle or more ale.

The food Mrs Mundy had prepared was unlike anything I had ever eaten. It was an array of meat and vegetables in sauces served with rice, and all of such barbarous hotness that I felt as though each mouthful was taking off the skin of my tongue. It was far more highly spiced than the mild *karhi* served at tiffin during my time in Madras. Since there was no possibility of conversation during the meal, the chief diversion was supplied by my discomfort with the highly spiced food, which entertained Mr Mundy so much that he roared with laughter until tears ran down his cheeks.

All the way through our meal, Mrs Mundy and the two children ate silently and watchfully, their attention fixed on Mr Mundy with a keenness that seemed slightly unhealthy.

It was nearing nine o'clock when I got up to leave. Abel Mundy had retired from the table to sit by the fire and smoke another of his infernal cheroots. I told him not to trouble himself to see me out. The daughter lit me to the door with a candlestick – the staircase by that time being as black as pitch. I looked up from the street to the lighted windows of their home. Naturally, I could see nothing from where I stood on the pavement, but I imagined Abel Mundy with his glittering eyes and his deaf family around him, breathing smoke from his nostrils as though the seacoal fire burned within him, instead of in his hearth. I swore from that moment to have nothing more to do with him, and I turned my back on that house and set off towards my own home with a shudder.

The reader will very likely wonder what on earth could bring me to such a drastic resolution after what must seem like a comical encounter with a family more remarkable for its oddness than its viciousness. But the short time I had spent observing the Mundys had been enough to inform me of the real state of marital relations in the household. It was quite clear that Abel Mundy was a wife beater.

For a number of reasons, this would not have been apparent to most visitors to the house. The style of Mrs Mundy's dress concealed all but her face and hands, and these were unmarked. The outward signs of the abuse were very few, though apparent enough to me.

I had noticed, when she was carrying dishes between the table and the kitchen, that, while she had the use of both arms, her left elbow was carried very close to her chest, and that she winced from the effort of lifting a heavy pile of plates. This disability would at least have occasioned comment in any normal house, but here it passed without remark. Secondly, though she was, I concluded, in some pain, it struck me forcibly that she was endeavouring to conceal it from me. It occurred to me that my presence was a kind of added torment for her — but whether this was her husband's motive for inviting me there, I could not say. The show of fortitude was a necessary charade, and I could easily guess the consequences for her if she let it slip for a moment. There is no victim more cowed than the one who conspires with her persecutor.

The final proof was in the eyes of her children. Even the younger, the boy, displayed an anxious wariness that was entirely in advance of his years, and which increased whenever Mr Mundy gestured to his wife, or when, in response to a gesture, she had to gather or fetch articles from the kitchen, all the time in pain, and all the time concealing it.

My story would be a short one if this single evening were the whole extent of my involvement in the lives of the Mundys. Even a determined rescuer would have had a difficult time overcoming the double isolation that afflicted them on account of their deafness and the strictness of their keeper. They could not have been more isolated were Mr Mundy their gaoler in fact, as indeed he was in all other respects, or were they living in solitude on an island, like Crusoe, in the South Seas.

But as it fell out, my curiosity pricked me on to discover more about their situation, and Providence – or whatever we may call it – had marked me down for their Friday, and the means of their deliverance.

I did not box the following week, and from this moment I date my inconsistent attendance and eventual abandonment of the regime. Instead, I took some pains in composing an invitation, ostensibly to reciprocate the hospitality the Mundys had shown me, which I delivered in person at the hour when I knew Abel Mundy would be occupied at Fernshaw's school of arms.

I guessed, rightly as it fell out, that there was no chance of my invitation being accepted, but that was hardly my purpose in extending it. I wanted the opportunity to test my impressions of the household in Mr Mundy's absence and, by passing on my name and address to the family, to offer Mrs Mundy my confidence. I gambled that the slim hope of deliverance might prompt her to communicate with me herself. My only misgiving was that her husband might hold her responsible in some way for my unexpected arrival and the consequence for her would be another beating.

This fear was confirmed by her behaviour on my return. My appearance seemed to cause her alarm at first, and it was a minute or two before I was able to convey to her the reason for my visit, and before she remembered her manners and gave me a cup of tea, brewed, as she indicated with gestures, in an Indian style with sugar and pods of cardamom.

The younger child having been set down for a nap, we were a party of three. Conversation on all sides was naturally limited, and though I consoled myself that I had accomplished my task simply by visiting, I knew that I would need to approach the subject more directly in order to assure her that I was an ally. Though I did not allude to it, it was immediately apparent that Mr Mundy had been less careful with his attentions since my previous visit, because his wife was marked with a black eye that was very noticeable in spite of her dark skin. It was a shocking detail, all the more so because I had seen what he was capable of in a boxing ring against a grown man his size and weight. I wondered then – I wonder still – that he had not blinded her.

Chance accomplished what my calculations had been unable to. The fire (much smaller in the absence of Mr Mundy) burning very low in the grate, the daughter was dispatched to the cellar to fill the scuttle. As soon as I heard her footsteps descending the stairs, I seized a pen and wrote on a piece of paper:

'How came you by your injury?'

To this, Mrs Mundy responded, smiling, with a well-rehearsed mime of a domestic accident.

With my heart pounding in case we were discovered by the daughter, I decided then to take an approach that would give her some idea of how much I already suspected. I took up the pen again and wrote: 'It is not right that your husband beats you.'

Mrs Mundy stared at it for a full minute without responding, until I was sure she found it illegible (my nerves had rendered the penmanship less clear than on the previous inscription). Then, surely anticipating her daughter's return, she threw the note into the fire of a sudden and fled from the room. When she returned, she had composed herself for her daughter's sake, but it was clear to me that she had shed tears in the interval. As, very often, a hardship that seems supportable during its infliction grieves us most painfully when someone aims to relieve it with tenderness, so I believe the mere thought of hope was enough to plunge her into fresh despair.

I took my leave of the Mundys shortly thereafter, with no very great expectation of seeing the mother and children again. I received by post Mr Mundy's regrets that he was unable to accept my kind invitation.

The following week I boxed as usual. I had a slight trepidation of seeing Mr Mundy, and had prepared an elaborate explanation for my having delivered the letter myself, which involved several unexpected errands across the city that had taken me into the vicinity of his home. As it happened, my explanations were unnecessary. Mundy was curt but civil, beat hell out of his opponent, and then left the gymnasium to do the same to his wife.

I heard nothing more for weeks after that, by which time my zeal to help had faded into the vague hope that my interference had not made Mrs Mundy's life worse than it was already. Then, on the two-month anniversary of my first meeting with Mrs Mundy, I received a letter from her. As she requested, I destroyed the original, but the substance of it remains with me, almost four decades later. 'Dear Mr Holmes,' it began.

'You gave me hope to suppose that you understood what kind of a man I am married to. Of whatever you believe him capable, I assure you the truth is worse. That he does not love me, I always knew; that he beats me, I must accept; but that he has forced my daughter to submit to the vilest attentions, I cannot. How you may help me, I do not know; it is more for the sake of my children than my own that I write. I am too weak to act on my own behalf, but I am fearful for my little one. I pray you to burn this letter.'

This was not the communication I had foreseen – I did not imagine that Mundy was capable of raping his own daughter – but in the months that had passed since my visit to Fenchurch Street, I had brooded on a number of outcomes; I had anticipated one that required abrupt and forceful intervention and made preparations for it.

I left my house immediately, going first to the home of the Mundys, where I found Mrs Mundy in much the state in which I had last seen her sans the black eye. Her expression was fearful but composed; I think the habit of terror was so strong with her that she never doubted but that she would spend her days in that hell until her husband killed her. She could not allow herself the possibility of hope. Her daughter made tea, but I could neither drink it, nor look her in the eye for thinking about the shame her father had inflicted on her.

I wrote quickly on a piece of paper to inquire what time her husband was expected home. She wrote down that he would not be back for some hours yet. In return, I counselled her that I would do what I could, but that, whether I succeeded or failed, she should never try to contact me again; and that, if her husband did not return home this evening, she should report his absence to the police.

'I hope,' she wrote in answer, 'that I may never see him as long as I live,' emphasising the vehemence of the sentiment by striking herself over the heart.

Then we burned all evidence of our conversation and I left.

I remembered quite well the place where I had encountered Abel Mundy by chance those months before, and made my way there as quickly as possible in order to attempt a repetition of that encounter, this time by design. It was much past the hour when we had met before and there was still no sign of him. I began to worry that he had left earlier on some business, or perhaps been working in some other place that day, or that I had deceived myself as to the location of his office. I had a flask of brandy in the pocket of my coat, and took nips of it as I waited. Finally, after I had all but given up hope, the door opened and two men emerged: one, by his bulk and stoop-backed walk, Abel Mundy; the other a tall man whom I did not know.

The truth is that I was sick at the thought of what I was about to do. It is one thing to imagine killing a man, it is quite another when the living, breathing man stands before you. The two men parted, and Abel Mundy made his way along the slippery pavement towards me.

At that instant, I began walking in the opposite direction, giving no indication that I recognised him, until our shoulders bumped and he stopped and looked in my face. This was my first miscalculation, for two reasons. Firstly, I should have known better than to attempt to convince him that a second coincidence had caused our paths to cross. He was a suspicious man, and this put him on guard for some mischief. I would have done better to concoct a reason for seeking him out in person, and indeed, many times when I had foreseen the meeting, this had been how I envisaged it. But somehow, at the crunch, my sense deserted me. The second mistake was to bump shoulders with him. I needed no reminder of the disparity between our strengths. I knew that in any fair encounter I would be the one to come off worse, and the thought of it put fear in me.

'Holmes?' said he.

'Abel Mundy!' I replied. The surprise in my voice sounded patently false to me. 'Just the fellow I need! Are you in a hurry, Abel? Can you spare me a minute?'

'I am somewhat pressed, Holmes,' he said, and I knew he suspected a trick.

Although I was armed, confronting him seemed like desperate folly, like throwing myself against a statue or a mountainside. I saw him pounding me slowly senseless with his big fists, and the fear of it swallowed me up like quicksand. I staggered forward and threw up at his feet.

'Christ, man, are you drunk?' he said.

Too indisposed to speak, I nodded weakly at him, and vomited again.

He lifted me up by the collar of my coat like a kitten, knocking my hat off in the process.

'On your feet, man,' said Mundy. Over my protestations, he marched me up the street and into a doorway some fifty yards from where I had been taken ill. I protested weakly, feeling like a condemned man on the trap waiting for the ground to drop away from my feet and to hear the snap of my own neck. Roughly, he bundled me inside the warehouse and dropped me on to a chair; then he left me.

My wits had deserted me. I sat mute in the darkness, gradually conscious of the rough boards beneath my feet and the smells of spice and river water that contended in the air. I did not think to run away: I could not see where I had come in. My mouth tasted foul, and my hands shook. I felt as weak as a baby.

I do not know how much later it was when Mundy returned and handed me a cup. 'It's been standing a while,' he said. I drank the water gratefully while he wandered over to the window and lit a cheroot. 'Better?' said he.

I nodded and wiped my mouth, even though he could not have seen me in the darkness.

'You young fellows,' he said with a laugh. 'All piss and swagger.' I saw sparks fly from the floor as he dropped his smoke and ground out the coal with a boot heel. 'Well, if you're convalescing, young Holmes, I need to be on my way. I would drink no more today, if I were you.'

'I'm not drunk, Abel,' I said.

'And I'm not Abel Mundy, neither,' said he. 'I could smell the drink on you.'

'I'm not drunk, Abel,' I said. 'I'm sick with fear.' He said nothing. 'I mean to kill a man,' I said, 'and the fear of it sickens me.'

'That's a queer way to talk,' he said quietly.

We sat silently in the darkness. The only sounds were the river lapping beneath us, and the rats rustling among the sacks and barrels.

'Who is this man?' he said finally. 'Who is he, Holmes? What in God's name are you talking about? You're full of drink and you're babbling, man. You're talking nothing but nonsense.' I could see him pacing in front of the window.

'I mean to kill you, Abel Mundy. Turn your face to that window, or by heaven, I'll shoot you dead,' I said, drawing a brace of pistols from my greatcoat.

'You, Holmes? A eunuch? A half-man, fit for the harem, to cook chocolate and dress dancing girls? Why, stow your nonsense, or I'll break you like a twig.' He stood stock-still, weighing up the odds against him, deliberating whether to charge me or to wait.

'I assure you, you will find threatening me a singularly unfruitful course of action,' I told him. 'Now do as I say.'

'What the devil?' was the mildest of the volley of imprecations he uttered, but he did as I commanded.

I told him that unless he agreed to leave the country immediately I would take his life on the spot.

He turned suddenly and sprang. The flash of the pistol lit the darkness. I felt the heat of it across my hand. In the panic, the other weapon fell to the ground. Mundy lay in the darkness groaning. I found the second pistol and placed the muzzle behind his ear. With a huge effort, I pulled the trigger, but my efforts were rewarded with a click. The mechanism had broken in the fall.

Mundy dragged himself upwards with a groan and I felt his huge hands close on my ankle. I took up the chair on which I had been seated and brought it crashing down on his skull. It felled him, but even then the man was so strong that he rose to his knees with a groan and grabbed at my hands. Again and again, I struck him with the chair with a kind of rising horror and pity, and a desperate wish that each blow would be the last of him. The chair by now having come apart, I was forced to belabour him with the parts of it, a chair leg, a spoke, whatever was left in my hands. He turned his face to me in the half-light as I struck savagely with the crude lumps of wood, black blood streaming from his nostrils and staining his teeth.

'For Jesus' sake, pity,' he groaned.

'Where was *your* pity, Abel Mundy? Where was *your* pity?' And I beat him until he moved no longer, until I knew he was dead, and then for a while after, because of the terrible darkness inside me.

Afterwards, I fumbled through the pockets of his coat for his cheroots and matches. As I placed one between my lips, I tasted the blood on my fingers and a shiver went through me.

All my preparations had come to this. I had planned to offer him exile, but I had beaten him to death with a trick and his blood was all over me. And yet, until I said the words aloud I did not believe them myself: *I mean to kill you, Abel Mundy.* From that moment, all the fear left me and I knew I would succeed, because, for all his strength, my will was stronger.

About the warehouse were several empty barrels into one of which, with much effort, I forced Abel Mundy's body. I had no means of sealing the barrel, and the corpse's hand continually dropped out as I rolled it along the floor, until I no longer bothered to push it back inside, so that it lashed the dirty ground with every revolution of the cask. I was some time wondering how I could make the barrel sink, and I further knew that the gas building up inside the dead man would tend to raise him, barrel and all, to the surface, unless there were a counterweight sufficient to keep him down. I was fortunate, indeed, to find a great stack of lead blocks each marked for half a hundredweight and used for weighing cargo.

I rolled the barrel into a skiff that was among several kept by on the wharf, and placed the blocks in after, as many as I could safely put in it, then fastened all with lengths of rope.

Fog had obscured the opposite bank and was closing fast, lessening my danger of being observed, but rendering my navigation more perilous. I took up the oars and rowed my cargo out to where I could see neither bank; here buoys were fixed in the deepest part of the river.

My ballast was so heavy that there was barely freeboard between the gunwales and the water, and I shipped a little water with each stroke. When I had reached what I took to be the centre of the river, I stove in the bottom of the skiff with a hatchet, until the river boiled up through it, sucking down the little boat and the barrel. The water was icy and dank, and all the harder to negotiate because of my heavy clothes and shoes. Having reached the farther bank, I struggled through the mud up to the nearest stairs, and as I reached out to steady myself on the stone, I saw my hands had been washed clean of blood, and with the darkening effect of the water on my clothes, it was impossible say which liquid was the Thames and which Abel Mundy.

I made my way home by back streets, and was helped by the weather, which had turned to rain and rendered my sodden attire less conspicuous.

Abel Mundy's body was never found. Suspicion fell upon Mrs Mundy, but she claimed, with justification, that her husband's disappearance was as much a mystery to her as to anyone else. By a circuitous coincidence, several months later my brother was employed by Abel Mundy's insurers to ascertain whether or not the man was indeed dead. This was a kind of loss-adjusting work well suited to deductive reasoning which he frequently undertook, but which was of more significance to his finances than to his hagiographers.

I had continued at Fernshaw's for a short while after, but found that I had lost the taste for combat. I grew lethargic and, after a while, ran to fat. An acquaintance from school had set me down for membership of the Diogenes Club, and I began to pass my evenings there, in the panelled silence of its library. It was here that I was summoned one evening to receive two visitors in the only room of the club where talking was permitted.

My brother was there, along with his lumpen sidekick. He had come, it turned out, to seek my advice about the Mundy case.

'I knew the fellow,' I said, before he had gone beyond the details of the disappearance. 'Boxed with him for a year or more.'

'You . . . boxed?' cried Watson, unable to conceal his surprise. I had, as I mentioned, run somewhat to fat.

'Took a Blue, old boy. Don't do it nowadays of course.'

'A Blue! As did your brother.' He made a note on a piece of paper which he had taken from his pocket.

'My brother boxed, Mr Watson, but he did not take a Blue.'

My brother looked slightly uncomfortable. 'What sort of a fellow was he?'

'You should be able to tell me that yourself.'

'Well, yes, of course. I merely meant to ask you for your opinion. Did he strike you as the type of chap who'd pull a jape like this? Disappearing into thin air.'

'The police found blood and traces of a struggle, did they not?' I said.

'Blood, yes. But whose blood? The blood of what? He wouldn't be foolish enough to disappear without an alibi. A clever criminal could have disposed of him without a trace of blood.'

'If I understand you rightly, brother, the absence of blood you take as evidence of a murder. The presence of blood you take as proof that no murder happened. If your reasoning is correct, we must be witnesses to a massacre. Why, look at my hands!' And I held up my fingers to him in the lamplight.

FINIS

TWENTY-THREE

I MUST HAVE FALLEN ASLEEP in the armchair. It had carried on raining during the night and I was vaguely aware of drops drumming on the window. I found the noise consoling. I woke up when it seemed to begin again, this time louder. Gradually, it resolved into an insistent banging at the kitchen door.

The pages of Patrick's stories were scattered around the armchair. I gathered them up quickly and put them on a high shelf. I assumed my visitor was Nathan, coming round to pick up the money I owed him.

Mrs Delamitri stood outside the kitchen door in a dazzling white jacket. It was already sunny and the light bounced off her clothes so that I had to squint to look at her. Seen in silhouette she looked like a quarterback, because of her huge shoulderpads and the way she pressed her handbag along the inside of her left arm like a rugby ball.

'I've changed my mind,' she said.

I remembered the unsuccessful pass I had made at her on the beach. What had seemed spontaneous and feasible then, now felt like a moment of toe-curling embarrassment.

'About the painting,' she said. She pronounced it without the *t: paining.* 'There's no need to look so worried. Oh my God, Damien, did you think I wanted to go to bed with you? You did, didn't you? Oh my. Go get dressed and I'll make us both some coffee.'

She had a way with the recalcitrant kitchen that made me realise just how well she had known Patrick.

'I was thinking it over,' she said a little later, when I had changed and the coffee was made. 'And do you know I thought that once you've left I probably won't ever come here again. I wanted to have something – a memento. I'm sorry I came by so early, but I was afraid you might have already left.'

I told her not to worry about it. I couldn't leave until I had got hold of a new passport. I mentioned that I had found some stories that Patrick had been working on.

'Stories? By Patrick?' She couldn't have looked more excited if I'd told her I'd found fragments of the true cross in the attic. There was a fervour in her voice – almost a tone of veneration. 'Where were they?'

'In one of the boxes.'

'I'd love to see them,' she said.

'They're in a very rough state.' I was reluctant to let her see the manuscript. I had found the implications of the final story too unsettling. There was something obsessive about the violence in it, as though Patrick had been trying to write one story but in spite of himself had written another.

'Damien, this is so exciting.' She put her cup down so quickly that a little of the coffee slopped on to the table. She didn't notice. 'Where are they?'

'I took them into town to have them copied.' I looked at my

watch. It was half past nine. 'Just got back about twenty minutes ago.'

'You left an original manuscript at a copy shop in Westwich? Oh, Damien. Was that smart?'

I tried to reassure her. 'They'll be fine,' I said. 'I gave them to Mr Diaz to copy. There's no way he'll lose them.'

'For a moment, I thought you'd just dumped them at some Korean grocery shop,' she said. 'What a relief.'

I told her I'd had trouble reading Patrick's handwriting so I didn't know what the stories were about. Her surprise was genuine, I decided. I don't think she had any idea that he had been working on the Mycroft stories.

She took the painting and began talking about the friend she was staying with up at the War Bonnet Cliffs. She said she was a sculptor, and began describing how she used driftwood that she collected from the beach.

I found it hard to concentrate on what she was saying. The coffee had revived me, but my thoughts were all about my uncle's strange story.

The tone was strangely confused – after a dark opening, it had reverted to jokes and soft pornography. But an unsettling mood had come over it with the arrival of Abel Mundy. It was a different atmosphere from the previous stories – the darkest they'd got was a kind of melancholy, the wistfulness of a self-described failure looking back on his life with regretful humour. This was something else: vengeful, active. It was almost as though there was too much anger for one character to contain. Mundy's violence seemed to infect Mycroft, and by implication, Patrick. I thought about what Mrs Delamitri had said about Patrick's baseless guilt. 'There was always this feeling that he'd done something awful.'

I began to wish Mrs Delamitri would go away so that I could reread the story and consider what I had found upsetting about it.

'It's a quality the light has here, apparently,' she was saying as she stood gazing out of the window over the garden.

'She came out here from Wisconsin and just fell in love with it.'

The detail that stood out for me was the deaf family. Although they had been transposed in time and place and re-upholstered as a different ethnic group, I felt they were still recognisably my neighbours, the Fernshaws. It wasn't just the deafness. The sexes and relative ages of the children were the same in both families as well. It meant Abel Mundy might be a portrait of their father.

'. . . built up in layers of impasto on scrunched-up news-paper. They'd make lovely gifts.'

'You know the Fernshaws, don't you,' I said.

'Excuse me?' Mrs Delamitri turned round from the window and let the lace drape fall back across the glass.

'You told Nathan to say hi to his sister.'

'Oh, sure. I met them a couple of times. They seemed like nice kids. Patrick got close to them after their father died. The girl is beautiful. She'd be more your type, Damien. Closer to your age, too.'

'She's got a boyfriend,' I said.

'Really? What's he like?'

'He's an academic. Name's Michael. Quite a bit older than her.'

'That figures,' she said.

'Why?'

'Oh, the old cliché about looking for a father figure, I guess.'

I refilled the kettle from the tap. 'What happened to her actual father?'

'Don't quote me on this, Damien, but I believe he drowned.'

Mrs Delamitri left before lunch. The pistols were in the chest of looted possessions that I had stored up in the attic. I wasn't sure what I hoped to learn from them, but I found myself examining them again closely. They did look like murder weapons. That was what I had found unpleasant about them in the first place. They had the same grubbily practical quality as

the objects in Ziploc bags that attorneys brandish in court-
rooms. They were cruel and ordinary – like a pair of bread
knives, or screwdrivers, like the chair legs Mycroft uses to
finish off Abel Mundy.

Nothing in the previous stories had prepared me for the violence Mycroft unleashed on the wounded man. It was
completely unexpected. It also seemed unnecessary. Surely
Mycroft the egghead could have come up with a more elegant
way of disposing of his man than bashing his brains out with
a lump of wood?

I cocked and fired the faulty pistol. Still no click. Had it
been damaged in a fall? Rust seemed a more likely answer. And
who in their right mind would plan to carry out a murder with
an unreliable antique? I told myself it was a prop from the cos-
tume box, not an exhibit in a murder trial.

I found it hard to admit to myself what the story made me
think.

Mycroft had said he was offering Mundy a choice: if
Mundy left the country, he wouldn't kill him. But the more I
reread the story, the less the offer seemed sincere. Mycroft had
planned to kill him all along. And the sinister part was that he
seemed to enjoy it. He was thrilled by the taste of the dead
man's blood. By comparison, the account of disposing of the
body was totally dispassionate. It had a weird detachment, as
though it were written by a character in shock.

Down in the basement, Patrick had saved copies of his
rage-filled letters like trophies, like so many scalps that he'd
taken from his victims. And to Patrick each of them repre-
sented a wrong righted, a humbug exposed, a slight avenged.
Mycroft would undoubtedly have approved. He was everything
Patrick felt about himself, raised to heroic size: the neglected
genius, the avenging angel, the scourge of the powerful, the
mould-breaking intellectual. And when Patrick was in a manic,
morally indignant frame of mind, he shared Mycroft's confidence that no problem was so complex that it wouldn't benefit
from his interference.

And even the more low-key Mycroft recalling his adventures in old age bore similarities to my uncle: the erudition, the reflective melancholy, the obssession with success and failure, the hinted-at burden of guilt.

But Mycroft was a murderer.

TWENTY-FOUR

MR DIAZ WAS SORRY when I told him I would be leaving in about a week. I said I might be back the following summer, but secretly I felt this would be the last time I would ever visit.

'I'll have it winterised,' he said. 'I'll get the police to stop by once a day. We don't want another break-in.'

'You might invest in a burglar alarm,' I said.

'I'll put it to the trustees.'

'There's something else,' I said. 'I came across this story while I was going through my uncle's things. I'd like you to read it. I'd like to know what you think of it.'

He looked at me with a slightly puzzled smile. 'May I ask why?'

'I'd rather not say,' I told him. 'I'd like you to read it with an open mind. I found it somewhere that makes me think Patrick felt it was important.'

'*Moby-Dick* important, or Headline Rate of Inflation important?'

'That's why I wanted you to read it,' I said, and he slapped my back and chuckled.

He met me the following afternoon at one of the harbour bars in Westwich. I had arrived slightly early and got a bowl of wilted-looking yellow popcorn and a pitcher of frothy lager.

'Well, what did you make of it?'

He took a handful of popcorn from the bowl. 'You trying to get me in trouble with my wife?'

'I'm sorry?'

'"Her hand roused my naked yard to stiffness."'

'I'm glad to hear it,' I said.

Mr Diaz snorted with laughter and a popcorn kernel got stuck at the back of his throat. 'I was quoting from the story!' he wheezed.

'I know, I know. I didn't want your opinion on his sexual braggadocio. What did you think of the rest of it?'

'Well, it's all kind of mixed up. I mean, one guy's called Fernshaw, but the Fernshaw character's called something else.'

'Mundy. He transposed the names.'

'Right. I'll tell you another thing, from what my wife tells me, it wouldn't take Sherlock Holmes to figure out Dicky Fernshaw was a thug.'

'How do you mean?'

'It was well known.'

'Really?'

Mr Diaz nodded.

'What happened to him?'

'Drowned, I think. I don't know too much about it. This is old island stuff. You should really talk to my wife. She was in high school with all the Fernshaws.'

I found myself too ashamed to admit to the thoughts I had been having about Patrick and had to resort to a fictional device to make me feel less uncomfortable.

'The thing is,' I said, 'I showed the story to an old friend of

Patrick's and she was quite upset by it. She felt that the story wasn't one hundred per cent fiction. I have no idea myself. She even – I know how ridiculous this must sound to you – she even thought Patrick might have been somehow involved in Mr Fernshaw's death.'

'You're kidding me.'

'No. That's what she thought. I didn't know enough about the background to it to tell her she was wrong.'

'I mean,, the story is ten per cent jokes, ten per cent porno, eighty per cent whatever. But it's not evidence that anyone's killed anybody.'

'It's not evidence you could use in court,' I said. 'But it's still a "confession".'

'That's right. "The Confession of Sherlock Holmes."'

'Mycroft Holmes, actually. Sherlock's older brother.' It somewhat undermined my confidence in Mr Diaz that he couldn't even get the title right and didn't seem to have grasped that Sherlock wasn't the protagonist.

'Well, let me ask you this,' he said. 'Do you think Dick Fernshaw's body is in a barrel at the bottom of the Thames?'

'Of course not,' I said. Mr Diaz was looking pleased with himself, as though this observation was conclusive. 'The point is the story made her feel uncomfortable, and so I thought it was worth running past you.'

I knew that the inference I was putting on the story depended on being selective about what was literally true, but I found this difficult to explain to Mr Diaz. He had a point, of course. Wasn't it either all true or all false? Then I would remember the haunting line in the story that began *And I beat him until he moved no longer* and get uneasy.

'That's my opinion, Damien. I majored in Business Administration, not English Literature. In fact, I got an F in Great Books. I can frame a legal document that's watertight, but if you want literary criticism you should be talking to someone else. That sound funny to you?'

'You remind me of someone,' I said, thinking of my father.

'I've lived on Ionia seven years. Fernshaw died before I even came to the island. I've never heard that there was anything suspicious in it. I'll ask my wife if you like, but I'd say you've been on your own in that house for too long.' He smiled at me to show it wasn't meant unkindly.

'It's not my theory,' I said. 'I'm sure you're right. I just wanted to be able to set her mind at rest.'

'If you really want the scuttlebutt on the Fernshaws, come by and talk to my wife. She's an authority on island gossip. She'll tell you what's true, what's not true, what might be true, and a whole lot besides.'

TWENTY-FIVE

I WOULD HAVE GONE to see Mrs Diaz sooner, but I had to go to the mainland to get a new US passport. I had promised Nathan that I would take him with me. He wanted to buy an inflatable boat from a shop in Hyannis. He had called it a turtle boat. I asked him what that was.

'It's a boat shaped like a turtle. It's got feet and a head, and on the bottom it says, "Help", in case it flips over, so the Coast Guard can come and rescue you.'

'And what if you don't need to be rescued?'

He shrugged. 'You flip it over and get back in.'

My motives for taking him weren't purely altruistic. I think I hoped to learn something from him that would allay my anxieties about his father. Whenever I was with him now, I found myself checking him over for psychological scars. Aspects of his behaviour which had previously seemed mildly eccentric began to strike me as neurotic.

Nathan was meticulous about his appearance. Whenever the slightest bit of dirt touched him, he broke off whatever he was doing and went to clean himself up – even when he would inevitably get dirty again, minutes later. He spent so much time traipsing across the lawn to wash his hands that I had bought him gloves for outdoor work, which he never took off. Each time I saw him, he was wearing fresh clothes, which was a reproach and an example to me, who tended to wear the same paint-splattered clothes for days. He had a horror of insects and anything rotten: he would go to great lengths to avoid touching decayed apples with his hands, generally spearing them with a stick to propel them into the marshes. Once he shuddered and turned pale after he brushed against some cobwebs in the garage.

Occasionally, I found my mind wandering off in directions that were just plain crazy. At one point, I envisaged a murder scene where Nathan was reluctantly assisting his mother and sister dispose of his father's body. Perhaps he had contracted his squeamishness from handling his dead father's severed limbs.

But as soon as I thought about the real Mrs Fernshaw – plump and friendly, moving gracefully around her kitchen – I knew she was incapable of a violent act and felt slightly ashamed of myself. I knew nothing about Mr Fernshaw's death. My idle brain had daydreamed a set of incidents that had no basis in reality.

At times, I wished I could unread the story. It depressed me. There was something grim and unforgiving about it – the way an intimation of death can make everything else seem foolish or inconsequential beside it. But like an ordinary depression, my anxious thoughts receded altogether sometimes. I had hours without thinking about it when I felt relatively happy. But I only had to remember the vivid and clumsy murder of Abel Mundy and the worries would begin again. As with the first fragment, something in the tone of it

was all wrong. The violent murder was as under-explained as
Mycroft's abandonment of Serena Eden.

My speculations weren't confined to Nathan. I tried to fit
his sister's behaviour into patterns suggested by the story.

I built my obsession on tiny details. The innocuous Michael
Winks made better sense as a partner for Terry if you considered that her father had been an ogre. Her insecurity, her
eagerness to please her boyfriend seemed to point to a fraught
relationship with the dead man. And she hadn't hesitated
about leaving me with Nathan on the day we went to the
cinema – I put that down to an abused child's antennae for a
potential abuser.

I know they don't mean anything – these observations were
trivial. You could turn them round and use them to support a
contrary argument. But the suspicion remained with me – like
one of those obsessive worries which defeat all attempts at reasoning – that it might be based on truth.

Winks had hurt his foot and couldn't drive. He was lying full
length on the sofa in the Fernshaws' TV room with his leg on
a pile of cushions. Terry and her mother had gone into town
to go shopping, he said.

'Back-to-school sales?'

'Yeah. Wish they wouldn't call them that,' he said, as he
flipped disconsolately between channels. 'Makes me feel like a
prisoner on furlough.'

'That looks like a bad sprain,' I said.

'Tell me about it. The Fernshaws are discovering that stoic
fortitude is not my strong suit. Personally, I think these shopping expeditions are just an excuse to get away from me. It's
Nathan's fault. We were playing wiffleball in the yard. I ran
backwards for a pop-up and must have stepped on the side of
my foot. Felt like I'd broken it.'

I told him I would be having a cookout before I left. It
would have been Patrick's sixty-fourth birthday in a week. I
wanted to mark that and my own imminent departure.

I liked Winks. I wished I could show him the stories: I would have welcomed his thoughts. He might even have been able to ease my worries by pointing out some trivial discrepancy between the fiction and reality. He would have been an ideal reader, but if any part of the story turned out to be true, it would have put him in a difficult position.

Did I think Patrick had killed Mr Fernshaw? It was a literal-minded explanation of the story, I told myself. Equally, that didn't prevent its being true. But what was truth in this case? I didn't think that Patrick had ever had a boxing lesson; I was sure Mrs Fernshaw didn't cook curry and had never been near the Indian subcontinent. I doubted Mr Fernshaw had ever had 'oakum' on his boots. Whatever that was.

But what was true was that my uncle was an isolated old man who was troubled by memories of the past. His neighbours were a deaf family, minus one father, who it seemed had been abusive to his wife and children. And these were all spelled out in the story.

It did violence to my memory of my uncle to think that he was capable of such an act, of course. I had never seen him so much as lose his temper, though I knew he was capable of it. I know that when his relationship with my father was at its nadir, my father was physically afraid of him. But this, I thought, was my dad being neurotic. It wasn't based on a rational assessment of Patrick's character.

To accept that my uncle would attack someone, hurt someone in a premeditated way, was to accept that I didn't know him at all. I hadn't accepted this, but just thinking about it, entertaining the possibility, made Patrick seem stranger and more remote. I wanted to exonerate him, if only so that I could have my image of him restored to its former innocence. Looking back, I suppose I was guilty of a kind of sentimentality.

When Patrick talked about writing, which he didn't often, because he was superstitious, he sometimes said that a story was a way of asking a question so loosely that the writer wouldn't even be aware of its real meaning. I think he was afraid of those questions, the ones he couldn't control, and which couldn't be answered with any of the vast array of facts that he had stored up in his cranium. I think that's why he had virtually stopped writing. Better to make lists, better to crack jokes, better to dazzle without any risk of self-exposure. It wasn't surprising that the stories had stayed on his desk. Mycroft was a dangerous character. He was capable of getting all of us into trouble.

It was another overcast day. The summer was already entering island mythology as one of the worst in fifteen or twenty years. I felt now that the Ionians were taking a grim pleasure in each fresh spell of rain and would be disappointed if the weather took a turn for the better.

Nathan stood at the aft rail of the ferry watching Ionia recede into the distance as the engines churned the sea into froth right under him. Judging by the look on his face, he didn't get off the island very much. I told him so. 'It looks small, doesn't it?' he said. I told him it was small, then felt bad for saying it.

'Which is bigger,' Patrick had asked once, 'Little England or Great Britain.' And then: 'Great Britain or the United States?' I got the answer wrong in both cases. The gross disparity in size between Britain and the United States had come as something of a shock to me. Since then, America has always struck me as some kind of bigger and more glamorous younger brother. I think the Portuguese must feel the same away about Brazil. The younger brother who went away and made his fortune, while the older one stayed home and looked after the family farm. One night, there's a knock at the door and it's young Brazil, or Yankee Doodle Dandy, in a sharp new suit, flashing his money around and full of advice about how to modernise the cowshed.

I often had the feeling, though I tried to deny it, that England was tired and second-rate, and that it was precisely its tiredness and second-rateness that fated it to be a significant part of my life. I could not identify with the superiority that Americans – even Patrick – took for granted. English people took pride in failure. 'Good losers', people said of the English – but that was because they had so much practice. Primacy was the American obsession. 'We're number one!' And its sportsmen had developed a repertoire of gesture – high fives, clenched fists, chest bumps – as complex as Ionian sign for signalling their superiority. In England, low self-esteem was part of the national character, although it was partly concealed by our grandiose insistence on our glorious past.

I bought Nathan his boat from a shop in the Cape Cod Mall, a better-stocked version of the one on Ionia. I tried to persuade him to buy one that was more nautical, with little rowlocks and oars, but he wasn't having any of it. I had to keep my own authoritarian tendency in check. I had a prejudice against the turtle boat. It was slightly effete. It was too young and gimmicky. It was a toy. I was being like my father, who refused to buy me the Wendy house I wanted for my eighth birthday and got me a pup tent instead. I realised that part of me wouldn't be happy until I had cajoled Nathan into a mapping expedition in the sand dunes.

We had two hours before the next ferry crossing, so I suggested we go to the flea market in Barnstable. I don't think Nathan even knew what it was, but he must have liked the sound of it.

It was bigger than I remembered. A faint drizzle lay heavily on the gathering; the air was thick and warm, like damp wool. The stalls were laid out in neat rows over several acres of wet grass. Nathan skipped off to examine a stall of rusty toy boats. Before he went I asked him to find out where we could buy some fleas. He gave me a pained look and rolled his eyes, and I watched him disappear into the crowd.

The vendors, who were retirees for the most part, sat in deck chairs behind their trestle tables, selling things that were not really antiques at all. A velvet reproduction armchair was sprouting springs through the ripped fabric of its seat. It wasn't antique furniture, it was senile furniture. There were little tins of gramophone needles, glass bottles, unloved LPs. If you were lucky, you might find a copper washbasin or a pair of snowshoes, but it would take a lot of searching.

This had been one of Patrick's favourite places. The flea market was guaranteed to get him on to the mainland. He'd sometimes show up at the house in Truro before seven in the morning to take us along with him. Or he'd appear afterwards, the boot of his car stuffed with treasures which he'd show my dad in the driveway.

I rarely saw him happier than he was then, or at the flea market itself, his eyes bright with the prospect of imminent acquisitions.

Occasionally, when we were with him, we saw a book we wanted and he'd urge us to haggle. 'Offer him five dollars for two.' 'See if she'll take fifty cents for it.' I had seen him walk away a hundred times from things he desperately wanted for the sake of a dollar or two, or because he found the vendor churlish. It wasn't exactly meanness. The arbitrary budgets acted as a brake on his desires. If he'd been a millionaire, there would have been something else he would have forbidden himself, as though a thousand small acquisitions could take the place of a single, inadmissible desire.

I had lost sight of Nathan. Big fat raindrops had started to wash away the remaining charm of the flea market. Eventually, I spotted him far off, wandering among the stalls. Small and serious, he moved with the peculiar invisibility of a well-behaved child.

Then, more than I ever had at Patrick's funeral or living in his house, I felt I had lost Patrick, and with him a chunk of my own past. It was strange that only a few months earlier my reaction to the news of his death had been: Patrick who? But in answering, or trying to answer, that question, I had indirectly found a new enthusiasm for my own life. I felt it was an insight that depended on understanding who Patrick had been, how unhappy he had been, and how close I had come to turning into him. That recognition was a relief. I felt I understood that I had to live and trust people, not because people were innately trustworthy, but because the alternative was to turn into Patrick.

My father had said he lacked ambition. It was a characteristically obtuse observation. I didn't believe it. I thought Patrick had been wounded in some way, and had surrendered to despair because he lacked the faith that anyone could help him out of it. It was how I felt about myself. Discovering that he'd saved my letters seemed to confirm our kinship.

But my reaction to his story, I realised, was a howl of incomprehension. Where did it come from, this violence? This violence that he tried so hard to legitimise.

If Patrick wasn't who I thought he was, my optimism was founded on deceit. The empathy I felt with him was wishful thinking. And just when I should have been happy and excited about leaving, I felt as though the dark wing of some nightmare bird had come between me and the sun.

The reason I didn't give up, then, and wash my hands of the whole business, was that I thought the truth might be more complicated. It was characteristic of me, and Patrick – and Mycroft – to know everything in advance. In my life, I have been trying to commemorate Patrick by becoming more unlike him. It's an ongoing and never wholly successful undertaking, but a key part of it is the effort to renounce damaging certainties, to try to know a little less every day.

TWENTY-SIX

MRS DIAZ WAS VAST, like a tiny planet – Mercury, maybe. She was standing on a chair holding a small green watering can up to a tier of hanging baskets. The fact that she was raised up into the atmosphere of the room – a conservatory that had obviously been added to the house – made her seem even rounder and bigger. She cut short the watering when she saw me come in. After stepping down with a nimbleness that belied her size, she sank into a huge wicker chair. She was squeezed into the seat like a coconut at a coconut shy.

'Don't tell my husband you saw me up there,' she said, 'but if I have to wait for him to water them, they'll be nothing but potpourri!'

She fanned her face with her hand. 'I can't bear this weather. There's nowhere for the heat to go.' She was very pale, except for her cheeks, where the red was unhealthily intense, as though they had been scrubbed too hard. Her light brown hair was very fine, like a toddler's, and had been cut short.

By way of small talk I mentioned that the bookshelf in her living room included two copies of *Peanut Gatherers*.

'Your uncle gave me one of those. I forget which.' She had the island accent, a pleasant low voice, and a fat woman's throaty chuckle. 'I was a big fan.'

'Of him, or the work?'

'Both. I used to run an auction house in Westwich – this is before I met Tony. Your uncle would be there every week. We had the auctions on Wednesdays. That's how I got to know him. His taste was very . . . eclectic.' She coughed. 'Excuse me. Could you slide that stool over?'

She propped her feet up on to the stool with audible relief. 'I used to put bids in myself for certain things, so I'd notice who bought them. Books mainly, and cup-plates. We liked some of the same stuff.'

It turned out that Mr Diaz – or Tony, as she Anglicised him – was her second husband. Her first husband had been older, a hard-drinking Ionian, who had run off, leaving her to bring up three kids. She began telling me how she had scratched a living from a restaurant she opened on the island. She sold it for a profit with which she bought a bigger restaurant, made a success of that, and then bought the auction house. It was an impressive story: she couldn't resist a digression on the hardships they'd all undergone along the way: eating scrapple, wearing homemade clothes – and a long account of her fifteen-year-old son's stepping in as auctioneer on the opening night when the real one showed up drunk. After twenty minutes I was starting to wonder how I could bring the conversation around to the Fernshaws without seeming rude. But the good thing about people who talk a lot is that sooner or later they touch on everything.

'My first husband was from an old island family like the

Fernshaws. He was a Cullity. They all came from up-island. Do you know what that means?'

I said I didn't.

'That's the west of the island – it's from sailing. Because it's "up" in terms of longitude. Harriet Fernshaw was from up-island, too. Now she was a Tregeser and a lot of them were deaf. I guess they carried the gene for it. Here, pass me that.'

It was a high-school yearbook from 1970 bound in rubbery dark blue plastic. A mortarboard and a quill pen were raised in relief on the cover.

'My brother's yearbook,' she said. 'I loaned it to your uncle. He got interested in the Fernshaws, too.'

I felt a momentary excitement at the thought that my uncle had passed this way: it was like coming across his footprint in a forest. 'What did you tell him?' I asked her. She was flipping through the glossy pages of the yearbook.

'I asked him which Fernshaw he wanted to know about.'

'How many are there?'

'Funnily enough, that's what he said.' She paused. 'Here we are. Dick Fernshaw.'

He was square-jawed, with a smart crew cut. Not much like Nathan, maybe a little like Terry in the eyes.

'Looks like the all-American boy, doesn't he? He was a nasty piece of work, though. My brother once saw him stuffing a kid into a gym locker. You know—' She mimed it with uncharacteristic ferocity. It sent her fine hair flying around her head. 'He stopped – at least this is how my brother tells it – he stopped and said: "You don't see anything, do you?" My brother just nodded and got the hell out of there. He was a bad kid. Grew up to be a bad man. No one was sorry to see you go.' This last sentence she said to the photograph itself. 'He's the father of Harriet's eldest.'

'He was lost at sea?'

'Him? Oh no, he was killed in Vietnam. Brave soldier too, by all accounts.'

'Killed in Vietnam?' I was confused. 'I've had it from two or

three different people that Mrs Fernshaw lost her husband in
an accident at sea.'

'That's right.' She took the book from me and turned the
page. There was no photo here, just an entry and a list of the
school associations of which Zachary Fernshaw had been a
member.

'There's no photo,' I said.

'He didn't turn up for it, I guess. A few people didn't. It
was a way of saying screw you to the school authorities. Zac
wouldn't have meant it like that. He was a good kid. I guess he
was ill or something. This one photo does for the two of
them.' She turned back to the previous page. 'Their mother
couldn't tell them apart.'

'Twins?'

'Yup. Zac was the elder by a couple of hours. A nicer guy
you could never hope to meet anywhere. He was an angel.'

The story Mrs Diaz then told me was like all stories – full
of what Patrick called 'pavanes and divagations'. I couldn't
remember her every digression, even if I wanted to, or the way
my questions prompted her to clarify and elaborate her original narrative. I'm sure there are more artful ways of relating
what she said – my uncle's story was, in a very lateral way, one
of them – but I'm more comfortable with a digest of the facts.

Richard and Zac Fernshaw were the only children of a relatively elderly island couple. They were identical twins, born
within an hour of each other, into a family where twins
occurred in every other generation. 'The Fernshaws had the
genes for *that*,' said Mrs Diaz, meaning, I suppose, that it was
a more benign legacy than the gene for deafness carried by a
disproportionately large number of island families in the nineteenth century.

I had the feeling that Mrs Diaz embellished her account of
their childhood slightly. She was making the point that while
Zachary was conscientious and good-natured, Richard was self-
ish, violent and eventually delinquent. She dwelled on this
contrast as though it were something essential in the boys'

natures – a Manichaean split; Cain versus Abel. I didn't say what I felt: that faced with a Goody Two-shoes of a sibling, behaving badly might be a necessary way of carving out your own identity.

There were no academic expectations placed on the two kids. Zac finished high school and joined his father's fishing business. Richard left home to hang out with a gang of self-styled hoods in town, where he got involved with petty crime and earned the disapproval of the town's elders and the sneaking admiration of their children. In a quiet town like Westwich in the early seventies, young men like Richard had the status of dangerous, glamorous outsiders. They were followed from afar by some of the town's good girls, who probably saw in them a vicarious way of chafing at the strictures of their own parents. Richard got one of these girls pregnant – a pretty, deaf teenager called Harriet Tregeser. Then he left the island to join the army.

From the way Mrs Diaz told it, I couldn't figure out if he knew about the pregnancy before he went away. She implied that he'd joined to evade his responsibilities as a father, but it seemed just as likely that he hadn't known, and had gone off to the mainland blithely unaware of the impending birth.

I don't think I had the reactions to her story that Mrs Diaz wanted. It was hard for me to think of Richard Fernshaw as a monster, even if he had upped and run when he heard about the pregnancy. He would have been more than fifteen years younger than I was then when he found out that Harriet was pregnant. Abortion was unthinkable in that close-knit island community. Richard Fernshaw was just a boy, panicky and inadequate, who had shirked responsibility ever since he had learned to walk. He disappeared.

He didn't show up until more than a year later. He walked into a Westwich bar in his uniform. He'd thrived under the army's benign discipline and, away from unfavourable comparisons with his brother, discovered he had a knack for soldiering.

Why had he come back? Mrs Diaz wasn't sure. Perhaps he just wanted a chance to show the islanders how he'd made good. Perhaps he wanted to take responsibility for his baby daughter. Perhaps he wanted to marry her mother and make a life together.

In any case, it never got that far. His brother, who had spent his life overcompensating for his twin's shortcomings, had married the woman himself.

Richard heard all this from one of his old friends. He found Harriet, who refused to let him in to see the baby, so he got drunk and went looking for his brother. Luckily – or unluckily, who's to say? – he never found him. Zac was away at sea. Richard went back to the mainland, swearing he'd come back for revenge.

'And did he?' I asked.

'Oh no. He got his. Fragged in Vietnam.'

'Fragged?' I wondered if it was like 'fagged' at English public schools. It would have been a justly bathetic end if this glamorous hood had spent the Vietnam War making toast for more senior officers and shining their shoes.

'As in "fragmentation bomb",' explained Mrs Diaz. 'It means he was killed by his own men. I guess he was too much of a hard-ass, a disciplinarian.'

As for Zac and his new bride and his stepchild, against the odds they were happy. He learned his wife's rare language and made a decent living fishing for tuna. 'They'd take the catch into P-town and sell it to Japanese buyers right off the dock. He made good money. I suppose the fish ended up as sushi.'

After ten years together, the couple had a child of their own, a boy named Nathan after Zac's dead father. But Zac himself didn't live to see his child turn one. He was hiking with a couple of friends along the coast at Nawgasett on the mainland when he lost his footing on a rock. A wave – not even a large one – splashed over his foot and caused him to slip into the water. He struggled against the current but like a lot of the older island fishermen he wasn't much of a swimmer. One of his friends ran to fetch the Coast Guard but Zac was dead even before he made it back.

This is the distillate of a conversation that bubbled on for an hour and a half until Mr Diaz came into the room with his wife's painkillers. Although I was never bold enough to ask her what was wrong with her, from hints she dropped I guessed that the operation she'd had had been a hysterectomy.

Seeing her with her husband, I noticed for the first time that she was older than him by about five years and possibly more. He was sweetly uxorious: bustling around her, fixing pillows and draping an afghan over her lap. She allowed herself to be a little crotchety with him, but in a way that suggested a deep affection. I took the interruption as my cue to go.

Something like nuclear fission had taken place. The fictional villain of my uncle's story had split into two people: Zac and Richard Fernshaw. There was no question of a murder, because there was no victim. What had seemed like a story about an abusive husband had its roots in a story about two brothers.

I had asked Mr Diaz to show the story to his wife. 'It's a what-if,' she said, when I asked her about it. 'It's kind of like the good brother never saved her. What would have happened then? What kind of a father would Dick Fernshaw have made? A terrible one, obviously. Luckily old Mycroft is around to take care of business.'

'Don't you think the violence in the story is excessive?' I said.

'Excessive?' The word sounded a bit precious when she repeated it. 'I suppose it is.'

I bought some flowers from a shop in town before I drove home, and put them in front of my uncle's self-portrait as an expiation. I told myself I'd visit his grave on the mainland before I left the country for good.

I understood that since there was no victim, there could be

no question of a murder, or a murderer. There was only a murderous rage, an anger without an apparent location that was the story's most troubling feature, and which had lured me into the false assumption that the events it described were real.

TWENTY-SEVEN

IT TOOK ME FOUR MORE days to get my affairs in order and make my arrangements for leaving the country. My flight was scheduled to leave Logan Airport just before midnight on a Sunday, three days before what would have been Patrick's sixty-fourth birthday, so I decided to have a barbecue to celebrate my last day on the island. It would be both a leave-taking and an anniversary.

I called Aunt Judith in Boston to invite her too and apologised for not having kept in touch. She mentioned that Vivian had been shooting something in Vermont and was threatening to pay her a visit in Medford. She didn't use the word 'threatening', of course. She would have been pleased to see him. I said to let him know he was welcome to come, too. Throughout our conversation I was thinking that Judith's reliable Christmas presents were almost all that remained of the invisible links that once held our family together.

I didn't expect my brother to turn up. I just wanted to send the message that, on my side at least, I was dismantling the barricades. I was realistic enough not to expect that we'd become bosom buddies – we're too different for that.

The Saturday before was overcast and humid. Nathan helped me manoeuvre the barbecue – the one with a tall black hood like a blast furnace – out of the shed and up the hill to the house. He had the idea of putting it in the pony trap to move it more easily. We laid the barbecue on its side and lashed it down, then each of us pulled one of the shafts of the trap. I told Nathan how Captain Scott and his team had pulled their sleds to the South Pole the same way. It struck me as I was telling him that I had heard the story first from Patrick: *The Worst Journey in the World* was one of his ten favourite books.

But talk of Antarctic weather was out of place the following day. By eleven it was clear that it was going to be one of the hottest days of the summer. The sky was a searing blue – like balloon silk.

The first guests to come were the Fernshaws, who brought with them a giant Tupperware bin of potato salad. Winks hopped across the lawn behind them on crutches.

I had invited everyone I could think of. Mr Diaz was there, Mrs Diaz sent her regrets, but Stephanie the paralegal came, as did Officer Topper, whom I invited on a whim. Mrs Delamitri brought her friend from up-island, who in turn brought some guests she had staying, including a whey-faced Englishman in his late forties called William Ricketts who worked for the United Nations and turned out to have been a pupil at my boarding school. 'I met your uncle once,' he told me.

'Yes,' I said, 'he mentioned you.'

Mr Ricketts insisted on reminiscing to me about our alma mater while I tried to cook the burgers and the chicken thighs on the barbecue.

It annoyed me that he singled me out as a co-conspirator.

Not only was I preoccupied with the temperamental barbecue, but I also thought his cliquishness compared badly with the geniality of my American guests, who were swapping anecdotes and doing their best to overcome the communication barrier posed by the Fernshaws' deafness. It was a reminder of what was waiting for me back in England – guardedness, reserve, insularity – and it was an affirmation of the regrettably English parts of my own character, because William Ricketts was the person at the gathering I most resembled.

But I was enjoying myself anyway, partly because the event was so improbable. I liked overhearing Officer Topper holding forth on genealogy to Winks, and seeing Nathan interpreting one of Mr Diaz's rambling anecdotes in gestures to his mother. And I liked the continuity that it implied with the celebrations I remembered here from my childhood.

I think a family is made up of people who are bound together by habit more than by ties of blood. My evidence for this is that a family can die while its nominal members are all still living. Mine did. But that afternoon, I got the feeling that I'd managed to reincarnate it. Its old habits had been revived – as though a group of people had got together and learned to speak a dead language.

I'd set up Patrick's croquet hoops on the flattest part of the lawn. It wasn't real croquet, it was a variant, a dialect of the game that Patrick had half remembered and half made up. But since we had never played anything else, it had always been croquet to us.

After we'd finished eating and had a short rest, I explained the game to everyone who wanted to play. Winks couldn't, Officer Topper had to go back to work and Mrs Fernshaw didn't want to, but everyone else was up for it. Only William Ricketts raised objections to the unorthodox rules, but he was too hesitant to offer an alternative and just carped quietly from the sidelines as I ran through my version of them.

I teamed up with Mrs Delamitri and Stephanie the para-legal; Nathan with his sister; William Ricketts with Mrs

Delamitri's artistic friend, whose house guests played as a threesome with Mr Diaz.

I suppose we'd been playing for about half an hour when the sound of an engine must have become audible from the driveway. I say 'must have' because I didn't hear it myself. I was wrapped up in the game and while I tried to retain a relaxed and casual appearance I was determined to batter William Ricketts' ball into the salt marsh.

There must have been the sound of an engine, logically, because a car was arriving. But the first I was aware of it was when I saw my Aunt Judith's head peering around the side of the house, shortly followed by her waving hand and then the rest of her body. Just behind her was her husband, Lynde, a retired high-school gym instructor, who had been a silent and unfathomable accessory at family reunions for as long as I could remember.

I was surprised to see them – I wasn't sorry, but I knew it must have been a long trip and I had invited them more for the sake of form than in the belief they'd really show up. But I was more surprised to see that my brother Vivian was bringing up the rear.

But I was pleased, almost in spite of myself, to see him loping across the lawn behind them. There was an uncomfortable moment when I forgot to detach myself from my croquet mallet to shake his hand, but the greetings over, I was able to conceal my awkwardness by officiously discharging my duties as host.

My brother had driven down with a friend – a bit of blonde eye-candy who was younger and more silent than Terry Fernshaw. My brother was looking tanned and muscular. I caught him admiring his own biceps as he held a cup of iced tea in front of him. Why a film director should want to emulate a leading man, I don't know. I would have thought that one of the perks of the job was being able to exude some status-related sex hormone without going to the trouble of breaking a sweat at the gym. Anyway, he made me feel very pasty and English.

It might have been my paranoia, but I think that a slight buzz went around the garden when he arrived. People are like that about celebrity; and they're noticeably less good at concealing their interest when the person in question is someone they think they ought to know but can't quite place.

'Was *October Conspiracy* one of your brother's?' William Ricketts asked me discreetly.

'Yes,' I said.

'Oh, that was jolly good. Yes, I enjoyed that.'

He worked up his courage to pass on the compliment to my brother, who was obliged to inform him that he'd had nothing to do with it.

Most of the guests began to disperse around four. Several were returning to the mainland as I was and had long journeys home. But the Fernshaws and Winks and Mr Diaz had gone down to the beach for a swim. I walked down to tell them I was getting a lift to Boston with Vivian.

I said goodbye and exchanged a wordless farewell with Mrs Fernshaw, who gave me a hug. As my cheek brushed the side of her head, I found myself looking at the silent zone around her ear. Even if we had shared a language, I wouldn't have been able to say much more than goodbye, or begin to explain that something I had found in her story was sending me across the world to find the conclusion of my own.

As I left the beach afterwards, I turned back for a last look. A mass of clouds had formed over the eastern end of the island – their undersides were just touched with pink as the sun dipped on the other side. Terry and her mother were scouring the lower part of the shore for sea glass. Mr Diaz and Nathan had taken the turtle boat into the water and were floating it in the shallows between the shore and the sandbar. Winks had rolled up his trousers and was hopping at the water's edge with his crutch. Occasionally he used it to point at something – the moat of water around the sandbar was full of starfish, sand dollars and flickering shoals of minnows – and the crutch cast a long whisker of shadow along the beach.

For a brief moment, there was one of those special con-
junctions of the season, and the weather and the company – all
of them, even William Ricketts – that brought the present into
sudden communion with the past. That could almost have
been Patrick playing in the water, or my grandmother collecting sea glass. It was as though the past had been brought to life
in front of me – the past that at all other times was no more
than a handful of August afternoons as faint and distant as the
lights of a remote constellation.

TWENTY-EIGHT

VIVIAN HAD SOME KIND of Japanese off-road vehicle that seemed only slightly smaller and less robust than the amphibious vessels they used for landing troops on D-Day. Even so, he cringed when I closed the passenger door and complained that I'd slammed it.

'Do you want to slam it a bit harder?' he said. 'There's a woman in Provincetown who didn't hear you that time.'

I opened the door and shut it again as delicately as a surgeon lowering a new heart into a patient's rib cage. 'Better?'

'I bet you don't shut the door of your car like that,' he grumbled as we turned out of the driveway of my uncle's house for perhaps the last time in our lives. 'Not that that shitbox would ever have made it as far as Boston.'

I began to regret having accepted the lift, but the alternative would have been a taxi and then the bus.

We drove mostly in silence to the ferry port at Westwich.

Vivian's prepubescent girlfriend fell asleep on the back seat with her feet on the sofa-sized armrest that separated me from my brother. She remained comatose all the way to Westwich, slept through the ferry crossing, and only opened her eyes briefly when we arrived on the mainland.

I felt a slight ache at the thought of leaving. The dense pine trees that stretched away on either side of the highway and the dusty golden light of late afternoon on the Cape seemed so familiar that I found it painful to think I might revisit it again only as a memory.

'Dad was ill,' Vivian said, apropos of nothing, as the car rumbled up Route 6 towards Boston.

'Judith didn't mention anything.'

'I imagine he didn't tell her. You know what he's like.'

'Is he all right?'

'He's over it now. I had my assistant call you at the time but she said some fucking Russian guy kept answering the phone.'

'You had your assistant call me?'

'You never return my calls anyway, so what difference does it make?'

'What was wrong with him?'

'He had a medical in Boston while he was over for Patrick's funeral – he must have felt he was next in line for the big guy with the sickle. He called me up afterwards to brag.' Vivian lowered his voice in an impression of my father's drawling mid-Atlantic accent: '"Blood pressure one forty over eighty-five, they said I had the eyes of a fighter pilot, I could have run on that treadmill all week. Nothing wrong with your genes, Vivian."'

I laughed in spite of myself. Vivian smiled. When he was funny, he was also strangely remote from me: it reminded me of the distance between us.

'Turns out he didn't quite get the all clear. They ran tests on everything, you know what American doctors are like: fingers up the back-bottom, checking the old chap, cholesterol levels, chest X-rays, blood sugar and God knows what else. He had some sort of discoloration on his arm and they wanted to check that out, too. Anyway, the stool sample showed up little traces of blood, so they had to have him back for a colonoscopy, and found a tumour.'

'Oh.'

'Yeah, that was my reaction. He was in hospital a week while they removed it. They did what's called a "resection" – they just cut out about fifteen centimetres on either side of the lump and then join the two ends together. The procedure itself is no big deal, actually. I went to see him a couple of times, including on the day of the operation. I was with him when they wheeled him into the operating theatre. He was all groggy just before he went under. I was holding his hand and he kind of whispered something to me. I had to bend down to hear it. I'll give you five hundred bucks if you can guess what it was.'

'"*Veni, vidi, vici*"? "It is a far, far better thing . . ."?'

'That's two guesses and they're both wrong.' He paused for dramatic effect. It was a serious story and my suggestions were unwelcome. He paused, as though waiting for my flippant remarks to disperse. 'He was whispering, "Bolder than Mandingo". Bolder than Mandingo! Remember that dumb game? He was making a joke. They could have been his final words. I was proud of him.'

'I'll have to ask him about it when I see him,' I said. I knew that Vivian hadn't been trying to make me feel like a disloyal son, but I did anyway. I wanted to tell him that I was going to see our father now, but I was afraid it would have sounded defensive, or like a boast.

Vivian stretched forward over the steering wheel and then settled back into the seat. 'This reminds me of when you slashed my arm with your Swiss Army knife,' he said.

I found myself repeating the explanation I gave at the time. I had been sixteen, and travelling up to Maine with Vivian and my father. 'It was an accident. I didn't mean to cut you. I was just threatening you with it.'

'Just threatening me? *Just* threatening me? Ha!' He laughed
to himself for what seemed like a long time. 'Just threatening
me. Did you hear that, honey?' Lolita in the back said nothing.
She was listening to a Walkman. 'I must remember that.'

I stared out of the window trying to think of a similar out-
rage that Vivian had committed against me so as to erase his
moral superiority, but I couldn't remember any. The cruellest
thing my brother had done had been completely unintentional.
He had grown four inches taller than me by the time I got
back home from my first term at university. And he not only
had usurped my height, but had taken on a kind of sneering
superiority in his way of speaking that can only have been an
imitation of me. Everything he didn't like was dismissed as
'sad' or 'tragic', which was slang for 'contemptible', and while
I still caught glimpses of the old, soft Vivian when I overheard
him talking to his friends, I never saw it again myself.

About a year after that, I found a diary in the drawer of his
desk when I was looking for a pencil sharpener and leafed
through it – pretending to myself that I wasn't sure it was a
private notebook – and found myself referred to as 'that weirdo
Damien'. I carried on reading it in the hope of finding something complimentary as an antidote, but only discovered
further remarks in the same vein and a couple of short sentences where he said I was so staid that he felt sorry for me. I
think I was hurt, apart from anything, by how little I featured
in his internal life, more than by the tone of my few appearances there.

'What was the kid's name?' my brother asked suddenly.

'Which kid?'

'The kid at your cook-out.'

'Nathan?'

'Nathan.' My brother pronounced it with a sonorous final-
ity, as though it were the tag on a folder of observations he was
tucking away into a mental filing cabinet. 'I'm hungry. There's
a couple of Twinkies in the glove compartment,' he said.

I opened the packet and passed one to him: sticky and

corn-coloured like a barely damp bath sponge. He stuck half of it into his mouth. 'Want one?' he said – except his mouth was so full it sounded like *Wampum?*

'No thanks.'

At the airport drop-off I hugged him awkwardly. 'Thanks for the lift,' I said.

'No sweat. Judy and I are flying back to LA in a week, but please look us up if you're out there.'

'Did you give her a sleeping pill?' I said.

'She's had a busy week,' he said.

'Up early for kindergarten?'

'Don't spoil it, Damien.'

'Sorry.'

We shook hands.

'I promise to return your calls if you promise not to have your assistant make them,' I said.

'Deal.'

He walked me to the check-in desk. 'You're flying to Frankfurt?' he said. 'Why the hell would you want to go there?'

'It's the transport hub of Europe, mate. Connecting flight to Pisa.'

He looked at me in astonishment. 'You're going to see Dad?'

TWENTY-NINE

MY FATHER'S HOUSE was an hour's drive from the airport. He had a big villa that looked out over olive terraces. I suppose the landscape had been chopped out of the hillside by the Etruscans, but the depth of my historical reference is such that winding roads and hills and vineyards mainly evoke a mythical location which I think of as Car Advert Country.

I parked on the verge and walked through the front gate. The housekeeper indicated in signs that Signor March was round the back, tending to his garden somewhere.

I found him at the foot of the slope, among his beehives. He wore one of those veiled hats and was moving an object that might have been a wooden tray, but that was obscured with teeming black bodies. Around him, the bees seemed to make solid shapes in the air, like translucent curtains being pulled this way and that by the wind.

'Stay where you are,' he said. 'I'm moving the queen.'

'No gloves, Dad? Don't they sting you?'

'They sting me – but it prevents arthritis, so I'm happy to put up with it.' His voice was slightly muffled through the layers of cloth around his face. 'I forgot where you said you were staying.'

'A schoolfriend of Laura's has got an old mill outside Lucca,' I said. I decided it wasn't really a lie, since the statement was true, even though the inference I expected him to draw was false. Laura and I had spent the New Year there ten years earlier, but I hadn't seen the woman since.

'Woman friend?' asked my father.

'Yup.'

'You should have brought her along. Is it a romantic entanglement?'

For some reason I thought of the moustachioed dragon who had studied my passport photo like a chess puzzle before giving me a room in her guest house. I smiled. 'No. Unfortunately not.'

When my father took off his hat, I noticed he had lost weight. It made his features more prominent. His hair had been cropped into an unintentionally fashionable style, and with his beaky nose and beady eyes I thought he bore a striking resemblance to a baby eagle.

'Vivian told me you'd been ill,' I said.

He waved his hand dismissively. 'Nothing worth bothering with.' Then he changed the subject. 'You've never been here before, right?'

'That's right.'

'Do you have time for the tour of the house?'

He showed me round briefly. His living rooms were plain and sparely furnished. His tiny study was dominated by a wall of legal textbooks. A big photograph of Vivian and me jumping off a sand dune in Truro hung above his desk.

I had come to take my father to dinner. He chose the restaurant, a local place called Il Vecchio Pazzo. I had made it clear that I would be paying, over his protestations. It made me feel more up to the task at hand to be in the driver's seat in this way. The power of being the giver amounted to a slight equalling of our respective positions. Although, when I worked it out, I realised that his dead brother's mistress's husband was the real sponsor of our reunion. But money's weird like that.

My father insisted on changing for dinner. I waited in his tiled sitting room, worrying that he would appear in an opera hat and tails as though dressing for the captain's table on some prewar Atlantic liner, but he put on nothing more formal than a navy-blue, brass-buttoned blazer.

The waiters clearly knew my father. I overheard one of them referring to him affectionately as 'Il Ingles', and he seemed pleased when I mentioned it. He introduced me to the maître d' and chatted away to him about the menu in Italian. Once his detailed inquiries had been satisfied, he turned to me and said, 'You could follow that, couldn't you?'

'I don't speak Italian, Dad.'

'Well, it's all basically Latin.'

'Never my strong suit, I'm afraid.' I helped myself to water from the bulbous carafe. My father was turning over the napkin in his lap slightly nervously. I remembered that there was always something distracted in his manner – he had a restless energy that was only still when he was at his desk working. But he seemed a little more twitchy than usual. He probably thought I wanted to interrogate him about his illness. Still, he was handling the situation with great aplomb.

He broke up a piece of bread and used it to sop up some olive oil. 'How's life at the Beeb? It's terrible what they're doing to the World Service.'

'It doesn't really apply to me,' I said.

'Well, of course, I know you work for the TV part.'

'I mean, I haven't been in London for a while. I've been on Ionia.'

'Ionia?' As he said it, I was struck by what a beautiful word it was. He repeated it softly; his surprise gave it a sense of wonderment and his sonorous voice lingered on the vowels. I remembered the sound the breeze made when it sprang up to rustle the pine trees in the late afternoon. 'Is the water still as cold as it used to be?'

'Most definitely.'

'I remember taking you and Vivian to the beach there before either of you could swim and having to watch you both like a hawk.' He pronounced 'hawk' *hock*; it was one of the Medfordisms he could never shake off.

'I saw Vivian a few days ago.'

'You saw Vivian there?'

I nodded. 'He told me about your operation.'

'How is he?'

'Strength to strength, I gather. I was staying at Patrick's.'

My father raised his eyebrows, but it could have been in surprise, or because, at that moment, the waiter was sliding a plateful of ravioli under his nose. I was having the same: it had a delicious, indefinably meaty filling.

'What is this, pork?' I said.

'*Coniglio.*'

I shook my head.

'Bunny rabbit.'

'It's good.' I tore up some bread and swirled it in the garlicky sauce. 'I figured I'd spend the summer there − swim every day − reminisce. Do a spot of painting. I couldn't think why else he would have left me the house.'

'He was a truly strange man, Damien. I say that as his brother. I could show you letters I got from him that would make your hair curl − abusive, deranged, cruel.'

'I know, I know. But I was talking to his lawyer about it. Apparently he told the guy that I'd know what to do with it. But what? After about ten minutes I realised I'm sure as hell not supposed to live in it. But I figured it out. It's a museum. It's an unofficial museum, and I was supposed to be the curator.'

'You're not eating your ravioli.'

I spooned a couple into my mouth and the waiter took my plate away. 'Tell him they were great.' I said. '*Delicioso*.'

My father murmured something to the waiter, who seemed to retire through the swing doors satisfied.

'I brought you something, by the way,' I said, passing him the envelope of photos I'd found in Patrick's library.

'Well, I'll be darned,' he said. 'This is from before your mother and I were married.' He went through the photos twice, pausing on each shot as though in front of a painting in a gallery, absorbing details of the figures, the composition, the relationship of the figures to one another. I sensed he was a million miles away.

'Well,' he said, passing them back to me.

'Keep them, Dad. I brought them for you.'

'I'm touched, Damien.' He sounded slightly abashed. I looked down at the crumbs on the table in front of me.

My father had chosen the wine for the main course, which was some kind of slow-braised lamb – shanks, I think. The wine was a deep, deep red and sat shimmering in the glass. The flavour was so full, it made me think of arterial blood – if that can be a pleasant quality in a wine.

'This is nice, isn't it?' I said. I wanted it to mean the whole thing – me being there, me and my dad, in Italy, eating dinner.

But my father chose to understand it less emotively. 'Yes, this was a great find. I'm very fond of this place. One of the things that I'm most proud of in life is that the chef here uses my honey on his baked figs. That's quite an accolade, I think.'

'It is. It is.' I took a sip of my arterial blood. I was thinking that my dad was – emotionally speaking – a fiddler crab, backing away into his tiny hole at the slightest approach, beadily scouring the beach, and impossible to dig out. He had to be stalked stealthily.

The main course arrived and we had to postpone our conversation while the waiters went through a little masque of giving my dad the best service in the restaurant. I liked the fact that he was popular with them.

'I was in the middle of telling you something,' I said, when they'd gone.

'Don't let it get cold.'

'Okay, Dad.' I ate some of the lamb – it was soft and aromatic from long cooking. I noticed he seemed preoccupied – maybe the photos? – so I decided to postpone what I had to say until after the meal.

We had the baked figs and the chef emerged like a deus ex machina from the bowels of the kitchen to drink a toast to my father's bees. Then we took our *vin santo* out to the terrace and sat staring at the darkened valley. The yellowy moon picked out the neat rows of vines in front of us.

'I made a big discovery on the island,' I said.

'On Ionia?'

'Yes. On Ionia.' I liked hearing him say the word almost as much as I think my father enjoyed saying it. 'I turned up a manuscript of Patrick's with some unpublished stories in it.'

'That *is* a find. What were they about?'

'It's called *The Confessions of Mycroft Holmes*. You know, Sherlock's older brother. Do you ever read Sherlock Holmes?'

'Not now, no. I'd have thought those stories were pretty well unreadable now, at my age.'

'There's some good stuff in them. I reread them when I was trying to get to the bottom of Patrick's stories. I had to do some detective work of my own. Do you remember the *Sign of Four*?'

'It's been years since I read it, Damien.'

'That's the one where Sherlock says: "How often have I said to you that when you have eliminated the impossible, whatever remains, *however improbable*, is the truth." That's good, isn't it? It sounds like a maxim of jurisprudence.'

'Say it again.'

I repeated it and my father said the words slowly to himself. 'Yes, that is good,' he said thoughtfully.

I took a sip of my wine. It gave me a thrill to think that it had grown in the earth which I could smell cooling below the terrace we were sitting on.

'What happens in the last story – briefly, so you don't have to wade through it. Mycroft – who's kind of a layabout – meets this fellow, Abel Mundy, who has a deaf wife and kids. Mundy's a nasty piece of work – this is, like, high melodrama – and Mycroft ends up topping him. Simple enough.'

'Simple enough,' my father agreed.

'But here's the weird part. Patrick really had some deaf neighbours. And being a little literal-minded, I thought: It's a confession! – maybe he's trying to tell us something. Maybe he's offed this bloke, Fernshaw–Mundy.'

'Who?'

'Patrick. It sounds ridiculous, but I really did believe it, I think, for a moment anyway. That he might have been capable of murder.'

My father shook his head. 'He was capable of a lot of things, but not that.'

'No, you're right,' I said. I took another sip of the wine and it seemed to leave a trail of stars across my tongue like the one above us. 'You're absolutely right. I looked into it further and it turned out that the villain in the story is actually a composite. He's based on two characters, two brothers, who have a pretty interesting story of their own.' I broke off. 'You know what? I think I left those photos indoors.'

'No, I have them right here. You gave them to me, remember?' My father patted the inside pocket of his blazer.

'Of course I did. My memory is going. What was I saying? This story. It was a basically a love triangle: two brothers in love with the same woman. I'm not even sure how the three of them met, but I have a feeling they were all foreigners abroad and just sort of fetched up in the same city. The brothers were close in age but quite different. The younger brother was rather conventional, hardworking and – not dull – what's the word? Prosaic. Maybe a little more prosaic than the other.'

'You don't mean "prosaic", surely?' said my father.

'Don't I?' I wished I'd held off the *vin santo*. Trust my dad to be listening to my tale of heartbreak with one eye on *Fowler's Modern English Usage*. 'Let's just say "prosaic" for now. I need to tell you about the other brother. I suppose I think of him as poetic, but he wasn't a poet. Actually, he was a bit feckless, and found it hard to keep himself to one thing for any length of time. They were both complicated people. I don't know about the woman, presumably she was too. But the older brother was definitely more glamorous, funny and unpredictable, and the kind of man women like to be with. Or this woman did, at any rate, because she was totally smitten with him, and probably didn't even notice the younger brother. They had that "hearts and flowers" phase of the romance and she got pregnant.

'So now, she's pregnant and looking for some help, but as I said, the older brother wasn't able to commit to anything and he just fucked off. He disappeared, went, I don't know, to Russia. He went away, God knows where. Poof! Just vanished.'

I was trying to sense my father's reaction to what I was telling him, but he sat there beside me in absolute silence.

'You can imagine the state the girl was in,' I said. 'This was a different time. Being pregnant and unmarried was seriously bad news. Oh yeah, and to make things worse, she was a Catholic – all three of them were, in fact.' I paused. 'You'll never guess what happened.'

He said nothing – the only sound was the slow sigh of his inhalation.

'The younger brother stepped in. He loved her anyway, and he may have had faults, but pride wasn't one of them. I mean, he didn't need to punish her for preferring his brother. And he was hard-working. It may sound strange, but I think he believed in hard work in the way some people believe in God – and that through hard work, he'd make her love him. More wine, Dad?'

My father shook his head – I sensed the movement in the darkness, but nothing else.

'To cut a long story short – although you might say it's a bit late for that – they got married and things worked out quite well and they had a second child together. Then she died suddenly. It was a terrible blow, but it had one surprising consequence which was that the brothers became friends again, tentatively. I think with all brothers there's so much similarity, you know, that even after a row, they continue to look at the world in the same way.

'So there was a sort of rapprochement. It was a bit tense, I gather, perhaps because the older son was never told about, well, what I've just told you. And in the end the strain grew – you know how old men get weirder as they get older – and the friendship became impossible to sustain.

'That's more or less the story. The reason I'm telling you is that I found it very touching. The younger brother never took credit for what he'd done. I can't imagine that he was ashamed about it. He brought the child up as his own, loved it in his own way, and had the usual parental failings, but didn't favour either of his sons, even got them mixed up at times, which, given the circumstances, is quite lovely, I think.

'One of Patrick's neighbours told me all this. She said to me, "Who was the older boy's real father, then?" I told her paternity's not the issue, is it? The younger brother was a father to both the sons. And it was a pity, in a way, that the older child could never know.' I had to stop briefly because I didn't want my father to hear the catch in my voice. 'It was a pity – imagine the love and gratitude if he'd known the truth.'

My father was silent for a long time. I began to think I'd made a terrible misjudgement.

When he finally spoke, there was more astonishment than anger in his voice. He had been turning over in his mind the one thing that he still hadn't been able to forgive.

'Not a letter,' he said, in a whisper. 'Not even a letter when she was dying.'

THIRTY

GETTING BACK TO LONDON was the strangest thing. The city was shabby and overcast but it also seemed as comfortable as an old couch – specifically, the couch I had chucked out to make room for Platon Bakatin's sofa-bed.

No one met me at the airport. I just kept walking past the phalanx of chauffeurs with signs, and expectant relatives, and for once I was in no hurry to get back to central London and a makeshift bed in Stevo's dingy studio flat.

Although I hadn't spent the night at my father's, he did insist on taking me back to show me round his vegetable garden. It was past midnight, but he had two ridiculous flash-lights that we wore on our heads. The beams glinted on the shiny skins of tomatoes and aubergines.

'*Solanum melangena*,' my father said.

I nodded. We both pretended not to notice each other's tears.

That our reunion was only tolerable because of a complicated charade that redirected our strong feelings on to members of the vegetable kingdom, I find both typical and unbearably moving. And that is how I most often remember my father – eyes glistening, torch sweeping the garden like the beam of a lighthouse, excitedly explaining the difference between white and purple aubergines.

He died a year and half later from a more virulent recurrence of colon cancer. We were deprived of a death-bed reunion by a baggage-handlers' strike at Heathrow. My wife was having a difficult pregnancy so I had decided to remain with her as long as possible. As it turned out, I had cut it too fine. I still regret not managing to say goodbye properly, but Vivian was by his side and once again reported that his last words were 'Bolder than Mandingo'. I wouldn't go so far as to call this a lie, but I think that Vivian may have been unable to repress his cineaste's need for a strong ending.

I have never been back to Ionia. I relinquished my interest in the estate and every year get a Christmas card from the two old priests who now live there. Father Donovan is the name of one of them. I can never read the other man's signature.

For a while I was so busy trying to put a life of my own together that I thought very little about Patrick, although I was always reminded of him when I saw that old guy outside Baker Street tube station dressed as Sherlock Holmes and handing out brochures to the museum.

Then Mr Diaz wrote to me two years ago. He needed my permission to open the house to one of Patrick's prospective biographers. I gave it, figuring that some lucky postgraduate student was welcome to make what sense he could out of the penny-banks, the ice-cream scoops, the crazy letters, and the unpublished writings. It's not a boast to say I was the only person capable of following Patrick's paper chase right through to its conclusion.

The biographer, Edwin Sapsted (D. Phil., Oxon.) has been in touch with me a couple of times over the past twelve months. He E-mailed me lists of questions on matters of chronology, stuff about the history of the house, and Patrick's relationship with my father.

I decided to be helpful but not too helpful, because although I wanted to unburden myself, I didn't feel right about it, even with my father and Patrick both dead. So I fended off his inquiries and when he asked me about Mycroft Holmes I told him all the books he needed were in Patrick's library. I didn't tell him my own conclusions about the stories. But his curiosity piqued something inside me, and I found my thoughts drawn back to Ionia.

I think the imagination roams widely over the world until it finds a predicament that reflects its own secret agonies. And if it lacks the will to move on, it roosts and broods, and pecks at old injuries. Mycroft can nail half of London Bridge to that barrel as ballast, but nothing will stop Abel Mundy's restless ghost pursuing him into his dreams.

Because the ugly secret of that final story – and of this story, perhaps of all stories – is that the author ultimately identifies with his villain. Abel Mundy, violent husband and failed parent, is a grotesque, but strip away the calumnies and he is only a husband and a parent – and I think that is why Mycroft murders him.

It's very late. Going over all this for the last time before I set it aside for ever, I see that I've tried many ways to approach Patrick – through the facts of his life, and his work, and the gaps in his work, and the impress of his personality upon the house and island that he definitely loved – and yet in the end, he has eluded me. Whatever he was, he is now too insubstantial for me to grasp, except fleetingly.

Mycroft comes closest to embodying something of him, but in spite of everything that Patrick wrote, Mycroft also remains frustratingly absent. So I'm resigned to the idea that my final approach to Patrick is a qualified failure. And after all, there is a quiet poetry in Mycroft's absence. It echoes the life of another absent man, someone who perhaps resembled his creations – Mycroft, Abel Mundy and the innocent protagonist of *Peanut Gatherers* – but who was, principally and biologically, my father, Patrick March.

MARCEL THEROUX

Damien March hasn't thought of his eccentric uncle for almost twenty years when he receives a terse message by telegram: *Patrick dead. Father.* Damien, a journalist for the BBC in London, is even more shocked to learn that he has inherited his uncle's ramshackle house on Ionia, an isolated island off the coast of Cape Cod.

Offered the choice between his own humdrum life and the strange isolation of his uncle's, Damien decides to make the swap. But his new future means moving circuitously into his family's past; rummaging through his uncle's possessions, he finds letters and writings that provide scattered clues to Patrick's solitary life. And when he discovers a fragment of an unpublished novel, *The Confessions of Mycroft Holmes*, the stakes in the paperchase become dramatically higher.

Mycroft Holmes, the older brother of Sherlock, is one of literature's most intriguing absences. A neglected genius who lived in obscurity, he bears a striking resemblance to Patrick himself. And as the parallels quickly grow more disconcerting, Damien realises the tale of murder and deception is taking on a sinister new meaning . . .

The Paperchase is at once an engaging mystery and an illuminating story about family secrets and identity.

ABACUS FICTION

U.K. £9.99*
*Recommended only

ISBN 0-349-11466-8

9 780349 114668